MW01492487

Guardians of the Second Son

Allen Kent

Guardians of the Second Son. Copyright © 2013 by Allen Kent.
All rights reserved.
Printed in the United States of America. No part of
this book may be used or reproduced in any manner
whatsoever without written permission except in the
cases of brief quotations imbedded in articles or
reviews, with attribution shown. For information
address AllenPearce Publishers, 16635 Hickory
Drive, Neosho, MO 64850

AllenPearce Publishers © ©

Library of Congress Cataloging-in-Publication Data
Allen Kent
River of Light and Shadow
Kent, Allen
ISBN 978-0615855714

Allen Kent © 2013

To

Charles Brewster

Allen Kent

Acknowledgments

I am most grateful to my team of readers, my wife Holly, Anne and Richard Clement, Diane Andris, Marilyn Jenson, and Paul, Jim and Erica Farnsworth, whose invaluable editorial assistance improved this book immeasurably. Special thanks to David Farnsworth who suggested the idea of "shared divinity" and stimulated much of the thinking that led to this plot. And thank you to my talented daughter-in-law, Jillian Farnsworth, who took a rudimentary cover idea and turned it into a work of art. Without all of you, this book would not have been possible

CHAPTER ONE

When he opened his eyes, J. Dixon Bartlett's first thought was of the ancient Chinese philosopher Chuang Tzu. After waking from a dream in which he was a butterfly, the venerable Taoist sage had wondered if he was a man dreaming he was a butterfly, or was now a butterfly dreaming he was a man. The apparition that floated above J. Dixon Bartlett was not one of a butterfly, but of a woman as beautiful as any Bartlett had ever seen. Her hair cascaded over her shoulders and was as black as the night that enveloped the room, framing a face of flawless cinnamon skin, full red lips, and dark eyes under perfectly shaped brows. From the red bindi on her forehead he knew she was Indian, a realization that added to his sense that he was still dreaming. Even six weeks ago when he was in India, the vision of such a beautiful woman in his bedroom would have seemed a dream. But he was now back in Charlotte and had gone to bed very much alone.

The woman smelled faintly of jasmine, a scent so real that he smiled to himself, marveling that a dream could be so sensory. The beautiful woman did not smile back, which surprised him. She should be smiling in a dream. As he struggled to decide which side of sleep he was on, she leaned over and spoke to him softly.

"You have betrayed us," she said, the words clipped and exact as is typical of Indian English. "We trusted you with that which is most sacred to us, and you violated our trust."

I'm having a nightmare, J. Dixon thought, noticing that the figure wore a sari as black as her ebony hair, leaving her beautiful face floating as a disembodied visage above him in the room. *My conscience is playing tricks on me!* He had been hesitant to announce his discovery, knowing that making it public would violate an oath he had taken nearly a year earlier. But for an endowed professor of religious studies, the announcement would vault him to the top of his profession and secure his legacy as a scholar. And what were the few Disciples of Thomas, so far away in Kerala, India, to do if he broke his oath? He had no plans to return to India's Malabar Coast. Still, he had delayed publishing his discovery, less out of concern for the believers in Kerala than for matters of professional ethics as a researcher. He had been wrestling with the ethical question when he dropped off to sleep and now his conscience had taken human form and was hovering above him in the room.

"You took a fragment, Professor Bartlett," the exotic vision said in the same soft, but very chilling voice. "And you plan to reveal what is in the letter. That was forbidden, and you knew the penalty. I am a Guardian of Thomas and I have come to hold you to your oath."

She reached forward with her left hand and placed it on the covers that blanketed his chest, leaning over him with a light pressure that seemed too temporal for a dream. But with the slow motion of dreams, she raised her right hand and pressed it firmly against the side of his head where his thick white hair had been flattened by sleep. The prick of the barbs penetrating his scalp was also too real, and a deadening numbness began to spread across the back of his head and down his spine. Suddenly he knew that the woman was not a vision, that he was fully awake, and for the very last time.

. . .

News of the sudden death of distinguished professor, J. Dixon Bartlett spread across the campus of Alexander Martin University with the speed one might expect from the resignation of the head basketball coach. Only a year before, few on campus beyond the Department of Religious Studies had even heard of Bartlett. But publication of his recent book *The Christians of Kerala* had not only made him the most talked about professor among the distinguished universities in North Carolina, but a darling of network morning news programs across the country. Controversy can be mother to celebrity, and Bartlett's book was the stuff controversy is made of. It claimed that the beliefs of a small group within the greater St. Thomas Christian community in southern India, a group that called itself the Disciples of Thomas, might express a doctrine that was closer to the original teachings of Jesus of Nazareth than any that existed in modern Christian thought. Fundamental to this teaching was a claim that Jesus and his disciple Thomas were biological twins and that although Jesus was indeed the son of God, so also was his twin, whom the Disciples referred to as The Second Son. As the twin of Jesus and off-spring of the immortal God and Mary, Thomas inherited both physical and divine natures that were manifest during his ministry.

6

When first published, *The Christians of Kerala* was believed to be an interesting anthropological study of a curious, but heretical off-shoot of early Indian Christianity. The Thomas "twin" myth was not new with the Disciples, but appeared in other early apocryphal Christian writing. Bartlett's book received only modest attention—and that only because the professor was known to be a thorough and responsible scholar. His critics attributed the doctrine of the India Disciples to writings dated to the second or third century that referred to Didymos Thomas as "the twin." The Thomas Christians of Kerala adopted this belief, the critics contended, after exposure to the ancient Christian community in Syria.

But when Bartlett announced that within a month he would produce proof that the teaching could be traced directly to Thomas—proof that before the Gospels of the New Testament were written, Thomas was presenting himself as Jesus' twin and was teaching this shared divinity— Bartlett became an overnight sensation. As his notoriety grew, so did the criticism, curiosity, and anger. But now, before that proof had been seen by anyone, J. Dixon Bartlett was dead.

The death of the endowed professor was especially troublesome to Associate Professor Nolan Lemay. Bartlett had helped Lemay acquire his position in the Department of Religious Studies at AMU, encouraged by J. Dixon's wife, Vivian, who had been a sorority sister at North Carolina with Nolan's wife Regina. The women still remained closer to each other than they were to their own siblings. Dixon Bartlett had also taken Nolan under his wing and championed Lemay's pursuit of a coveted tenured position on the university faculty. But Nolan was not a strong or particularly imaginative scholar. Nor was he naïve. He knew that he had lived on Bartlett's hand-me-down projects since he entered the university. When J. Dixon came across an idea that had research potential but lacked the scholarly cachet to capture his imagination, he passed it along to Nolan. But even with this help, Nolan's record of research and publication hadn't earned him an endorsement from the departmental committee on tenure and promotion. The dean had passed it along to the university president with a recommendation that tenure be denied. At AMU, being denied tenure was a death knell. It meant a one-year continuance to get your affairs in order and seek other employment, then out the door.

Enter Regina Lamoreau-Lemay and the not-too-subtle influence of the

Charlotte Lamoreaus. Through a twenty million dollar gift to the university, Colonel Charles Whitaker Lamoreau had endowed not only J. Dixon Bartlett's position at AMU, but eleven other professorships across campus. Few faculty at the university and even fewer students knew much about Alexander Martin, representative from North Carolina to the Constitutional Convention of 1787, after whom the university was named. But they all knew about Colonel Charles W. Lamoreau. Three buildings on campus bore his name and a life-sized bronze statue of the colonel graced the quad in front of the library. The Lamoreaus were an institution in Charlotte, and Charles W. Lamoreau had chosen AMU to showcase his wealth and influence. After a call from the colonel to the president's office, the dean's objection to Nolan's tenure was overturned, and as long as Nolan didn't commit a felony or some other egregious moral offense, he was professor for life.

But Nolan's extorted professorship was 'employment without distinction' in a family of almost unparalleled recognition in North Carolina. Since pre-Civil War times, Lamoreau had been synonymous with wealth, military leadership, and political power. To be a Lamoreau without these attributes, even if only by marriage, was tantamount to failure. Regina and the colonel had done their best to boost Nolan into a position that, if it failed to enhance, at least did not embarrass the family reputation. But Nolan knew that to a large degree, what little success he enjoyed as an academic was as an acolyte of J. Dixon Bartlett. And now the distinguished professor was dead.

As Nolan hunched in his high-backed desk chair and gazed out over the azalea-lined walks that separated the building housing Religious Studies from the Charles W. Lamoreau Library, he could see promotion to full professor slipping silently into the grave with J. Dixon Bartlett. He knew the colonel and Regina would not interfere in a promotion decision to full professor. Dismissal from the university because he had not been granted tenure was one thing. It would stain the family's honor. But being relegated to an obscure corner office within the department was only a minor inconvenience—a bit like a business holding that was unproductive, but couldn't be unloaded because one of the family was too heavily invested.

The one possible salvation in all of this, Nolan mused, might be Marcus Branscomb. Bartlett's graduate assistant was two years short of completing the research needed to complete his dissertation and the young acquisition from Duke University's master's program was one of the brightest students Lemay had seen. Nolan's classical language expertise was in Aramaic, particularly the dialects of first-century Palestine. But Marcus Branscomb read and wrote Aramaic, Greek and ancient Pali, the language of the early Thomas Christians of southern India. He was better versed in New Testament texts of the first four centuries than Lemay could ever hope to be. If Nolan could pick up Branscomb as his own assistant and the graduate student's research led to periodic publications, Nolan could insist on co-authorship and might be able to build a publications record worthy of promotion. As the thought began to percolate through Nolan's brain and restore a glimmer of hope to his gloomy morning, the phone buzzed loudly on the desk. He pushed aside a pile of unread essays from his Early Christian Writers course and grabbed the receiver.

"Doctor Lemay."

"Nolan, this is Vivian. Do you have just a moment?"

Nolan straightened in the chair and leaned over the desk. "Of course, Vi. Anything I can do to help. Is Reggie with you? She was going to call this morning to see if she could be useful ...."

"She's been and gone." Vivian Bartlett's voice was as strong and calm as Nolan had ever heard her. "Everything is pretty well taken care of, but Reggie's going to help with lunch following the service. She's such a dear."

"So, what can I do to help?"

Vivian had called the day after J. Dixon's death to invite Nolan to be a pallbearer. He learned then that she had found Dixon dead in his bed when the maid called him to breakfast and he didn't respond. Bartlett and Vivian hadn't shared a room for nearly ten years but always had breakfast together in the sunroom. Dixon read *The Observer* and the *New York Times* while she commented, largely to herself, on what she had seen in the Charlotte *Observer*'s society section before he came down to breakfast. Nolan wondered if they still cared for each other at all and from the tone of Vivian's voice, the answer seemed to be "very little."

"There is one thing you could do for me ...." Vivian paused as if she expected Nolan to ask before she told him.

"Of course. Anything ...."

"I need someone to go through Dixon's things—both here and at the University. Someone who will know what needs to be kept and to whom some of his papers and books should be given. I would like you to keep what you think is useful, and decide if there are other books or papers that should go to a library collection—or just be thrown away. Could you help with that?"

"Of course." Nolan's thoughts went immediately to J. Dixon's orderly office—one of the tidiest on campus. His books were shelved by topic and century, his files numbered and catalogued in a neat ledger he kept in the center drawer of his desk. The task would be relatively simple and could be rewarding. J. Dixon had an enviable collection of early Christian texts.

"I think you might want to start at the house," she suggested. "His most valuable books are here in the study, and he has something locked away in the safe that he's been very secretive about. I think it may relate to the announcement he planned to make ...."

Nolan's heart leapt into his throat. Dixon had said nothing to anyone about the nature of his "proof." When Nolan had prodded a little after a recent faculty meeting, his colleague smiled enigmatically and said, "Just wait a few days. This will blow your socks off."

"I have classes through the afternoon, Vi," Nolan said, "and don't want to disturb your evening. But my day is open tomorrow. Can I come by about 9:00?"

"That would be perfect. Dixon's sister is flying in from Richmond and will be staying at the house, but that shouldn't be a problem at all. We'll just close you in the study and let you see what's there."

"Do you have access to the safe?"

"I know where he kept the combination. I'll give it to you when you come."

"Perfect. I'll be there at 9:00."

·   ·   ·

At one end of the stone room the baptismal font stood empty, unused since the Disciples had initiated the American professor into their society. At the other end, three women sat stiffly on straight-backed wooden chairs facing five elders across the bare chamber. The men also sat on plain wooden chairs with nothing separating them from the women. The room was cool and the women wore long silk shawls over their heads that draped down over colorful saris. Three of the men wore white caps and a fourth, a woolen shawl pulled tightly about his shoulders.

"You did your work well, Kanta," the senior of the elders said, addressing the woman on the right of the trio. She appeared to be in her mid-twenties and was strikingly beautiful, with an oval face framed by glossy black hair, large dark eyes over a slightly aquiline nose, and full lips that now showed the slightest frown.

"Thank you, *Babaji*" she said. "I had hoped never to have this responsibility, but our training prepared me well. I was able to enter and leave the home without notice and the toxin worked as you said. Very quickly and apparently without detection."

"We were concerned about your ability to travel inside the country," one of the men said. "You are becoming such a celebrity."

"In India, perhaps," she said. "But outside of the Indian communities in America, no one knows our film industry and its celebrities. The small bit of fame helped with the visa but once there, I was like every other foreign woman. The documents you provided got me from New York to Charlotte and back with no one knowing I left the New York hotel."

"Did he see you?" another of the elders asked.

"He awoke and looked puzzled rather than surprised," she said. "I told him he had broken his vow and I was there to exact the penalty. I think he understood just before the serum began to act."

The five men nodded solemnly.

"And you, Meera—you have also had to fulfill your role as Guardian when Ashok left us and began to talk openly."

The woman in the center bowed in acknowledgement, but said nothing. She was smaller than the first with short dark hair and a face marked across both cheeks and chin by adolescent acne. But she returned the gaze of the elders with the quiet confidence of a woman who was comfortable with herself and with her world.

"I hope we will not have need for your talents, Manisha, "the senior elder said, turning to the third. "We have been fortunate that all others in our society have remained faithful."

The third woman bowed slightly to show her respect and spoke softly to the row of men. "I am ready if needed, *Babaji*. I feel most blessed to serve as a Guardian."

"And here we are on the day of St. Thomas," the senior elder said, standing before the three women. "Each of you was selected when you were young because we saw in you the mind and courage of a Guardian. You were chosen also because you are women and, regrettably, women still move through our society largely unnoticed—even when very successful. We have given you the education you need for that success and the training you need to carry out your responsibilities as Guardians when called upon. When you turned eighteen, each of you replaced one of the former Guardians, though they were unknown to you and you remain unknown to them and to this community beyond our council."

He paused and studied the three women in front of him. Each sat without expression, hands folded in her lap.

The old man lowered his voice as if in prayer. "Today is the day we celebrate the departure of St. Thomas into the world. It is also the day we meet together each year to renew your vows. You have known from the time of your initiation that you can choose at the beginning of any year to forsake your vows and return fully to your former lives. Should you choose to leave, it will be without disgrace or recrimination. The Guardianship is a covenant of choice." He turned to the striking young woman to his right.

"Do you, Kanta, choose to continue as Guardian of Thomas?"

Kanta bowed slightly and murmured, "I do, *Babaji*."

"Then kneel," the elder said and Kanta moved forward and knelt before the five men.

"And you, Meera. Do you choose to continue as Guardian?"

"I do, *Babaji*," she said, and rose to kneel beside Kanta.

The same was asked of Manisha who murmured her acceptance and knelt beside the others. In one movement, the three women uncovered their heads and lowered their eyes to the floor.

The five men stood and formed a half-circle in front of the Guardians with the senior elder in the center. Those to his right raised their left arms to the shoulder of the man beside him and placed their right hands on Kanta's head, with those to his left locking right arm to shoulder and placing a left hand on the head of Manisha. The old man in the center leaned slightly forward and placed both hands on the short dark hair of Meera.

"On this sacred day of St. Thomas each of you has come to this place to renew your vows as Guardians of the Second Son. Thomas, our master, instructed as he left us that we should guard his secret as the Light that remains in the world until the return of the Messiah. You have been chosen through the inspiration of that Light to be Guardians of the Second Son. Does each of you now accept this responsibility of your own free will and choice?" His voice had risen to be clear and strong and echoed in the cool stone chamber.

"I do," each of the women said.

"Do you swear during this time of service to remain chaste and pure, virgins in the service of the Second Son?"

"I swear it," they said.

"Do you swear to follow the directives of the elders of the Disciples of Thomas, in all matters related to protecting the divine mission of the Second Son, without question and without remorse?"

The three women repeated in unison, "I swear it."

"Do you swear to keep secret from all others, including your own families, your sacred callings as Guardians of the Second Son?"

"I swear it," they murmured.

"And do you swear to protect with your own life the divine calling of the Second Son, that he may remain undisturbed as the Light that shields the world from utter darkness and destruction until the return of the Messiah?"

"I swear it," the women said as one voice.

"Rise, then, Guardians of Thomas," the old man said. "May God bless and protect you."

The three women rose, bowed silently to the five elders with hands pressed together below their faces, then left the room. Each again pulled her shawl up over her head and one-by-one exited the small church, walking in different directions to where they had parked their cars.

When the women were out of the building, the senior elder turned to the others, his face reflecting a deep sadness.

"I had always seen the Guardians as largely symbolic," he said to his brethren. "But twice within this year they have been called upon to act. I fear we may have relied too much on trust to keep our secrets safe."

"Ashok was the first to leave the order," one of the men replied. "And Meera acted quickly and without raising suspicion."

"Ashok died in a hotel room, apparently of over-exertion with a prostitute," one of the others observed. "Do we have reason to believe that Meera has broken her vow of chastity?"

"I have not asked her directly and she swore her oath of purity tonight," the senior said. "If I know Meera as I believe I do, she would arrange for someone else to seduce Ashok. She is a very enterprising woman."

The others nodded their agreement.

"We had no history of deceit or betrayal beyond Ashok," one of the elders observed. "It seemed too much to believe that one of our own would betray us."

"True," the senior elder agreed, "yet it was one of the First Son's own who betrayed him. But I have no reason to believe others will reveal our secret. We keep it even from those within the community until they have demonstrated commitment and maturity." He paused and bowed slightly to his four companions. "I know now that we should never have trusted an outsider. I bear full responsibility and am ashamed for having vouched for his sincerity."

"We all believed him to be an honest and sincere seeker," another said. "We all share the blame."

"Perhaps we are too casual about the security we have in this building," a third suggested. "The letter is protected only by two locks that any good amateur could open."

"The greatest security is ignorance," the senior said. "No one looks for something that is not known to exist. To add greater security is to add suspicion. Until we have reason to be concerned, I suggest we continue to rely on the power of our own sacred oaths."

The men nodded their agreement and one-by-one, left the chapel.

CHAPTER TWO

Vivian Bartlett lived in a stately two-story brick bungalow on a quiet cul-de-sac in the Elizabeth District of central Charlotte, not far from Independence Park. Nolan pulled his silver Mercedes to the curb in front of the walk that led across a shaded lawn to the Bartlett's columned porch and sat for a few moments looking at the house. He and Regina had visited the home a dozen times since Nolan joined the AMU faculty, but always as guests of both Vivian and J. Dixon. It seemed unnatural to enter the house without Dixon being there and it occurred to Nolan that the loss of a friend didn't really begin to sink in until you went somewhere the friend had always been, and he wasn't there. When he and Reggie came as a couple, Nolan spent little time with Vivian and wasn't sure he really knew her very well. Dixon rarely talked about her at work and when he did, it was in an abstract, detached "She rarely tells me what she has planned" sort of way. Vivian was Regina on steroids. She was a Brighton, one of the few families in Charlotte that rivaled the Lamoreaus, and she accepted station and deference as an entitlement. Nolan had always been a little afraid of the woman and to be in the house with just Vivian would be—well, uncomfortable.

He forced himself from the car, walked the thirty paces to the high white-framed door, and twisted the antique handle that served as a bell. A moment later the door was opened by a woman who looked to be in her late fifties, dressed in casual slacks and a waffle-patterned grey pullover. She smiled at Nolan and ushered him into the spacious entryway, extending her hand.

"You must be Nolan. I'm Allyson March. Dixon's sister. Vivian asked if I could meet you and show you to the study."

"Vi's not home?" Nolan hoped his voice didn't reflect relief.

Allyson's smile twisted slightly to reveal a trace of annoyance. "Oh, she's here. But she's busy with a number of other things. She asked me to take care of you."

"I'm deeply sorry about Dixon's death," Nolan said, following Allyson down a hallway to the right that skirted the parlor and ended at Dixon's study. "He was a dear friend and colleague."

Allyson's brow furrowed and she shook her head as she ushered him into the walnut-paneled room. "We knew he was having some heart issues—and he'd been cautioned to lose weight. But this was so unexpected ...."

"A real loss to us all," Nolan said awkwardly, looking about at the shelves of books and file boxes that lined three walls of the room.

"Well—I'll let you get started. Vivian asked me to give you this, and the wall safe is on the other side of the fireplace in a niche that has a bust of Constantine in it. Just put the statue on the table there ...." She indicated a side table beside a brown leather recliner and handed Nolan a slip of paper with a four number combination.

"Has anyone been through any of these things?"

"I think Vi looked in the safe. She said it has one of Dixon's research journals and an envelope. I don't think anyone else has been in here." Allyson looked quickly around the study and pulled the door closed behind her as she left. "Give me a shout if you need anything. I'll just be in the kitchen."

"Will do," Nolan said absently, examining the row of numbers in his hand.

As soon as the door closed, he found the alcove and moved the bust to the side table. The safe's door filled the entire back of the niche and with the statue covering the dial, was designed to look like a plain section of wall. Not entirely hidden, but not obvious. He followed the directions on the slip and the door swung open, revealing only a black, leather-bound notebook and a large manila envelope. Propping the notebook upright against the safe's interior wall, he carefully removed the envelope. It was closed only with a fold-over metal wing-clip.

Nolan walked to the door and pressed in the lock button below the bronze lever handle, then carried the envelope to Dixon's richly polished walnut desk. The desktop was empty except for a blotter pad and an engraved pen and pencil set with a small plaque that announced that J. Dixon Bartlett had been selected as Charles W. Lamoreau Endowed Professor of Religious Studies. Otherwise, there wasn't so much as a fingerprint. Nolan sat in the rolling chair that served the desk and pulled it forward, placing the envelope on the blotter. He was almost hesitant to open it, afraid its contents might not equal the excitement of his expectations and would again push him beneath the cloud of depression that Dixon's death had left hovering nearby. But he folded back the clasp and extracted the three sheets of paper that were its complete contents, turning each over and finding writing only on one side.

The first was on letterhead from the University of Arizona's Radio Carbon Dating Laboratory; a report on a papyrus fragment J. Dixon had submitted for analysis the previous September. Nolan scanned it quickly, noting that the fragment was identified only by catalogue number MP-12-1723 but was dated by the test to be from between 50 BCE and 100 CE. A brief footnote at the bottom of the page explained to those not familiar with international dating nomenclature that BCE referred to "Before the Common Era" and CE to "Common Era." The abbreviations were used rather than BC and AD so as not to connect the dating process to any particular religious or cultural tradition. Nolan didn't need the footnote. BCE and CE were standard among scholars of religious studies.

He set the page aside and wiped his fingers on his pant legs, feeling his palms moisten and his mouth become dry. This first page only added enticement, and if the tested fragment came from an ancient Christian manuscript, these dates placed it among the very earliest.

The second sheet was less formal—a letter from a Dr. Felix Bingham, professor at the Center for Hebrew and Semitic Studies at England's Cambridge University. It stated simply that Dr. Bingham concurred with Dixon's translation of two partial sentences that read *"peace be with you through the spirit of God and through our knowledge of the good news of our Lord, Jesus Christ. By his word I have been called ...."* Bingham noted, however, that one line from a manuscript was not much to go on when attempting to provide paleographic analysis, an assessment of a document's age and origin based on examination of the writing. The professor agreed that the script was certainly early Aramaic, and appeared from its stylistic conventions to be first century Galilean Judeo-Hebrew. A more accurate analysis might be possible if more of the script were available.

Nolan's heart rate stepped up a beat. A first century document written in Aramaic. Surely this was the proof Dixon had been promising. He glanced at the door, adjusted himself in the chair, and uncovered the bottom page.

The top portion of the third sheet contained a colored photographic image of a papyrus manuscript with all but the first four lines covered by what appeared to be a white cloth. The papyrus was ragged at the edges and yellowed over most of its surface, but the carefully formed script was fully legible. Nolan bent over the page and studied the writing. It was clearly early Hebrew and he began at the right, reading slowly across the page, then noticed that below the photograph on the bottom portion of the sheet, J. Dixon had handwritten a translation:

From Thomas, twin of our Lord Jesus in the flesh, and faithful servant in the spirit, to our brother James who ministers to the saints in Jerusalem. Peace be with you through the spirit of God and through our knowledge of the good news of our Lord, Jesus Christ. By his word I have been called ....

Below the translation was a brief note: "See pages 47 thru 81 of journal 7/10/12."

Nolan dropped the page onto the blotter and leaned back in the desk chair with an audible release of breath. "My God!" he muttered. So this was Dixon's bombshell! A manuscript attributed to Jesus' disciple Thomas and written to James, head of the church in Jerusalem, dated to the first century of the Christian era. And .... Nolan re-read the lines, translating them himself. ...and identifying Thomas as literal twin of the Christian Messiah.

"My God," he said again, shaking his head slowly as his mind struggled to get itself around what he was reading. There was an ancient Christian myth, based on references in the *Gospel of John* and the apocryphal *Acts of Thomas*, that Thomas, called *Didymos* or "the twin," was a twin of Jesus. But this assertion had been rejected as heresy from the earliest centuries of the Christian era. If this papyrus were real, an authentic first century manuscript that in its opening line affirmed Thomas' literal kinship to Jesus as his twin, this was more than a bombshell. This was a theological tsunami, bound to sweep away two thousand years of Christian doctrine!

Nolan leaned forward, again studying the photo. That was clearly what it said, *"From Thomas, twin of our Lord Jesus in the flesh ...."* He slipped his hand into the manila envelope, checking to be certain he had not missed anything. Where was the papyrus? Dixon must at least have had access to it, if able to take the photograph and obtain a fragment that could be dated. But it would be far too valuable to keep in his home. His eyes fell again on Dixon's handwritten note at the bottom of the photocopy. "See pages 47 thru 81 of journal 7/10/12."

The black notebook was still leaning against the wall of the safe. Nolan retrieved it and returned to the desk, examining the leather cover as he crossed the room. It displayed no title, date, or inscription. He glanced again at the locked door, sat in Dixon's leather chair, and carefully opened the journal. The first page was blank except for an abbreviated date – 7/10/12 – and the location, "Kerala, India." This was obviously the volume referenced by the note and Nolan flipped through it, searching for page 47.

J. Dixon had started each day's entry on a new page and page 46 was dated *July 27, 2012*. As if shielding it from prying eyes, Nolan looped an arm around the notebook and crouched over it, starting at the top of page 47.

Finally, after three years of working with the Disciples, they appear to have taken me into their confidence. Tomorrow I am to be ceremonially accepted into the faith, the first non-Indian, to my knowledge, to receive this honor. I have hope upon hope that this may give me access to the sacred "truths" they talk about so enticingly. I was told about one such ceremony during a visit in 2009 and it included a ritual baptism, followed by the swearing of an oath. I was not allowed to witness either, assured by Father Venkatesan that the reason for the exclusion was not that the ritual or oath was secret, but sacred, and should not be profaned by sharing it with those outside the faith. It is a fascinating example of the constant interplay between the secret and the sacred, and I must remember to suggest an exploration of this relationship to one of my graduate students. A topic worthy of a dissertation ....

Bartlett had not made an entry on the 28th, but the first words on the page for July 29th indicated that Dixon had been through the ceremony.

I am now numbered among the Disciples, and though I have taken an oath not to reveal what I have learned, I must write it here for the sake of my failing memory. I admit that I feel a bit disingenuous, having professed a belief in the true apostolic calling of Didymos

Thomas and in the divine nature of Jesus of Nazareth. I am not certain that I fully accept either—but neither can I reject them—so I have chosen to profess a belief to see how I can further knowledge about this fascinating sect. Though I know their faith in Thomas is something akin to the strongest manifestations of Mariology, I could not have guessed at its origins. I am completely stunned at what I have learned and have been promised that this is only the beginning of a new personal enlightenment. But first things first ....

Nolan noticed that the hand that rested on the desk had curled into a tight fist and he consciously tried to relax, feeling the telltale flush in his face that signaled climbing blood pressure. He stretched his back, drew a couple of slow, deep breaths, and returned to the journal.

The baptism was simple and followed the practices of the early church to immerse. I was given white clothing and taken to a small, non-descript church in the hills north and west of the city of Coimbatore, inland from Kochi on the other side of the Western Ghats. The church is built against the hillside and behind its sanctuary, additional rooms are carved right into the rock cliff. Within one of these rooms is a stone baptismal font, also carved into the living rock and measuring about a meter and a half square and of the same depth. I was taken down into the water, but rather than a single prayer and single baptism, I was immersed first in the name of the Father, then again in the name of the Son, and a third time in the name of the Holy Spirit. As I prepared to climb from the font, the priest continued again and baptized me in the name of the Tumha Tanaya, the "Second Son!" I was so stunned that I was unable to speak, but Father Venkatesan simply nodded knowingly and instructed me to dry myself and get changed.

Nolan rocked back in the chair and locked the fingers of both hands behind his head. Dixon had never said a word about this initiation. They had talked about aspects of his research in India almost daily since his return and he'd never mentioned the baptism. Why would he keep something this uniquely interesting to himself? Nolan hunched back over the journal.

Some fifteen members of the Disciples were present, mostly older men. After changing, I rejoined them in the room that held the baptistery where they formed a circle around me, each placing his right hand on my shoulder, back, or chest. I was instructed to repeat after the Priest and pledged upon penalty of death never to reveal what I was about to be told. Once this pledge was made, I repeated a liturgy in which I accepted my new position among the Disciples of Thomas and in so doing, acknowledged him as Jesus' twin—not born as mortal—but sharing in his divine nature. I acknowledged that as second-born, Thomas did not inherit the birthright to the Throne of David, but a position of giving service to his brother and Lord—a service that Thomas did not fully understand until he saw with his own eyes the risen Lord and felt of his wounds. The Priest instructed me, and I professed knowledge, that in later meetings with the resurrected Jesus, Thomas was told that he also possessed power over death. The liturgy ended with a declaration that Thomas still lives and has never tasted death. As a Disciple, I pledged to keep this sacred knowledge in trust so that the world might not profane this truth or seek to expose the Second Son while he continues his earthly mission. I have been promised that tomorrow I will see what the Disciples call the akaca apadisa, or "pure witness." I am still trying to fathom what I have been told. It cannot, of course, all be true. But it brings new credulity to early suggestions that Thomas was, in fact, the twin of Jesus, and may have been privy to information that was not shared with the other disciples, as suggested in Thomas' Gospel. Absolutely incredible!

Nolan leaned on his elbows and gazed in astonishment through the study window. "Incredible indeed!" he said under his breath. As a variant of doctrine, Dixon's discovery was even more unsettling than Nolan had imagined. According to what the journal said about the Disciples' beliefs, rather than negating the divine birth of Jesus, Thomas shared in it! Nolan knew of the early scriptural references to Thomas as a twin, but both were silent about whom he was brother to. But if Nolan remembered correctly ....

He scanned the study's shelves until he found a section labeled *Nag*

Hammadi and pulled a book containing a collection of the ancient Coptic writings from among two dozen volumes Bartlett had cataloged under the heading. If there was a piece of early Christian history where Nolan approached expertise, it was Gnosticism, the early mystical variant to Christian orthodoxy. The name Gnostic came from the Greek word for knowledge, *gnosis*, and covered a variety of early Christian philosophies that shared beliefs that the material world was essentially evil and corrupting, and that salvation came through gaining secret knowledge that could free the soul from the shackles of this mortal life. Jesus was often seen by the Gnostics as God appearing in the semblance of a physical being to impart the *gnosis*, the secret knowledge required to free humankind from the temporal world. And the writings found at Nag Hammadi formed the core of surviving Gnostic literature.

Nag Hammadi was a city in upper Egypt where in 1945, a year before discovery of the Dead Sea Scrolls, a collection of earthen jars was uncovered containing some of Christianity's earliest writings—scripture that remains relatively unknown because it was declared heresy by the early Christian fathers. To the degree they were able, leaders of the "orthodox" church during the first four centuries destroyed every Gnostic record, but the hidden collection of Nag Hammadi survived the purge.

Nolan turned to the index of the volume he had selected and found the page numbers for *The Book of Thomas the Contender,* thumbing quickly through the text until he found the book. The preface explained that *Thomas the Contender* was purportedly written by the disciple Matthias who overheard a conversation between Thomas and Jesus while walking with the brothers. Nolan found the passage he was looking for in the third paragraph in which Jesus said to Thomas:

Now, since it has been said that you are my twin and true companion, examine yourself and learn who you are, in what way you exist, and how you will come to be.

"Amazing," Nolan muttered. "This is *Da Vinci Code* all over again!" Evidence that the conviction of the Indian Disciples could be true—that Jesus had a mortal twin who shared in his divinity. He left the book open and looked back at Dixon's journal. Where was the manuscript? And what did it say beyond those enticing opening lines? Surely Dixon wouldn't have entrusted something that valuable to his house safe .... As he turned the page to the journal entry for July 30, the doorknob rattled and Nolan jumped from the desk, hurrying to unlatch it. Allyson March stepped into the study and looked at him curiously.

"Are you needing to keep the door locked?"

"Habit," Nolan said. "When I'm working in my own study, I always lock the door to keep from being disturbed."

"What did you find in the safe?"

"It's actually turning out to be pretty useful. Dixon and I were working on a joint project related to his work in India and the envelope contained some of the documentation I didn't have copies of."

"That merited being locked in his safe ...?"

"Original copies. If they were to get lost, it would set our research back until we could get to India again and make new ones."

"You probably should have copies of your own—for just this kind of eventuality."

"Just what I was thinking .... Do you need some help with something?"

"No. Just seeing how things were coming along. I have some bagels and cream cheese out here. Do you want anything? Coffee?"

"Ate just before I came," he said. "I'll give you a holler if I need anything."

She backed out of the room, pulling the door closed behind her. Nolan left it unlocked and quickly returned to the desk and Bartlett's entry for July 30.

This day has surpassed the last in excitement and mystery! I was taken again by the elders to the small church near Coimbatore. During this journey, I paid closer attention to the building and was struck by how intentionally non-descript it is. There is little to distinguish it from the row of simple homes that press against the stone face of the hillside in a tiny village I would guess to be no more than seven or eight kilometers from the city. As we entered this time, I noted that the chapel is a rectangular room that runs parallel to the rock face and that the room containing the baptistery is actually cut back into the rock. In the rear corner of the room, behind one of a number of ornate screens that I had taken the night before to be purely decorative, was a thick plank door with a heavy iron lock that opened still farther into the hillside. Beyond this door was a passage about twenty paces long that made a sharp right turn halfway along its length. We entered the passage using electric head lamps strapped about our foreheads and at its other end came to another hefty wooden door, similarly locked.

As we proceeded along the passage, I noticed a marked drop in temperature and humidity from the outside, which is already much cooler and drier than the coastal plain around Kochi. Here, the Western Ghats siphon moisture from the air as clouds cross the mountains, leaving this area semi-arid. The distance into the hillside further dried and cooled the air until I was chilled without a jacket. Father Venkatesan unlocked the inner room with a key suspended from his waist on a tether and we entered by the light of the head lamps. As far as I could tell, there was no other source of light in the room.

As Nolan turned the page, he felt the flush deepen in his cheeks and his heart rate quicken to the point of thumping in his chest. He was hunched over the journal like a starving man over a bowl of warm soup, unable to eat fast enough to satisfy his hunger. He moistened his lips, glanced at the unsecured door, and scooped again into the bowl that was Dixon's journal.

In the center stood a stone dais, carved from the rock with a square depression cut into its top. This space held a shallow rectangular box that appeared to be made of fired, but unglazed earthenware. As we entered, four of the five accompanying elders stayed outside, but pointed their lights into the room, and Father V accompanied me into the chamber. He asked that I remain by the door while he removed a stone cap, then the inset top from the earthenware box, and laid a light linen cloth across much of what the box contained. He then invited me to step forward. The box was lined with a dried plant matting of some kind that I was later informed absorbs moisture, as does the unglazed clay of the box. The papyrus pictured in the photograph was lying on the mat, partially covered by the cloth. A few small fragments have separated from the edges but otherwise it is in remarkably good condition. Father V gave me a pair of cotton gloves, said that I could touch the sides of the box but not the papyrus, and asked that I not remove the cloth from the lower part of the manuscript. "We will tell you what it says," he said. I asked if I could study it for a few moments and he allowed me the time, going to the door to speak with the other elders.

As I read the text my entire body began to tremble! This was beyond imagination and was made all the more incredible by the fact that it was in Aramaic and on papyrus rather than palm leaves, which would have been the traditional medium for early Indian Tamil writings. I was able to regain my composure long enough to slip my cell phone from my shirt pocket and with my head lamp lighting the manuscript, quickly photograph the papyrus as the elders visited. Then (forgive me, my anthropologist colleagues!) I wet a gloved fingertip and, with hands along the side of the box, touched and retrieved one of the small fragment pieces that had moved to the edge of the container. This went back into my shirt pocket with the phone. I know that I was violating the elder's trust and every rule of preserving fragmentary evidence, but I do not intend to reveal the contents of the box—only to determine its authenticity. The priest gave me a few minutes to translate what portion of the script I could see, though I should be able to render a better translation after I get the photograph.

When I had been allowed to study the papyrus for about five minutes, Father Venkatesan returned to me, withdrew the cloth, and again covered the box. We joined the rest of the group who had moved to the outer chapel and I was asked if I had questions. My brain was swimming, but I first asked about the content of the rest of the letter and why they kept it covered. Father V explained that the remainder, addressed to James, revealed that Thomas did initially doubt the divine nature of his brother Jesus and did not fully accept the Lord's power over death until he saw the risen Christ and felt of his wounds. It was then revealed to him in conversations with the resurrected Lord that he, too, shared this power and would not taste of death until he chose to give up his life. These, apparently, were the three secret truths Thomas referred to in the Gospel of Thomas, when he wrote that Jesus "took him and withdrew and told him three things." Thomas then told the other disciples, "If I tell you one of the things he told me, you will pick up stones and throw them at me; and a fire will come out of the stones, and burn you up." The Kerala manuscript reveals those three "truths": that Thomas shared in the divine nature as the Second Son, that he was not subject to death until a time of his choosing, and that in him, the light and the life of the world would remain on earth until the Master returns. These truths always remain covered, Father V explained, because of their sacred nature.

The food served up by Dixon's journal was almost too rich for Nolan's starving stomach. He rocked back in the chair, breathing heavily, and tried to digest what he had just consumed. The twinship of Jesus. A shared divine nature in the Second Son. An explanation of the cryptic statements in the *Gospel of Thomas* about three secret truths. Dixon's announcement would indeed have rocked the religious world— if this letter could be authenticated.

He returned to the journal.

I asked where the letter had been written and when told it was written in Kerala by Thomas, asked how it came to be on papyrus and why it hadn't been delivered. One of the five, the youngest among the "elders,' explained that Thomas had either carried papyrus and ink with him or obtained it from merchants who frequented the coast from ports along the Arabian Peninsula. A courier had attempted to deliver the letter, but found James to have been martyred in Jerusalem and, instructed not to give the letter to anyone else, returned with it to Kerala. By the time the messenger returned, Thomas had departed and his followers kept the letter as a sacred testament to his teachings and holy nature.

I expressed my dismay that the keepers of such an incredible treasure had not chosen to share it with the rest of the world! If the manuscript could be validated as first century, its contents would be the most important Christian revelation since the appearance of Jesus to his followers after his death.

"But to what end?" one of the elders asked. Thomas apparently

acknowledged in the letter that as second born, he inherited no birthright to the Kingdom, acceding that to his brother whom he recognized as lineal King by being firstborn. To announce to the world that there is a second divine son and that he may still be living to await the return of his Lord is to invite first ridicule, then a frantic effort either to validate or dispute the letter. And finally a worldwide hunt would begin for the remaining son of God in the flesh.

"And it would do little to change doctrine," the youngest elder observed. "Most people would go on believing as they do, but thousands would flock here with a desire to become part of our group—just as they do to every new Saint or Messiah. That is not what we, nor our leader Thomas, would wish for his disciples."

Nolan turned the page but found only two brief sentences on the following sheet.

I am so overwhelmed with what I have seen and heard that I must wait to say more. When I have had an opportunity to authenticate the manuscript, perhaps I will know what I must do.

Nolan thumbed through a few more pages and found them blank. From Dixon's announcement before his death, he must have decided to make his discovery public but write no more about it in the journal. Not surprising. An announcement like this would have made J. Dixon Bartlett the most celebrated religious scholar in... in the world! But now, Dixon was dead and only the Disciples of Thomas—and Nolan Lemay—knew the secret. And Nolan had taken no oath.

CHAPTER THREE

Marcus Branscomb had two consuming passions: early Christian history and football. On this particular Sunday afternoon he was combining them by watching a muted Bears-Lions game on his iPad, a Rams-Saints game on one of his computer screens, while running a computer-generated textual comparison of two early Tamil texts on the other. When Marcus was ten, his mother's religious faith had temporarily been bruised by a lecturer who had assured her that the *Epistle to the Ephesians* could not have been written by the hand of the Christian apostle Paul. Since that day, Marcus had been consumed by understanding who had written what parts of the New Testament and how anyone could determine such a thing two thousand years after the fact.

His mother's bruising had occurred one sweltering August afternoon in a lecture hall at Phillips Community College in Helena, Arkansas, just a few days after Marcus' tenth birthday. He and his mother lived in a small prefab house on Adams Street, one step above a double-wide trailer, just north of Helena's downtown riverfront and within spitting distance of the levee that separated the community from the Mississippi River. His father had died in an accident at the tire factory when Marcus was four, and Gloria Branscomb promised that she would give her only son all the opportunities that seemed to elude so many other black children growing up in the Delta. To her, that meant education, and when Gloria Branscomb set her mind to something, it usually happened. She enrolled him in Helena's KIPP Delta College Prep charter school where he soon led his class, and whenever the local community college offered special lectures, she and Marcus walked the mile and a half to the campus to listen to the presentation.

This particular guest lecturer, a professor of religious studies from Claremont College in California, was discussing textural criticism of early Christian writings as part of the college's New Horizons Lecture Series. Gloria returned home shaken to the core by the professor's claim that half of the letters attributed to Paul did not stand up to critical examination for authenticity when vocabulary, use of idioms, sentence structure, and common phrases were compared with letters known to have been penned by the great Christian missionary.

"I just don't know what to think," she muttered during the forty-five minute walk home. "It's just more than a body can fathom. How can a person come to know such a thing?" Marcus decided that evening that he would try to find out.

As he now glanced at the scores of the two NFL games and watched the latest version of his personally-designed computer program run a beta test, he knew that he was doing exactly what he had dreamed of doing since that day—other than becoming a pro football player. But his college years had demonstrated that he was a better scholar of ancient languages than wide receiver. He now enjoyed his one love vicariously by watching the on-field heroics of Calvin Johnson, while he compared textual elements from two early Christian treatises written 150 years apart in the south Indian language of Tamil.

It wasn't that Marcus lacked the tools of a great wide receiver. At 6'6" and 230 pounds of lean muscle, he had been accepted as a walk-on by the Tar Heels of North Carolina. But the rigors of leading his class at the KIPP charter school had kept him out of high school football, and on the practice fields at Chapel Hill, he simply couldn't compete with the more experienced college recruits. But he learned quickly that even for a young black man raised in the Arkansas Delta, the NFL didn't hold the country's only draft. The innovative textual comparison models in Greek and Aramaic he developed as an undergraduate student in Religious Studies positioned Marcus as one of the most sought after graduate student recruits in the country. After personal visits from distinguished professors from Dartmouth, Stanford and Berkeley, he had chosen the master's program at Duke. Two years later, Dr. J. Dixon Bartlett recruited him to AMU for doctoral work, much as he might have recruited a wide receiver—visiting his home in Arkansas to talk personally with his mother. Much to Marcus' embarrassment, Gloria Branscomb had pulled a copy of a letter of recommendation from one of Marcus' North Carolina professors out of a drawer and walked Dr. Bartlett through it line-by-line.

"And this is the most important part," she concluded, pointing to a sentence she had underlined in the final paragraph. "He tells you right here that 'Marcus is one of the nicest young men you could ever ask to meet.' Now, if he goes away to your university, when he comes back, that's the part I don't want to change."

Dr. Bartlett had assured her that if he attended AMU, Marcus would remain a 'nice young man,' and the Professor could assure her son opportunities that wouldn't be afforded him anywhere else. Bartlett had delivered on his promises.

During his first summer at the university, Marcus had accompanied his advisor to southern India. While the distinguished professor researched a small sect called the Disciples of Thomas, Marcus studied Tamil and Pali, the ancient languages of southern India, and worked on a model to date early Indian writings. But now J. Dixon Bartlett was dead.

One of the perks of working with Bartlett had been a small office of his own, deep in the bowels of the building that housed Religious Studies. Marcus now sat with his back to the open door, listening to water gurgle in the exposed pipes overhead and watching one of two computer screens on his desk begin to display the words, phrases, and expressions that appeared differently in the two Tamil manuscripts. The computer also analyzed changes in spellings of the same words and differences in letter formation as the language evolved over a century and a half. By examining a series of texts from the same two periods he could determine if a change was common, or simply the unique style of an individual writer. He was beginning to compile a small dictionary of stylistic conventions that typified both eras and saw in the project the beginnings of a very promising doctoral dissertation and scholarly career. As he leaned forward to select the print command to copy the pages of description, he heard footsteps at the door and turned to find Professor Nolan Lemay leaning against the door jamb. Marcus quickly clicked "print" and stood to meet his visitor.

"Doctor Lemay. Come on in." He lifted a sheaf of printouts from a chair and pushed them onto a corner of his army green metal desk.

Lemay was eight inches shorter than the graduate student and appeared to Marcus to feel the difference as he entered the room. The professor was of average build, but beginning to show the effects of a sedentary academic life about his mid-section. He had a longish straight nose, strong chin, and bright hazel eyes, with thinning brown hair combed straight back from a high forehead to cover a balding spot on his crown. Marcus thought his face always showed the flush of a man who drank or worried too much.

Lemay pushed away from the door frame and stood for a moment, glancing up at the exposed plumbing in the basement room and sizing up the towering graduate assistant whose head seemed almost to reach the pipes. Then he turned to the printer and watched it list the number of times a specific Tamil symbol was used in the text, with variations in the ways it was shaped. After a moment of awkward silence he moved to the chair and sat a little too stiffly to appear comfortable.

"Looks like an interesting study," he said, smiling casually. "One of the Indian languages, isn't it?"

Marcus glanced over at the humming printer, then back at his guest. He couldn't remember Lemay ever visiting the basement office or expressing any particular interest in his work.

"Yes, sir. Tamil. I'm running a textual comparison of works done in the late twelfth and early fourteenth centuries."

"Just why I'm here," Lemay said. "Terrible thing about Doctor Bartlett's death. He was a good man and a great colleague." He paused awkwardly. "But I was wondering what you plan to do now that Doctor Bartlett is no longer here to work with you."

Marcus settled back against a corner of his desk. Lemay's visit during the same week as his mentor's death took him a little off-guard.

"I'm having a hard time getting used to the idea that Doctor Bartlett is gone. He was a great advisor and very good to me ...."

Lemay flushed a shade deeper. "I understand completely. We were very close friends and I know he thought highly of you. He would want you to be well cared for by the department."

 Marcus shrugged. "It puts me in an awkward spot. I've completed my coursework, so it would be hard to move somewhere else without having to repeat a lot. But I want to continue this research and need to find someone with Doctor Bartlett's expertise."

"Well, I've had some similar thoughts. I'm very familiar with Dixon's work and could offer you an assistantship equivalent to what he was providing ...."

Marcus sat further back against the metal desktop and smiled nervously. "I appreciate that Doctor Lemay, but I'm hoping to find an advisor who's a recognized specialist in the Christian community in India."

Lemay nodded. "I understand, but as you know, there aren't many.

I'm considering continuing Doctor Bartlett's work in Kerala. My area of specialization is Gnosticism and though this would take me in a somewhat different direction, it's certainly related. Before his death, Dixon invited me to join him in one particular bit of his research that I plan to continue, and I could extend some of the same opportunities he was giving you. I have a sabbatical coming up in the spring and plan to spend it in the region where you were working with Doctor Bartlett last summer. I'd be happy to have you work with me there and perhaps you can become that new expert on the Thomas Christians."

Marcus studied the professor for a long moment, running a 'replay' in his head about what he had heard about Lemay. Students joked about his "uniform": the short-sleeved blue shirt with button-down collar, khakis, brown slip-on shoes—and the ever-present blue Carolina Panthers ball cap. Lemay didn't wear the cap to class, but always sported it when walking across campus or sitting at his desk. One of the other African-American students in the program, a first-year doctoral student from New Orleans, always referred to Lemay as "The Cat in the Hat."

Marcus had taken Lemay's Gnostic Literature course and found it interesting and challenging. But Lemay was viewed by most of the grad students as being a bit too casual; a decent lecturer, but not an impressive scholar. His advisees felt he treated them with benign neglect and let them do pretty much what they wished. Not what Marcus had in mind in a mentor.

"I can make this worthwhile for you," Lemay said, seeming to read his thoughts. He stood to look more closely at the computer printout. "I'll cover your graduate tuition for the semester, pay your expenses to accompany me to Kerala, including travel and accommodations, and give you a monthly stipend of $1000. I doubt you'll find an arrangement like that anywhere else."

Marcus' brow arched involuntarily. "Hmmm. That's *very* generous." He knew the professor was right. This went well beyond generous. "What would you want from me as your assistant while we're working there? And would the department approve expenses like that?"

"Some of this would come out of personal funds ... and as for expectations, I would primarily be looking for translation assistance every now and then. I know nothing about Tamil or Pali. But you could spend most of your time working on whatever research you wish. I'm anxious to keep you in the department."

"I'll definitely give this some thought," Marcus said. "When do you need to know?"

Lemay turned back toward the door. "I'm feeling some urgency about this and am starting to make travel arrangements. Can you let me know within a week?"

Marcus nodded. "That sounds fair enough. I need to decide for my own planning anyway. And thanks for the offer—one way or the other."

"Very good then." Lemay paused awkwardly and shook Marcus' hand, then eased sideways out of the room.

"Interesting guy," Marcus mused. One of the attractions of this offer was that if Lemay took him back to India, then showed that same benign neglect, Marcus might have all the time he wanted to work on his own projects. And who knew? Maybe he could do something to turn the professor into that scholar his students deserved.

CHAPTER FOUR

Regina Lamoreau Lemay was less than enthusiastic about Nolan's plan. She listened half-heartedly without looking away from her television program about the homes of the rich and famous until he mentioned India. Then she punched the 'off' button on the remote and looked at him sourly.

"You can't be serious."

"I'm very serious."

"Why India? I thought we were going to use your sabbatical to lease a villa in Italy."

"A sabbatical's supposed to be used to further my research, not take a vacation. And while I was going through Dixon's papers I came across something that looks like it could have real promise ...."

"Since when did you become serious about research?" Regina smirked. "Til now, if one of your grad students didn't do the legwork, it didn't get done. Or is that colored boy going to take care of that for you?" She leaned back on the settee and studied him with that look Nolan occasionally thought was begrudging admiration, but usually read as disgust.

"I wish you wouldn't say 'colored.' It's disrespectful."

She ignored him and reactivated the wide-screen above the fireplace. "So you're taking over Dixon's ideas and his graduate assistant. Where are you going to find his energy and intellect?" There was no mistaking the tone this time. It was disgust.

"I just hadn't found something that really excited me before," he said. "This does."

"Good to see you get excited about something," she muttered. "But if you're going to India, you're going alone. The place is so ... *dirty*."

"I didn't know you'd had experience with India," he shot back, trying to regain some element of self-respect. "It's one of the oldest civilizations in the world—and has one of the earliest Christian communities."

"Well ... there are Christians, and then there are *Christians*. And Vivian tells me it's overrun with urchins tugging at your sleeve and animals wandering loose in the streets. And it's infernally hot ...."

"Charlotte's hot. And what does Vivian know about India? She didn't ever go with Dixon."

"That's why," she said, as if it settled everything. "And you'll be going alone too if you choose India. I may lease a villa in Italy anyway and take Vivian with me. Who knows what kind of fun we might have while you're pretending to be a scholar."

"It'll take some money," he said, trying not to sound pleading.

She again clicked off HGTV. "My villa, or your research?"

"My salary will cover living expenses, but I need to cover support for Mr. Branscomb and may have access to some valuable texts—possibly make some purchases."

She looked at him coolly, the smirk curving into a frown. "How much are we talking about?"

He straightened and swallowed the lump that was rising in his throat. "I'd like to have access to a hundred thousand. One-fifty would be better. This could be a career-maker for me."

The frown curled back to openly display her disdain. "You are pathetic. We essentially bought your position and now you think you can buy a career. How is this going to work? You're going to pay the colored boy or some Indians to write something scholarly for you?"

"I may not need it at all," he said, feeling his back again begin to slump and realizing that contempt had become their single shared emotion. "But if the right manuscripts become available, I want to be in a position to make an offer. And that much money is nothing to you. Think of it as paying for three months during which you can do whatever you damn well please."

She arched her thinly penciled brows and feigned new interest. "Now, there's something to be said for that! So you're set on this India thing?"

He nodded. "It's the best opportunity I've had while I've been here."

Regina turned the set back on and watched silently as some young actress showed the television crew through her home in Malibu and out onto a veranda overlooking the Pacific.

"Look at that view!" she muttered absently, then turned back to Nolan. "You have your account. Won't that cover things?"

"There's not enough in it."

"Then when you leave, I'll add some money. But my accountant will want a careful record. If you use it as you say, it should all be a deductible business expense."

"I won't touch it unless I absolutely have to," he said, feeling his spine collapse the rest of the way.

.   .   .

The lab report on Dr. Nisha Pillai's desk both frightened and confused her. Though she worked in general practice, her advanced medical education was as an internist and she tried to stay current. When she saw the raindrop-patterned discoloration on Jaya Muduva's palms and on the soles of her feet, she thought immediately of an article she had read by Dr. G.N. Guha Mazumder, a medical researcher in Kolkata. He reported the same pattern on villagers suffering from arsenic poisoning from contaminated water in Bangladesh. The lab report that sat in front of Nisha was on Jaya's hair and nails and confirmed her suspicion. Her patient was suffering from arsenic poisoning and might already be running out of time.

The confusion came from the fact that Jaya wasn't alone. For the past week, Nisha had puzzled over an array of symptoms that were showing up in four of her patients without explanation: vomiting, diarrhea, dizziness and signs of anemia, accompanied by debilitating fatigue. In the two years she had served as the only doctor in this remote village in Kerala's Palakkad District, she hadn't seen anything like it. She ran the standard blood, urine and fecal tests, checked calcium and albumin levels, kidney function, and levels of immunoglobulin. But when Jaya Muduva arrived at the clinic from her village that bordered the Parambikulam Wildlife Sanctuary with raindrop hyperkeratosis on her palms and feet, Nisha thought she knew the answer. She clipped samples of Jaya's hair and nails, drove to Coimbatore, and sent them overnight to a diagnostic lab in Gurgaon. The results confirmed heavy levels of inorganic arsenic in the woman's tissue—higher than the levels that had prompted the water studies in Bangladesh. India had its own arsenic hotspots—places where the poisonous element occurred naturally in ground water. But none were in Kerala and she didn't remember any in the bordering province of Tamil Nadu. Since the poisoning wasn't limited to one patient or household, this wasn't contamination from some household item or a crude attempt at domestic homicide.

Nisha found a collapsible tripod for holding intravenous fluids in her supply closet and put some empty sample jars, two units of O+ blood and a solution of dimercaprol in a cooler, then changed quickly into blue jeans and a grey Sunkam Clinic T-shirt. Leaving the clinic in the hands of her nurse, she strapped the tripod and cooler to the back of her new Suzuki Hayate motorcycle and headed south toward the Muduva village. Jaya lived in a small collection of huts on the northern edge of the wildlife sanctuary and most of the road to her single-room shack was a rutted dirt track. The bike had been purchased for just this kind of travel—and because Nisha loved the rush of opening the Suzuki up on the paved roads between Kochi and Sunkam. Even during the soaking heat of summer, there was something soothing about feeling the wind whistle against her streamlined red helmet and press her shirt against her body.

It was a jarring thirty minute ride to the cluster of wooden and corrugated metal shanties that lined the washed-out gravel path that ran through the hillside village. She dismounted beside the shallow ditch in front of Jaya's door, stretched the cramps out of her back, and walked the bike across a narrow plank footbridge. Propping the Suzuki against the wall of the shack, she slipped her helmet over the handlebars and cast a threatening glance at two gangly young boys playing in the dirt between houses who ran over to inspect the shiny silver bike.

"Fifty rupees to each of you if you watch this while I'm visiting," she said. The boys nodded and took their posts on either side of the bike, stroking its smooth cowling and black leather seat as Nisha unloaded the cooler and fluids stand.

Kerala was one of India's most prosperous states but it still amazed Nisha that so many people, particularly those indigenous to these hill villages, continued to scrape a subsistence living out of the rainforest and small garden patches in the remote rural highlands. There had been tremendous pressure on local villagers to preserve the forest through production of non-wood products, but for many families that meant small plots of yams, ragi or rice, and hand-made crafts peddled to tourists who visited the wildlife sanctuary. The shanties that lined the narrow path were over-hung by coconut palms and most had small garden plots of carefully tended cassava and sweet potatoes. A spindly cashew tree cast a thin shadow over the door to Jaya's single-room hut and the door was open, allowing a light breeze to move through the house.

Nisha knocked on the outer wall, then stooped into the dark interior as a feeble voice called for her to enter. Jaya Muduva was stretched on a woven mat against the back wall, her head propped on a folded blanket. An old woman wearing a loose, cream-colored sari crouched beside her. Jaya's face was pasty grey and her wasted body seemed no more than a framework of bones under her own cloth wrap. Nisha murmured a greeting, then knelt beside her patient and took her frail hand.

"How are you feeling, Jaya?"

The woman smiled faintly, but didn't speak.

"She is so tired," the old woman said. "She has no husband and her children have all moved to the city. The others who are ill have family here but Jaya has no one. I try to care for her the best I can."

"The others that are ill?" Nisha asked.

The old woman nodded. "One or more in every house at this end of the village. A child in the house next to this one died last week."

Nisha sat back on her heels. "Why haven't they been to the clinic?"

"Some have been. Abjini and Balbir. But there are others."

"Balbir and Abjini live in this village?"

"In this end of the village," the old woman said. "All of the sickness is in this end of the village."

Nisha leaned forward again and gently touched Jaya's forehead. "I'll come back in a moment" she said, then turned to the old woman. "Come show me where the sick people live." She followed the woman out onto the dirt path. "Which are the homes of those who are sick?"

The old woman waved a hand in front of her, her sweep indicated a dozen shanties clustered on both sides of the path. "All of these. People are sick in all of them."

"You said 'in this end of the village.' What did you mean by that?"

The woman pointed down the path to where a shallow stream crossed as the track bent left out of sight into the trees. "Beyond the stream there is more village. Those people are not sick. But they are Malasar, not Muduva."

"You mean they are of the Malasar tribe? And the families at this end are Muduva? Don't the groups mix with each other?"

"Oh, yes," the woman said. "For some things. But the Malasar are not sick. They say that Mallung has protected them."

"Do the Malasar have their own gardens, their own pastures for their animals? Do they get their water from the same place ...?"

"We all have gardens, and our animals graze together. Each tribe has its fields of tea and rice on the hillside but they are close together. But the Malasar use the spring that comes down on that end of the village."

"And the Muduva families. Where do they get their water?" Nisha interrupted.

The woman turned and gestured back along the path in the direction Nisha had come on her bike. "There is a path just there that goes up the hill to our spring."

"Is it far?"

"Not far."

"And the spring of the Malasar? Is it far?"

"Not far," the woman said. "They both come together to make the stream."

"Let me see what I can do to help Jaya," Nisha said. "Then one of the boys can take me to the Muduva spring."

She returned to Jaya and examined her thoroughly, deciding it was too late to try chelation therapy with dimercaprol. Much of the tissue damage had already occurred and trying to draw the arsenic out of her body would be futile. She gave her two units of blood to try to rebuild her red cell count, then went back to the path with the old woman.

"Go to the other houses at this end of the village. Tell them to empty all of their tea and water and get new water from the Malasar spring."

"The water is bad?" the woman asked.

"I don't know. But we need to start there."

"The Vendari may not allow it."

"Who or what is the Vendari," Nisha asked impatiently, beckoning to one of the boys who still stood beside the Suzuki.

"The Malasar headman. He may not want the Muduva drinking from their spring."

"I will talk to him." Nisha turned to the boy. "Take me to the Malasar Vendari—then show me the Muduva spring."

CHAPTER FIVE

They decided to take the train from Mumbai, partly because Nolan had seen the film *The Darjeeling Limited* and wanted to experience India by train, and partly because Marcus thought it would be a wonderful way to see the fabled Malabar Coast. After looking over the first class car and who was in it, Nolan realized that their accommodations acquainted them with a part of train travel most Indians never experienced: a two-berth air-conditioned compartment. The dining car was filled with Europeans: older French and Belgian couples on their way to Goa as part of a rail package. As for the Malabar Coast, it was as exotic and exquisite as it had been described—beaches lined with colorful fishing boats, and nets suspended on long, tripod poles; thick-shouldered water buffalo with hand-carved wooden yokes, pulling single-bladed plows across emerald fields of rice; rainforests rising away from the coast into a mist that gave the distant hills the appearance of floating on a vaporous sea.

Nolan also wanted the time on the train to decompress before reaching Kochi. Regina had ramped the level of her sarcasm up a notch over the past two months, seemingly intent on sending him off completely emasculated. His only reprieve had been that she and Vivian *had* taken a villa south of Naples and left the week before he and Marcus departed. Nolan had dutifully taken her to the airport and was spared the embarrassment of her choosing not to see him off. And to a degree, the train had served its purpose. Passing through this fascinating country without her—knowing he was experiencing it and she was not—gave Nolan the first glimmer of independence he had felt in a long time.

But the twenty-seven hour journey helped Nolan understand why Indians who could afford first class train accommodations generally chose to fly. The constant sway and the hypnotic click-clack of the wheels against steel rails created a kind of monotonous stupor that eventually made even the scenery seem much the same. Somewhere after passing Goa, Marcus began complaining of stomach cramps and was soon dashing from the compartment to the WC at the end of the car. After the third trip, he didn't return for twenty minutes and Nolan balanced his way down the swaying corridor to the lavatory door and knocked hesitantly.

"Everything okay in there?"

The door eased open and Marcus leaned out, shook his head miserably, and looked down the aisle of the car.

"Does someone need the toilet?" He looked remarkably pale for a man with chocolate skin.

"I don't think so. I was just worried about you."

"I don't dare leave. If someone else gets in here and I have to go, I'll be in big trouble." He smiled sheepishly. "Must have eaten something that didn't sit well. Maybe the salad. I knew better, but it just looked so good."

"I think it was the shrimp," Nolan muttered. "I had the salad but I don't like shrimp. Only you had shrimp."

Marcus nodded absently then bent forward, lifted an apologetic hand, and snapped the door closed. After nearly an hour he returned to the sleeper.

"Nothing left in me," he said. "But I'd better not eat anything. I'm still feeling pretty punky."

"I got you a lemon soda from the dining car. You might give that a try."

Marcus sipped at it gratefully. "Thanks. That does feel better."

While Marcus had been in the toilet, Nolan spent the hour wondering what he was going to do when they reached the Kerala Province's city of Kochi. He had been in touch with Dixon's principal research contact, a Dr. Eldho Pillai, who had offered to meet them and introduce him to important members of the Nasrani, the St. Thomas Christian community in the Kerala region. Nolan knew he would have to show interest in the broader group, but he needed to connect as quickly as possible with this sect that called itself the Disciples—needed to find out where this manuscript was, and how he might be able to get to it. It had taken Bartlett years to gain the confidence of the Disciples and Nolan had only until mid-August. And he had no plan. What he did have was money, and Nolan worked on the principle that in the right hands, money could make up for a lot of time.

Just after 8:00 on the morning of the second day, the train slowed into the sprawling station at Ernakulan Junction in the suburbs of Kochi. What had been a double track for most of the journey spread suddenly into half a dozen lines clogged with blue passenger cars and blocky orange diesel engines, some belching clouds of black smoke into the humid June air, but most sitting idle. For the past forty-five minutes the tracks had been lined on both sides by grey corrugated metal buildings that, as they entered the station, gave way to long, narrow platforms teeming with a colorful cross-section of south Indian life: men and woman carrying bright bundles or pushing handcarts loaded with what looked like small bales of cotton; men in business suits and women in saris of every hue. Soot-stained awnings stretched to the sides of the track, shielding the crowd from the hazy morning sun. Marcus leaned uncomfortably against the window and gazed at the mass of humanity.

"I hope we can find Doctor Pillai and get inside quickly," he muttered. "I may need another bathroom."

Nolan stood as the train groaned to a stop, each car bumping into the next as the tension that had pulled them suddenly released. Marcus groaned and made his way to the open compartment door.

"I suggest we just get off and stand still," Nolan said, pulling their cases from beneath the sleeper bunks. "You'll be the only person out there who's six-six, and we'll just wait for Doctor Pillai to find us." They stepped from the train into air so warm and heavy that for a moment it took their breath away.

"My God," Nolan grimaced, removing his Panthers cap and wiping his forehead with the back of his hand. "It's like a sauna out here—and whew!" The humid air was thick with lingering diesel fumes and the sweat of men and animals, mixed with traces of baking bread and simmering curries that drifted from a small restaurant beside the platform.

Marcus frowned at him uncomfortably. "Better get used to it. I told you summer temperatures would be in the nineties and it will be humid every day through July. Then it starts to rain." He turned to look over the heads of the throng that packed the platform, then relaxed. "Here comes Doctor Pillai. Looks like we were right to just wait."

A heavy-set man with neatly-trimmed black hair greying at the temples and wearing a dark business suit pushed toward them through the crowd.

"I could find you anywhere, Marcus, my friend," the man said as he elbowed his way beside them and extended his hand to Nolan. "Doctor Pillai. But please call me Eldho. We were so sorry to learn of the death of Doctor Bartlett. He was a dear friend. But we are delighted to have you here with us, Doctor Lemay, and welcome you to Kochi. And Marcus, so good to have you back with us. Here—let me find a porter...." He turned and looked toward the station building, calling and waving to a group of men in blue coveralls who clustered beside the smoke-stained wall. Nolan noted with some surprise that in the hot sticky air that was already beginning to soak his shirt, Dr. Pillai seemed remarkably fresh.

"My car is just outside and I live only a short drive from the station," he said. "We have apartments arranged for you, but for the next few days you will be my guests. It is our custom and will give you time to get settled."

Marcus shuffled uncomfortably on the edge of the platform. "I may need to find a pharmacy. I ate something at dinner last evening that didn't agree with me ...."

"Ah, nothing more uncomfortable when traveling," Dr. Pillai said as a porter loaded their bags onto a red pushcart and used it as a plow to open a path to the station entrance. "But you are in luck. My daughter is here in the city staying with us. She is a physician and will know what you need. And there is a Chemist—what you call a pharmacy—not far from our home. We can get something after she looks at you."

"If you have family staying, we shouldn't impose," Nolan said, but Dr. Pillai waved the comment away.

"We have plenty of room. And she will want to meet you. She has a clinic in a village near Tamil Nadu and finds the languages there fascinating. Some are close to ancient Tamil." He smiled over at the tall black man. "You can discuss it while she treats your stomach."

The Pillai home was impressive, even by Charlotte standards—what Marcus would have called a mansion when he was growing up in rural Arkansas. It was a sprawling two-story white stucco manor with a pink terra cotta roof that reminded Marcus of pictures of the American southwest. It was near Jawhar Nagar Park, only a thirty minute drive from the train depot, but seemed a century removed from the industrial buildings that surrounded the station. The street on which the Pillais lived was lined with similarly impressive homes, packed together with small, beautifully manicured front lawns and narrow walks between houses that suggested that for even the wealthy, land was expensive.

Mrs. Pillai met them in the spacious central hallway in a gold-fringed blue sari, her black hair pulled into a neat roll on the back of her head. Marcus had met her before and remembered her as a quiet, elegant woman whose face seemed to bear a faint, perpetual smile that gave the impression of being completely at ease with the world. She greeted them warmly as a servant took their bags and disappeared up a wide staircase that rose to the left of the entryway.

"You may want to put on these slippers," she said, indicating a row of low shelves near the door where 'outside shoes' sat in a neat row below an equally neat row of assorted household slippers. Marcus led Nolan to the shelves, removed his shoes, and selected the largest slippers from the rack.

"This will be the custom in every home," he whispered to the professor. "Sometimes no slippers. Just socks."

Mrs. Pillai led them through a door into a formal sitting room where another maid was arranging small plates of English biscuits, cashews, and what looked like small petit' fours around a rose-patterned porcelain tea service. As they entered, a young woman in black pants and a white silk blouse rose to meet them.

"My daughter—the other Doctor Pillai," Mrs. Pillai said with obvious pride. "She is here for a few days and has been looking forward to meeting you"

"Nisha," the young woman said, extending her hand first to Nolan. "How nice to be here when you arrived. And you must be Marcus ...." She came only to his shoulder and looked up at him with a direct curiosity that made him feel the blood rise in his face.

"Yes, ma'am. That would be me," he said awkwardly. She was slim-figured with a pretty round face and short, stylishly-cut black hair that was parted in the middle and pulled back to partly cover her ears. But to Marcus, she seemed all eyes—large, dark, beautiful eyes that seemed to smile with the same contented assurance he had seen in her mother.

"Please—sit and have some tea." She indicated a long floral-patterned sofa. "I understand you are a specialist in languages and I would like to hear more about your studies."

"He had something on the train that disagreed with him," her father interrupted. Before he eats anything, you may want to suggest something that will settle his stomach."

Nisha seemed to switch immediately from hostess to doctor and took Marcus' arm, steering him toward a door that led deeper into the house.

"Let's go into the kitchen and I'll see what I can find. Please excuse us, Doctor Lemay. Enjoy some tea with Mother and Father and we will be back in just a moment."

Marcus followed her through a formal dining room and into a spacious kitchen that looked out onto a small, but equally manicured back garden of flowering bushes and expertly pruned fruit trees.

"Tell me about your symptoms," she said with a directness that added to the flush on Marcus' face. "Nausea? Diarrhea? Have you been drinking plenty of fluids?"

"All of the above ... except the drinking. A little lemon soda—but I've been afraid to put anything in my stomach. It's just coming right back up."

"And this occurred shortly after dinner?"

"Within an hour. We think it may have been the shrimp."

"Are you allergic to shrimp? Any swelling, hives or other reaction?"

"Been eating them all my life," Marcus said. "Shrimp or crawfish at least once a week since I was a boy. No allergies."

Nisha reached into a cupboard above a long counter that stretched beneath the rear windows. "I think we just need some antibiotics. If you were in the U.S. they would give you Cipro, but I have something I like better. It's Norfloxacin and is an old antibiotic that is very effective for lower GI problems. I use it because I think it may help us avoid some of the resistance we are developing to newer drugs. Take two now and one with breakfast for the rest of the week. And lots of fluids—especially in this heat. That should clear up your problem." She poured Marcus a glass of water from a large blue bottle beside the sink and handed it to him with the tablets.

He tossed them in his mouth and swallowed them with the water.

"Thank you. Whatever the doctor orders. I don't know when I've felt this miserable ...."

"Well, no sense going back in there and having to be sociable," Nisha said, leaning against the counter and shifting back into hostess mode. "Tell me about your interest in Tamil. I work in some villages east along the border with Tamil Nadu, and some of the people there still speak a form of the language mixed with Malayalam."

45

Marcus pulled his attention away from her captivating eyes and studied the rest of Nisha's face. She was pretty without being beautiful in the classic way he had seen in some Indian women. Smooth skin the color of dark honey and full, perfectly shaped lips, even without lipstick. Very nice. He returned his thoughts to her question.

"Speaking of language, your English has a touch of American influence. Did you study in the U.S.?"

"Medical school here, then a residency in internal medicine at Mayo in Rochester. You'll hear an upper-Midwest expression sneak into my speech every now and then—like, 'well, alrighty then!' And your home is in ...?"

"Eastern Arkansas in the upper Mississippi River Delta. A town called Helena—like in Montana. Ever heard of the King Biscuit Blues Festival?"

Nisha smiled and shook her head. "Don't know much about Blues. And I can only generally remember where Arkansas is in the U.S. But that seems a long way from studying classical languages."

He told her about his mother's experience with the lecture at Phillips Community College. "That got me started thinking about how experts go about deciding who wrote what, and when. But when I began working on textual criticism, I learned a lot had already been done with early Greek texts. Doctor Bartlett introduced me to some of the Tamil writings of the Thomas Christians—those early manuscripts that have survived the climate and have been hard to date. My work is in critical analysis of how languages change over time. By identifying unique language characteristics in texts that have accurately been dated in other ways, we can find those same characteristics in undated texts and determine when they were written." He smiled self-consciously and looked over her head out into the back garden. "Better not get me started on this. I could talk about it all day and you'd be bored to death."

"Oh, no," she said. "In fact, it really fascinates me. In addition to English I speak Malayalam, which probably came from early Tamil. When I visit the people in the villages I serve, I hear all kinds of variations. Some, I suspect, have been isolated for centuries and probably speak a form of Tamil that is closer to ancient Pali."

"I'd love to record them," Marcus said, thinking at the same time that he would love to have Nisha Pillai take him to the villages.

"I'm here waiting on some water tests that should be ready tomorrow. I don't know what your plans are for the next week, but you should be feeling better by morning and we keep a guest room at the clinic. If you'd like to come up with me, I would be glad to take you to some of the more remote villages. I need to get to one of them as soon as I get back anyway."

Marcus nodded. "I'd like that. I don't think Doctor Lemay has anything for me right away and said I could pretty much spend my time on the language project. I'll check with him but for now, let's plan on my going."

"Very good," Nisha said. "Now, perhaps we had better be sociable."

As Nolan sampled the tray of biscuits and sipped at his tea, he surveyed the family pictures and wall hangings that decorated the Pillai living room. Several of the photographs were of a young couple marrying in what was obviously a Christian ceremony.

"I had limited opportunity to visit with Doctor Bartlett about his work here before his death," Nolan said to Eldho Pillai. "But Marcus indicated that in addition to your academic interests, your family is Thomas Christian. I understand there are several variations in the region."

"Kochi as a whole is very diverse," his host said, setting his tea aside and smiling at his guest. "We have had a large Jewish community since before the time of Thomas—perhaps the reason he came here. And there is a shrine to the Hindu God Shiva near here that I will show you tomorrow—and in Mattancherry, a Jain temple. But yes, we belong to one of the groups of Thomas Christians and, I am proud to say, of the Malankara tradition."

Nolan nodded to indicate that he was familiar with the tradition, but could tell from Pillai's expression that the Indian guessed he was not.

"Tomorrow I will also take you to the Coonan Cross. It is an important symbol of our history. In 1599 through the Synod of Diamper, the Portuguese tried to force our ancestors to join Latin Rite Catholicism, but a group resisted and took an oath to remain aligned with the Eastern Church. Some Thomas Christians did follow the Roman Pope and among the seven million Christians in the Kerala region, there are still many Catholics. But we Malankara view ourselves as being from the purer Thomasian tradition."

Nolan nodded, this time with more confidence. "My friend Dixon was particularly taken with a group who call themselves the Disciples of Thomas. He said they consider themselves the purest of the pure."

Dr. Pillai's smile broadened. "And he was correct. My family and I are among the Disciples. Dixon was very close to us."

"From what Dixon said—and in fact wrote in his latest book—you consider Thomas to be the literal twin of Jesus and to have shared in his divine nature."

"Ah ... very true," Dr. Pillai nodded. "And that particular belief separates us from the rest of the Thomas Christians."

Nolan hadn't expected the conversation to move this quickly to the doctrines of the Disciples but his host seemed comfortable with the direction and he decided to press forward.

"I know that some of the Gnostic literature identifies Thomas as Jesus' twin, but may I ask what the Disciples base this belief upon?"

Eldho Pillai was thoughtful for a long moment. "You are familiar, I'm sure, with the *Book of Thomas the Contender* in which Thomas is referred to as Jesus' twin."

"Yes. Quite familiar."

"And these books were all declared heresy by the early Roman church and destroyed as completely as possible. But this was no more than an attempt to protect what was becoming orthodoxy, and orthodoxy was no more than the majority opinion of the emerging leaders of the church in the West. Our belief is that they were in error, and that the truth of Thomas' twin nature—both physical and spiritual—was intentionally purged from Western religious literature. It is no accident that virtually all of those early manuscripts were destroyed, and that in those that became part of the Christian canon, Thomas is referred to as 'the doubter.' The discovery at Nag Hammadi was entirely the result of some early Christians burying records they thought were important, because they knew the emerging church leadership was trying to purge them."

"Even so," Nolan observed, "this twin-ship is a rather extraordinary claim."

Dr. Pillai arched a questioning brow. "Again, extraordinary is a matter of perspective. Is believing that Jesus had a twin who shared in his divine nature more extraordinary than believing in that divine nature in the first place? Than accepting an immaculate conception, or a resurrection of the soul? One religion's 'extraordinary' is another's core belief. In our case, the divine twinness of Thomas is central to our doctrine. We believe that when the scripture states that Mary 'brought forth her first-born son,' it refers not only to Jesus being Mary's first child, but the first of twins she bore that holy night."

Eldho Pillai rose from his chair and walked to a wedge-shaped glass cabinet that stood in one corner of the sitting room. Nolan had seen cabinets like it in the homes of Charlotte's privileged, displaying expensive china, collections of porcelain figurines, and treasured knick-knacks. His host unlocked the glass door and lifted out a small mahogany chest similar to the one Regina used for her jewelry. He placed it on the coffee table in front of Nolan and unfastened a simple brass clasp.

"And Thomas left this with us," he said, raising the lid. "Like his brother, he was a carpenter and though he did not make this chest, it was made by one who passed along the traditions of his craftsmanship. It is marked here on the inside with the seal Thomas placed on all of his work—the sign of the Second Son."

Nolan leaned forward and looked at the inside of the lid where Eldho pointed. In the top left corner, carefully etched into the blood-colored wood, two fish faced each other with heads overlapped, sharing a common eye. The one on the right was sharply formed with smooth even curves, the other more roughly chiseled.

"The sign of Thomas, the Second Son," Dr. Pillai said reverently.

CHAPTER SIX

Since most foreigners and a good many Indians from the northern part of the country had trouble pronouncing his full name, Tiruchirappalli Vishwanathan Hem simply went by "Hem." His name followed the south Indian tradition of indicating the place of family origin, the family's surname and then his given name. But the tradition was rapidly disappearing, and Hem had never been one to closely follow tradition. He moved from Tamil Nadu into Kerala Province as much to get away from family as to find a better way to make a living than working in the family business. His goal in life was to avoid work altogether, and serving as a driver and guide for the American professor, Dixon Bartlett, was as close as he had managed to come to complete idleness. He was now committed to securing the same position with the new American.

Hem hung around the Department of Culture and Heritage at Cochin University of Science and Technology until he learned that a new professor was returning to India with the same tall black assistant, then followed Dr. Eldho Pillai as the Indian educator searched for apartments for his new guests. When the flat was selected, Hem had no trouble persuading the landlord to allow him to leave his business card on the kitchen counter with a brief note explaining that he had served Dr. Bartlett as driver and guide. He was available and interested in providing the same services, should the Americans need his assistance. The ploy worked as he had hoped and Dr. Nolan Lemay called Hem the day the professor moved into his new digs.

Hem was particularly relieved to find that the big black man was not with Lemay when he met with the professor at the apartment. Marcus—if he remembered his name correctly—had never trusted Hem, something Hem took as a personal insult though he knew it probably showed discerning intuition on the part of the professor's assistant. Fortunately Marcus had taken the week to visit villages in eastern Kerala with Pillai's daughter, leaving Hem to work the professor without interference.

"I know everything about Kerala," he assured Professor Lemay. "And I have connections with all the people you will want to know. If there is anything you want, I can get it for you."

This new American seemed less interested in references and past experience than Bartlett had been and hired Hem on the spot at one hundred U.S. dollars a day, for four days each week.

"Why don't we begin today and you can drive me around the city and show me the Church of St. Francis and the Santa Cruz Basilica," Lemay said. "I also understand Vasco da Gama had a home here near the Church of St. Francis. We can discuss our arrangement as we drive."

Unlike his predecessor, Lemay liked to ride in the front and seemed only moderately interested in the shrines at which they stopped. The American found the day oppressively hot and humid and wore sunglasses and a blue cap displaying a panther's head whenever they left the car, but preferred the air conditioning of Hem's Toyota. As they walked the short distance from St. Francis Church across the intersection to the Vasco House, Hem's instincts told him Lemay was in Kerala for some specific reason that hadn't yet been mentioned. Instinct also suggested that Hem would benefit from learning about this reason before Marcus returned from his stay in the villages.

"We can look in parts of the Vasco House," he said as they approached the 500 year old edifice, "but it now serves as a guest house. Mr. George won't let us look into the guest rooms if they are occupied. Generally the place is booked months in advance. But tell me, what is it specifically that you are here to research? I am certain I can find the right connections for you."

The professor stopped beside the road and studied the long white stucco house with its aged tile roof, mopped his forehead, and seemed to think it might also be good to broach the subject while the two were alone.

"I have a special interest in one of the groups Doctor Bartlett was studying—the Disciples of Thomas," he said after a moment. "He mentioned that they had a small church near Coimbatore where they held special services but when I asked Doctor Pillai about it, he seemed not to know what I was referring to. Said there was only the church here in Cochin where the group meets each Sunday. Do you know anything about this Coimbatore sanctuary?"

Hem knew nothing about the church but it was just the kind of problem he needed to solve to gain Lemay's confidence.

"The Disciples group is known to be secretive. But if there is such a place, I will learn where it is. Have you spoken to anyone about it other than Dr. Pillai?"

Lemay shook his head. "I thought if anyone knew of such a place, Doctor Pillai would—and that if it exists and he chose not to tell me about it, it would be wise not to ask more."

"Very wise, I think. But let me see what I can learn. Perhaps we can make a side arrangement on this and I will search for it on the days I am not working with you. If I find it, would it be worth another, shall we say, five hundred dollars?"

"Sounds fair to me," Lemay said with so little hesitation that Hem realized he could have asked more—and that this church was of more than casual interest to the American.

"I'll see what I can learn," he said and made a mental note to raise his prices for future services.

CHAPTER SEVEN

On the fourth day of his week with Nisha, she found what she was looking for. They were spending each morning in small villages bordering Parambikulam Wildlife Sanctuary with Nisha treating patients while Marcus recorded samples of the local language. In the afternoons they trekked in the humid heat through the forests along the northern edge of the park, looking for the source of the contaminant that was poisoning the Muduva spring and village.

The first three afternoons yielded nothing but aching muscles and soaked clothing for Marcus, and growing fear and frustration for Nisha. She amazed him with her stamina but as they struggled along one faint forest trail after another, some no more than an impression in thick, tangled undergrowth, her mood darkened.

"This has got to be coming from somewhere up among these hills," she said as they started east on the fourth afternoon, guided by one of the boys from the Muduva village. "We'll look a little farther north today— away from the park. But Pati says the paths are not as good this way. The hiking will be more difficult."

"That must mean no path at all," Marcus muttered. "And shouldn't we be worried about snakes?"

"They are more afraid of us than we are of them," she said, pushing forward without hesitation.

"They must be pretty afraid then. What kinds are there anyway?"

"Of the poisonous kind? Cobras—and what we call Malabar pit vipers. But the only people I treat for snakebite step on them when working in their fields. We'll be lucky if we even see one."

"I don't want to be so lucky," he said.

She smiled back over her shoulder. "They'll get Pati before they get you."

It was the first sign of good humor he had seen for two days and he pushed after her into the brush, the sweat already starting to trickle down his forehead and back. Monkeys chattered above them in the canopy and rather than retreating as they approached, followed them overhead as they worked their way up a densely wooded hillside. They saw no snakes and Marcus was beginning to feel reasonably safe, struggling along behind the nimble Nisha and Pati. Size, he decided, was no advantage in these forests and while Nisha and the boy slipped between dangling vines and low-hanging branches, he crashed his way along, stopping to get untangled before he could again push forward to catch up. As they paused partway up the slope for him to join them, Nisha turned again with a smile.

"Don't worry about snakes," she laughed. "Every animal within a kilometer knows you are coming."

"I hope you weren't planning to sneak up on anyone," he said dryly. "Maybe you and Pati should be doing this without me."

"Would you prefer to stay at the village?"

He shook his head, pushing his fists into the small of his back and arching backward to stretch out the cramps. "I think I make the villagers uneasy when I'm not with you. If you can put up with the noise and my speed, I like being along. But can I ask you something?"

She sat on a moss-covered rock and took a long drink from her water bottle. "Sure. Ask anything you like."

He squatted a few feet away, wiping perspiration from his eyes and neck. "The villagers seem a little nervous when they see us together. Is it because you're single and I'm staying at the clinic? I don't want to do anything that might compromise you or your work with them."

Nisha put the bottle back in the holder that looped about her shoulder and glanced at Pati who had stopped a few yards farther up the trail and didn't seem to be paying attention. "That may be part of it, but not most. You're a religious scholar. What do you know about *varna*?"

"It's the term used in some of the early Hindu texts to refer to social caste."

"Very good," she smiled. "But it essentially meant 'to sort' or 'divide by characteristics or qualities.' I don't know what you know about caste in India today, but you can often distinguish a person's caste by two characteristics—name and color. The family name can be an indication, but it is also true that the higher the caste, the lighter the skin color."

"Sounds familiar," he said, pulling up the tails of his long T-shirt to mop his forehead. "And castes still don't mix freely?"

"Much more than they used to. But less in rural areas in the South. The early Dravidians were in this part of the country and the hill peoples are their descendants—the dark people. They became the lowest caste or,

54

in some cases, the outcastes. The *Pariahs*."

"So these people are surprised to see you mixing with a dark person."

"Tradition is a powerful thing."

"Powerful enough to make you uneasy?"

Nisha shrugged. "For me, just the opposite. Just powerful and destructive enough to make me want to do something about it."

"Does your family feel that way?"

"Father, yes. Mother? Not so much. She is much more traditional."

"You mix well with the villagers and they seem very comfortable with you ministering to them ...."

"Does 'ministering to someone' strike you as suggesting equality?" she asked, her dark eyes studying him closely.

Marcus remembered how grateful and resentful he had been when he and his mother stood in line while the white Rotarians of Helena in their blue and yellow caps served them Christmas dinner. "I see what you mean," he said. "Thank you for siding with your father. You're a brave woman."

"It's not brave to do what's right. Like finding whatever's causing this pollution." She jumped back to her feet and watched with amusement as he unfolded from his squatting position. "You're also a foot taller than any of these people and they aren't sure how to classify you. So I think we're alright."

As they crested a long ridge near mid-afternoon, the impression in the undergrowth that served as a path opened suddenly onto a rough road—two worn tire tracks that wound along the ridgeline, disappearing into the trees in both directions. Nisha moved to the middle of the track, looked first one way and then the other, then pulled her cell phone from her pocket and poked at a couple of icons.

"That's east," she said, pointing to her right along the road. "This road must come along the northern edge of the Indira Gandhi Sanctuary in Tamil Nadu. It runs up against this preserve and I'm sure there are no roads that go north out of the park." She looked west along the track to her left. "I suggest we go this way."

They were able to move quickly along the cleared roadway and in thirty minutes found the road's end, a wide turn-about on the edge of a brush-filled ravine that dropped steeply to their right. The undergrowth was broken and scarred where the road touched the edge of the drop-off and Nisha paused for a moment, then plunged over the side into the ravine, sliding on her seat down the steep slope.

Pati cast Marcus a puzzled look then slid after her, disappearing into a screen of broken ferns, coarse grass and broad-leafed bushes. As Marcus considered the wisdom of following them down the slope, Nisha shouted from below.

"Down here, Marcus. I think this is it. Be careful coming down."

He stepped over the edge and immediately lost his footing on the matted grass, sliding feet-first into the bushes and pushing his way downward until he reached Nisha and the boy. They stood in an overgrown streambed looking at a pile of a dozen black plastic barrels that Marcus guessed to be about the size of fifty gallon drums. Each had a small fill cap in the lid that was overlaid with a hard yellow sealant. Otherwise the barrels were unmarked. A sharp metallic odor rose from the pile.

"This has to be it," Nisha said, pulling a pair of latex gloves from her pocket.

"Maybe you shouldn't be touching them, then," Marcus suggested. Something's obviously leaking. Should we be breathing this stuff?"

"I just need to get a sample and we'll get out of here." She pushed against one of the barrels and it didn't budge.

"Do you have any more of those gloves?" Marcus moved around the pile to stand beside her. She pulled another pair from her pocket and he wrestled them over his large hands.

"Judging from the smell, I'd guess the leak is down here," he said, pushing one of the heavy barrels aside to look deeper into the pile. "Be careful as I move these that you don't get splashed. If this is the stuff you're looking for, I don't think you want it on you." He rolled another two drums off the stack and peered between them at a barrel on the bottom of the heap.

"Here it is. This one hit something sharp as it rolled down the hill. It's punctured about half way up the side."

Nisha pushed beside him and peered down at the ruptured drum. "We need to get a sample," she said, pulling her backpack around to the front and fishing inside for a small bottle. "Do you think we can roll that one a little and see what comes out?"

"Doesn't sound smart," he said, looking around at the same time for a broken limb to use as a lever.

Nisha scrambled onto the barrel closest to her and leaned forward. "If we can just roll it a little .... That V shape in the bottom of the gash will act as a spout. I think we can collect a bit without getting any on me."

Marcus pushed his way along the bottom of the ravine until he found a limb that had been washed down the side by spring monsoons, carrying it back to where Nisha stood impatiently with her bottle. He thrust the branch behind the ruptured drum and pulled slowly forward. As the barrel tipped, clear liquid seeped from the open gash.

"Looks like water," he said. "Maybe the rains have washed in and filled it."

"It doesn't smell like water," Nisha frowned. "Hold my belt and I'll lean in there and get a sample."

Your belt?"

"Yes. Here." She patted the back of her jeans. "Grab my belt and I can lean in there."

Marcus braced the limb to keep the barrel in position, signaled for Pati to hold it in place, then slipped his fingers under Nisha's brown woven belt. She leaned over one of the intact drums and he eased her forward, almost holding her suspended as she slipped the edge of the bottle under the trickle of liquid.

"Got it," she said, pulling the bottle back and capping it. "I've got some wipes in my pack. Could you get one for me? And a couple of those plastic bags"

He eased her back onto her feet and retrieved the supplies. Nisha carefully wiped the small jar and placed it in one of the bags, then peeled off her gloves and put them and the wipes into the second.

"No markings on these drums to show where they came from," she said as they scrambled back up the slope to the dirt road. She fished again into her backpack and found a small black box attached to a Velcro strap.

"Game camera ... and a good one. It uploads a digital image when it takes a picture and sends it to my computer. Even better ..." she pulled a second one from her bag, "... I can mount two of these along the road and they signal me only when the same image passes both. That keeps me from being alerted by everything that moves in front of one of the cameras."

"You just happen to have these with you?" Marcus asked with amused curiosity.

"I hike in the Sanctuary all the time and my goal is to get a picture of a tiger. There aren't many left and they're very elusive. So I have half a dozen of these in various places around the park."

"Do you have them paired like this? Just to catch a tiger?"

"No—this is a more sophisticated set-up. I don't transmit signals from the tiger cams because there is so much activity in these forests. I just come download them every couple of weeks"

"How do you keep track of where they are?"

Nisha held up her smart phone. "GPS coordinates." She manipulated an icon on her phone and jotted numbers in a small notebook. "Now— we just need to get these strapped to a couple of trees with a good view of the road and the turnabout ...."

"They may have dumped all they're going to," Marcus suggested. "In that case, it will be pretty hard to figure out who they are."

"Maybe this will tell us," Nisha said, holding up the plastic bag that held the glass bottle. "Looks like another trip into Kochi."

CHAPTER EIGHT

It took Hem less than a week to locate the Disciples' small chapel near Coimbatore. When he wasn't escorting Professor Lemay around Kochi, he staked out Father Venkatesan. On the first afternoon following Hem's conversation with Lemay about locating the building, the priest left his home in Kochi and drove up through the Palakkad Gap toward Coimbatore, turning north before reaching the city. In a small village nestled along a steep rock hillside, he stopped in front of what looked like a white stucco house, distinguished from a row of other homes that pressed against a sheer stone cliff only by the symbol of two interlocking fish carved into the weathered lintel above the door.

A second car waited in front of the building and as Venkatesan pulled to a stop, a young family climbed from the car and greeted the priest. Farther up the street a blue Mahindra van also unloaded its passengers; an older couple and another young family with two children. The priest seemed particularly attentive to a girl of about ten who was the only child with the first family and wore a white dress that came to her ankles. A chain of white flowers was woven into her black hair and after unlocking the door to the building and speaking briefly with the older couple, the priest squatted in front of the girl, took both of her hands in his own, and talked to her for four or five minutes. Then he stood and led her into the church with the others following.

Hem sat in his grey Toyota Etios watching the building for nearly an hour before the group emerged without Venkatesan. The girl had changed her clothing to a light blue frock and Hem guessed she had been the object of the visit—a ceremony of some kind. The priest followed thirty minutes later carrying what appeared to be a laundry bag and paused long enough in the open doorway that Hem guessed he had not set an alarm. After feeling through his pockets to insure he had not left keys inside, the Priest locked the church behind him and left the village.

From where he sat, Hem could see that there were two windows across the front of the building on either side of the door, with another round window centered above the door below the ridgeline. The lower windows were curtained and each was covered by a black wrought iron grill, partly for security but partly as a reflection of Portuguese influence on the architecture of the region. The wall on the right that abutted the stone hillside was without windows, though other houses along the street all seemed to have side windows.

Hem crossed the street and knocked sharply on the door of the church, knowing that no one would answer. After a few moments he walked casually to the left side of the building and looked down the walkway that separated it from the adjoining house. As he had guessed, there were no windows on this side either. The only access was from the street and in any practical sense, through the front door. He returned to the door, noted the locking system, and returned to his car. An easy $500. But Hem guessed Professor Lemay's interest in this building went much farther than knowing where it was.

·   ·   ·

When he met with Father Venkatesan the following morning, Lemay wasn't yet aware of Hem's discovery. The priest had accepted an invitation to meet with Nolan at his new apartment and Hem wasn't expected until later in the afternoon. His guide had called the evening before to say that he had some "good news" and Nolan suspected the church had been found. That made his meeting with Venkatesan all the more important.

From his few days with the Pillais, he had learned that guests were to be greeted with tea and some other form of refreshment, and plates of nuts, biscuits and dried fruit were on the table in front of the sofa when the priest arrived. Nolan tried to take the requisite time to be a good host, engaging in casual conversation about his first week in Kerala and his impressions of Indian life. When the Father placed his teacup aside and leaned back into the sofa, Nolan felt that he could get to the point of the visit.

"I appreciate your willingness to help me better understand the beliefs of the Disciples," he said, also settling back into a chair that faced the priest across the small sitting room. "My colleague Doctor Bartlett had a deep interest in your faith and told me some of the principles and doctrinal points that separate you from the rest of the Thomas Christian community. And I have read his book, of course. I am interested in continuing his research, but there are several points about which I'm not clear. I hope you can enlighten me."

"Of course," the priest said, bowing slightly.

"The major point of difference, as I understand it, is your belief that Thomas was the literal twin of Jesus—and to at least some degree, shared in his divine nature."

"That is correct. We accept Thomas as the Second Son—not co-equal with Jesus, who had a Messianic calling by birthright, but sharing in the divine nature."

"I know that several early writings refer to Thomas as 'the twin'—one even intimating that Jesus was the twin—but I'm curious as to how this doctrine of shared divinity arose in your community?"

"It came to us from Thomas himself," the priest said. "It is part of the secret knowledge the Lord entrusted to him, and has been handed down from generation to generation within our community."

"It's just an oral tradition then?"

"To begin with, all of our Christian tradition was oral," the priest affirmed. "As far as we know, Jesus wrote nothing, and nothing he said was recorded during his lifetime, but was passed along orally for half a century."

Lemay nodded. "And did Thomas have any special mission as the Second Son? Did his sharing in the divine nature give him any unique responsibility?"

"A thoughtful question," Venkatesan observed, "and one that takes us into areas of doctrine that many believe separate us completely from the rest of the Christian community. But you seem to know something of the Gnostic literature. One of its recurring themes is that our physical state is transient and corrupt. Agreed?"

Nolan nodded. "This is often paired with a belief that the creator God was a cruel and capricious God. Do you share that belief?"

Venkatesan shook his head. "We accept the nature of creation as expressed in the *Gospel of John* ... that Jesus as the Word was Creator. But we do accept that matter is corrupt and transient by nature, which raises the question of what sustains this creation?"

"I'm not sure I follow."

"This is something of a crude analogy, but you are in the land of the Hindu. What do you know of Hinduism?"

"I teach a freshman course in the world's major religions so am reasonably familiar with the essentials."

"Then you understand that in Hindu thought, what is referred to as God has three general manifestations in worship: through Brahma as the Creator, Vishnu as the Sustainer or Preserver, and through Shiva as the destroyer. In Hinduism, these three manifestations of the divine represent the cycle of being, as the physical realm comes into and passes out of existence. If we were to apply this to Christian theology, we see Jesus the Messiah as Creator and giver of life—both in the physical and spiritual sense. You may recall that in the writings of Isaiah we find reference to a third son—the Son of the Morning, who is also called Lucifer. It is this same Lucifer who in the *Book of the Apocalypse* is cast down from heaven, taking a third of the host of heaven with him. He was denied an opportunity to enter the physical realm and in his anger, became the destroyer, committed to thwarting the work of the Creator and life-giver."

"You lost me somewhere there," Nolan said. "Are you suggesting that Jesus is the First Son, Thomas the Second Son, and Lucifer the Third Son? And that they are all manifestations of God in some respect? If so, what is it that Lucifer is trying to thwart?"

The priest smiled. "You are taking me very quickly into the deepest parts of our theology, parts we often choose not to share because they tend to draw ridicule. But I wish you to understand. We accept it as true that there is a Father God who shared with these three sons in the creation of this world. We were all part of that primordial host of heaven and this world was to be a learning place for each soul to experience mortality—or, thinking again in Hindu or Buddhist terms, to gain the discipline and strength of spirit needed to resist and slough off the corrupting influences of the physical world."

"Why experience the physical at all?" Nolan inquired. "Why not stay in some spirit state of eternal innocence?"

"Perhaps we were not so innocent," the priest suggested. "As the Revelator explained, there was war in heaven and the Third Son rebelled and was followed by a third of the angelic host who were cast out. Perhaps for the remaining two-thirds, passing through mortality serves as a refining process that is important to some future ability to fully experience the eternal."

Nolan considered this for a moment. "We have described the roles of the First Son and the Third Son. How does the Second Son fit into all of this?"

"The cycle of the host of heaven passing through mortality introduces the concept of time, as generation after generation procreate and bring spirit children into the world. But they enter a world that is by nature corrupt and transient. If left to its own devises, it would self-destruct and the Third Son seeks to hasten that destruction. The First Son, Jesus, came to provide a bridge back to immortality for those who can resist the corrupting influences of this world but in so doing, he had to leave this mortal state. In a realm of corruption and transience, what sustains it until all of the myriad host of heaven have an opportunity to pass through?"

"The Second Son is the Preserver or Sustainer?" Nolan knew that his voice reflected his incredulity.

"Exactly."

"What has he preserved? I wouldn't say the world is exactly a place of peace and harmony."

"Perhaps it only requires one place of peace and tranquillity. As God said to Lot, find me one righteous man .... It may be that it takes only one place of peace to keep us from utter destruction."

"A place sustained by Thomas? But by tradition, Thomas died here in India—and by some accounts is buried near Chennai. Others say his body was taken from here to Syria ...."

"That is indeed what tradition says," Venkatesan agreed.

"But the Disciples believe ...?"

"The Second Son is the Preserver," the priest said. "I will just leave it at that."

CHAPTER NINE

Her camera alarm buzzed just after midnight and Nisha struggled awake and squinted at the monitor through bleary eyes. Over the last four days she had recorded almost every animal common to the sanctuary: guar, tahr and sambar. But no vehicles. She was finding it harder and harder to force herself awake in the middle of the night to check the screen. A large male guar, the massive red-brown buffalo that inhabited the park's forests and grasslands, made a solitary pilgrimage along the road at about the same time each night, triggering the cameras and jolting her awake. Shaggy brown sambar deer wandered the park at night, grazing back and forth between the cameras and sending a new picture every time she fell back to sleep.

But tonight the image pulled her abruptly from her bed and she reached instinctively for her cell phone, punching the autodial as she pulled on jeans and a loose USC sweatshirt.

The "hello" that answered was groggy with sleep.

"Marcus, we have a delivery. A white panel van. I'll pick you up in five minutes."

Marcus was waiting in front of the clinic when she pulled up and hunched into the Honda's passenger seat as soon as Nisha came to a stop. He had insisted on spending a second week among the villagers, claiming he needed more language samples. But Nisha knew he was intrigued by the arsenic mystery and seemed to be enjoying his days with her—a feeling she shared with this man who was twice her size, could lift her over a small stream as if she were a child, but could converse intelligently about any subject she wished to talk to him about. When the first week ended and he asked to stay longer, she knew she wanted more time together as badly as he did.

Marcus began to ask questions before she was out of the clinic's small parking lot.

"What did you see?" he asked, pulling the seat belt across his broad chest.

"Looked like a Mercedes Sprinter—the cargo model. It was just pulling up to the turnaround when I called. I think we'll be able to get to the junction with Highway 49 before they come out."

"And then what's your plan? Just follow them?"

"We need to learn where the barrels are coming from," Nisha said as she wheeled onto the road leading south from Sunkam. "It has to be one of the textile plants—probably in Coimbatore. The solution is a mordant used to fix color into fabric, so must come from one of the textile mills."

"I hope you found the right intersection. We should have followed that road back up into the jungle to see if it ended at the dump site."

Nisha glanced at him with mild irritation. "I know it's the right junction. The coordinates are right."

When they returned from the hike that had led them to the pile of barrels, she had used the GPS data from her smart phone to find the spot on Google Earth, then had taken the computer image down to the 5000 foot level where the forest road's turnaround point was clearly visible among the trees. Moving back along the ridgeline she found places where the road broke out of the forest into open grassland often enough that she could follow its path across the northern edge of the Anamalai Tiger Refuge to the point where it joined the highway to the city of Pollachi. With the coordinates of the highway junction in hand, she and Marcus drove to the spot and found the faint track emerging from the trees onto the paved road. It had taken them twenty-seven minutes. They estimated that if they left the clinic at the same time a vehicle left the dump site, with the speed the van would have to travel to navigate the forest road, she and Marcus could be at the junction when it emerged. Tonight they would find out.

As they reached the blacktop that led to Pollachi and turned left, the midnight traffic was light and Nishi accelerated to 110 kph. She could feel Marcus tense and clutch the side of the seat, knees jammed tightly against the dash.

"It's not going to do us any good to spot them at the dump if we kill ourselves on the way to intercepting them," he muttered.

"Be glad you aren't on the bike," she said grimly. "Then I'd be going fast."

"It won't do us any good if you get stopped either."

"You said you wanted me to call you. I called. And this isn't some back road in Arkansas. I drive like this all the time and I've never been stopped."

He apparently decided it wasn't worth arguing, but didn't relax.

"My cell's in the center compartment in the dash," she said. "Pull it out and select the GPS app. I don't want to miss the junction in the dark."

He did as she asked and watched the numbers change as they sped along the highway. As they approached the coordinate she had jotted on a piece of note paper taped to the back of the phone, he cautioned her to slow the Honda. They were in a long sweeping turn to the right and the dirt road exited to their left midway through the turn. Nisha pulled onto the shoulder and glanced back.

"We need to go back to where we can just see this spot," she said. "We'll see their lights when they come up to the highway, but don't want them to see us. I'm guessing they will turn left toward Pollachi, so we should be able to fall in behind after they get on the highway." She made a quick three-point turn and drove two hundred meters back the way they had come, turning around again where the car could sit in a wide spot on the shoulder. She switched off the lights and engine and leaned back, suddenly much more aware of how dark the night was and how large the man beside her seemed in the cramped Honda.

"Now we wait," she said, feeling his closeness in the seat beside her.

Marcus had relaxed back into the seat and was fingering the cell phone with his long fingers. During their treks in the forest he had been hesitant to talk about his personal life and she struggled now for a question to keep the silence from becoming awkward. As one of the few cars on the highway zoomed past, she glanced over at him and thought how much his profile reminded her of the American athlete Michael Jordan. In fact, that was who he reminded her of in general. He was big, but graceful in a long, flowing kind of way that captivated her as she watched him stride through a village with the young boys running beside him. He seemed constantly at ease among the villagers but remained very private, asking her practically nothing about her own life and offering her even less. It was as if he felt he had no right to probe into her past and was a little embarrassed about his own.

"Did you play basketball at university?" she asked finally.

He looked over at her in the dark and seemed relieved to have the silence broken. "A little in high school. Football in college, but they didn't allow us to play two sports. They worried we'd get hurt if we played another sport."

"American football, I assume?"

"Oh ... right. I played some soccer when I was in junior high, but by high school the smaller guys were better at it and I stayed pretty much with basketball. No football where I went to high school, so I had to pick that up when I got to college. American football."

"I'm afraid I don't understand the game," Nisha began but stopped in mid-sentence as lights appeared through the trees to the left of the highway where the forest path joined the road. She switched on the engine and they watched in silence as the van's lights bounced up to the edge of the pavement, paused briefly, then swung onto the highway moving away from them. Nisha waited until the van was around the sweep of the curve, then turned on her own lights and started after them.

"With the traffic this light, they'll know we're following them," Marcus observed.

She responded by accelerating until she could pass the van, then drove just fast enough to keep the lights comfortably in sight behind them.

"They won't expect a car that's following them to be ahead," she said.

As they neared the outskirts of Pollachi the van suddenly made a left turn and the lights disappeared between two long metal industrial buildings. Nisha spun the wheel into a jolting U-turn and sped back to where the van had turned down a narrow lane that separated the structures, but the lights had disappeared. She turned into the alley and doused the Honda's headlights, easing the car to the back of the buildings.

In front of them the alley widened and was bordered on either side by storage lots filled with agricultural machinery, each surrounded by a high chain-link fence topped with coiled razor wire. Loading docks stretched along the backs of both buildings, with sloped ramps that descended to a platform and rows of sliding metal doors. On both sides of the Honda, a shoulder-high concrete wall shielded the nearest loading bays.

"They may have turned down the back of one of these buildings," Marcus whispered, as if they could be heard beyond the closed windows. "I think we should back out of here and wait to see if they come out."

Nisha responded by edging the car forward, looking both directions along the backs of the buildings. For no particular reason—probably to keep the loading docks on her side of the car, she turned right around the end of the safety wall. From the loading bay closest to her, tucked in beside the shielding barrier, the van lurched backward on squealing tires, slamming into her door and driving the Honda sideways into the high fence. She felt her head and shoulder slam against the side airbag and Marcus' head bang against her left shoulder. She jammed her foot onto the accelerator to force the Honda out of the trap, but the front right tire had crumpled under the impact and a steel fence post pressed tightly against the front of the left fender. As she struggled to release her seat belt, she heard the door behind her scrape open and felt cold metal press against the back of her head.

"Turn the car off," a male voice barked in Malayalam.

Through the corner of her eye she saw Marcus turn and heard the voice say, "Keep your eyes straight ahead, black man." But the words were also in Malayalam and Marcus continued to turn. The spot of cold steel left her head and she saw the barrel swing across onto Marcus' forehead and he reeled back against the car window.

"Speak in English," she shouted. "He doesn't understand."

There was a pause as the men appeared to examine the damage to the Honda.

"When I tell you, I want both of you to climb back over the seat and get out on this side," the voice said in English. "We have guns on you, so do not try to be heroes."

Nisha leaned over and touched a growing knot above Marcus' right eye that seeped blood from an inch-long gash.

"Can you move?" she asked and he nodded. "You climb out first," she said, "and I'll follow."

He struggled through the gap between seats and out of the car, with Nisha clambering out behind him. Two men with scarves tied tightly below their eyes faced them in the dark: a short stocky man in a khaki shirt and dark pants, and a taller man with the boat-shaped turban of the Sikhs. He was dressed in what looked like the green coveralls commonly worn in auto repair shops. The stocky man reached onto the floor of the back seat and picked up Nisha's handbag before pushing the door closed, then turned them to face the smashed side of the Honda.

"Hands behind you," the turbaned man ordered, and Nisha felt strips of what she judged to be duct tape wrap her hands and wrists. He leaned forward and spoke directly into her ear in Malayalam. "Why were you following us?"

"We weren't following you. We just saw the van turn down between the buildings and thought it seemed suspicious this late at night."

"You are lying. We saw you when we reached the highway near the park. You were waiting for us. When we turned in here, you came back to find us." As he talked, the shorter man patted Marcus down, pausing to pull his wallet from his rear pants pocket.

"This man is American," he said in Malayalam to his partner. "He has a driver's license from the U.S." He turned to Nisha's bag and sorted through it quickly. "And this woman is a doctor. There is an identification tag from a clinic in some place called Sunkam—and one for a hospital in Kochi."

"Why were you following us?" the man in the coveralls repeated.

Before either could speak, their captors grabbed them roughly by the arms and pushed them to a side door of the van.

"Inside and lie down," the Sikh ordered and as they stretched on the floor of the Mercedes, his partner strapped their ankles together with the wide tape.

"What are we going to do with them?" the shorter man asked.

"Get the plates off the car and clean everything out of it, including the boot. I will call and see what they want us to do with them while we get out of here."

"We have to get rid of them," the stocky one said. "They must know where we are dumping the waste and will tie it to the company. If they contact the police or the Ministry of Environment, it will mean prison for us."

"I know where we can put them until we figure this out," the taller man said. "But you are right. I am certain the company will want them to disappear."

. . .

At 1:30 a.m. Hem parked in the shadows of a side street two hundred meters from the Disciples' church and sat for thirty minutes watching the dark street. A quarter moon was shrouded by high overcast, bathing the broken pavement in a hazy grey, but there were no streetlights. Nothing but a thin, slumping mongrel dog moved during the thirty minutes, zigzagging across the street in search of something to eat. When it finally disappeared, Hem pulled on thin leather gloves and lifted a black satchel from the passenger seat. Checking the street again and seeing nothing, he slipped from the car and walked along the front of the houses opposite the church until across from the Disciples' chapel. A life spent roaming the streets during the wee hours of the morning had taught him that the stillest part of the night was between 2:00 and 3:00 a.m. Late revellers were home by that time and the early morning merchants had not begun to stir. It meant no one was likely to see him—but if anyone did, he would raise immediate suspicion.

Hem's meeting with Lemay had been brief and to the point. As he had anticipated, the professor wanted more than directions to the church. When Hem informed him that he had found the sanctuary, the American took the crude map, studied it in silence for a moment, then asked, "Did you go inside?"

"No. There was some kind of family ceremony going on."

Lemay drew a long envelope from his pocket and handed it to his guide. "Good work," he said. "Do you think you could get inside?"

"When no one else is there, I assume ...?"

Lemay didn't answer immediately. "There's an old manuscript in there I would very much like to have," he said after a few moments. "I would be willing to give you $5,000 if you can get it for me."

"Not worth it," Hem said without having to consider the offer. "There was no risk in finding the place. Breaking in—very much risk."

"What would make it worthwhile for you?"

Hem had decided on a figure as he drove back from Coimbatore, weighing the risks against what he thought the professor might be willing to pay. "Twenty-five thousand—U.S. dollars," he said without hesitation.

"I can't afford twenty-five thousand, but can probably come up with fifteen."

"Twenty-five, or find someone else. You now know where it is."

Again Lemay paused, studying Hem with suspicious eyes. "When could you do it?"

"Within a few days. Do you know where the manuscript is?"

"Not exactly. But from what I understand, there are rooms cut back into the hillside. The manuscript is in a stone box in one of those rooms."

"And when you get this manuscript, what will you do with it? If it is unique and you announce that you have it, you will be charged with the theft."

"I'll claim I was approached by an anonymous source who sold it to me, and I had no idea where it came from. Once I have it, I'll photograph it, take a small sample so I can determine its age, then return it to the Disciples when they claim it was stolen."

"Why not just photograph it and take a sample to begin with—and leave the manuscript where it is?"

"I would then be admitting that I had someone get the photograph and sample. Plus, I need to be able to demonstrate that the sample and photo are of the manuscript in the Disciple's church."

Hem nodded thoughtfully. "So if I get it for you, what assurance do I have that you will not identify me as the person who sold you the manuscript?"

"You've been working for me since I arrived. Who would believe that I didn't hire you to steal it?"

Again Hem nodded. The professor had given this considerable thought. "For twenty-five thousand, I will get it. Any less, and you find someone else."

Lemay frowned. "That's more than I can afford but I have no other contacts. If you bring it to me in good condition, twenty-five thousand. It should be about the size of a legal sheet of paper and may be fragile. You'll need some way to carry it without bending or damaging it."

Now, as Hem looked at the church across the dark street and imagined rooms cut back into the rock face and handling a fragile manuscript, he wondered if $25,000 was worth the risk. Pulling a set of picks from a zippered side pocket of his satchel, he crossed the street and easily unlocked the deadbolt, slipping quietly inside. The interior was cool and pitch black, the pale light from the moon blocked by curtains covering the barred windows. Hem locked the door behind him, drew a small flashlight from his bag, and walked quickly to the back of the sanctuary, working his way along the rear stone wall. Behind a screen at the left of the chapel he found the second door, this one secured by an ancient ward lock and newer padlock that looped though welded plates, bolted from the inside. Though sturdy, the padlock was a simple pin and tumbler type and Hem opened it easily with a thin pick and tension wrench. Another ring contained a series of five long picks that looked like sections of a thin Celtic cross. Hem tried them one at a time in the ward lock, then in pairs until he found the right combination. The old lock clicked open and he removed it and pushed into the second room.

The chamber was of solid stone and stretched across the back of the outer chapel with a waist-deep pool cut into the floor at his far right. Directly across the room from the door Hem had entered, another entry was cut deeper into the rock, secured only by a ward lock of the type he had just opened.

"Not much security," Hem murmured as he opened it with the same pick combination and pushed it noisily inward. Beyond was a narrow passage just higher than the door frame that extended three or four meters into the rock cliff, then turned right for the same distance before ending at a third door, identically locked. With each penetration into the cliff side, the air cooled and dried, and as Hem entered this final vault a chill shivered along his back and down his arms. At the center of the small chamber, a square stone pedestal rose to waist-height with what appeared to be a fitted stone cap. Hem paused as he stepped into the room and ran the beam from his flashlight around the chamber. Other than the low stone stand, it was completely bare. He walked to the pedestal, held the flashlight between his teeth, and gently lifted the stone lid. It was lighter than he had expected and he propped it on the floor against the side of the pedestal.

Inside was an earthenware box of light reddish brown that reminded him of the massive jars used by villagers to store water. He gingerly removed its top, placed it against the stone cover, and flashed his light into the open square.

Hem knew immediately that he had asked too little of Nolan Lemay. He knew nothing about manuscripts, but the one that lay in the pedestal box reeked of value. It was written on some form of fiber parchment in a language Hem didn't recognize, its edges yellowed and frayed with age. The faded script was neatly formed, with a small hole breaking one of the lines about a third of the way from what he judged to be the top. He took the flashlight in his right hand and with his left, carefully fingered the edge of the course mat that lay beneath the manuscript. It was also made of fiber, about three millimeters thick. He eased a fingernail along the side and gently lifted the edge of the mat. It was tough but flexible and he slipped the mat and parchment to the right until it touched that side of its earthenware container. With the manuscript where he wanted it, he stepped back until the circle from his flashlight illuminated the full page and stood studying it for several moments.

What was this document that was worth $25,000 to the American? Lemay knew it was here and that it was in a stone chamber carved back into the hillside. From what the professor had said, Hem guessed the Disciples were not aware Lemay knew about the manuscript—so his knowledge of it came from elsewhere. From his American colleague? Bartlett? The man who had died only months before Lemay showed up looking for the document? Hem's larcenous mind worked through the possibilities and the more he thought, the more valuable the manuscript became.

He stooped to the satchel that also leaned against the base of the pedestal and drew out a legal-sized manila folder and a flexible plastic sheet of the same dimensions. Moving in slow motion, he slipped the plastic beneath the left edge of the fiber mat, sliding it down and under the manuscript until he could fold the plastic slightly to make it rigid, then lifted the mat and parchment from the box. With equal care he eased them into the folder and when the manuscript extended beyond the folder's edge, drew a second from his case and with clear plastic tape, strapped the folders together to create an enclosed envelope. From the appearance of the parchment, he knew that if he dropped or jarred it, the contents of his folder might disintegrate into small pieces, so he lowered the satchel on its side and gingerly slipped the thin package into the case, keeping it horizontal.

With the job complete, Hem became suddenly aware of the absolute silence of the stone chamber. As he had worked on lifting the manuscript from the box, even his breath had stilled and he could now hear the fierce pounding of his heart in the oppressive quiet of the room. Moving swiftly back into motion, he replaced the earthenware top and hoisted the stone cover back into place. Quickly he scanned the room to insure that he had not dropped anything, retrieved the case from the floor and, holding it with arms extended like a pan of hot soup, retraced his steps back into the main chapel. As he passed through each door, he eased the satchel to the floor and locked the door. In the sanctuary his feet creaked on the plank floor and he moved as quickly as caution allowed to one of the front windows, parted the curtain with the side of his head to survey the street. When comfortable it was still clear, he slipped from the building, bolting the main door after him.

The moon had disappeared, taking with it the pale haziness that had been the only outside light. Hem again moved directly across the street, then left along the house fronts to the alley where he had parked his Toyota. Opening the passenger door, he laid the satchel flat on the floor in front of the seat, then hurried around to the driver's side. A dog barked somewhere beyond the church and a square of light played out onto the surface of the street from an open doorway. The early morning people were beginning to stir. He drove without lights until nearly a kilometer from his parking spot, then flipped on the low beams and pulled into a light flow of early traffic on its way into Coimbatore. He had booked a room there before driving to the church and planned to sleep a few hours. Then he would call the American professor and discuss a new arrangement.

CHAPTER TEN

Marcus felt only pain. Pain and wet. The throbbing spot on his forehead from the pistol whipping in the car had somehow spread throughout his entire head and down into his shoulders and back—and into his left arm. The rest of his body seemed too distant to have any feeling at all. He struggled to open his eyes but when he thought they were open, saw only blackness. He feared fleetingly that blows to his head had blinded him, then realized that he was lying on his left side with his face pressed tightly up against something soft—and he was lying in a shower.

He attempted to push up with his left arm but a searing jolt of pain surged downward from his shoulder, and the arm refused to move. His right arm was against his side and he forced it forward, getting a grudging but less painful response. His hand groped at whatever was pressed against his face and he felt the small, soft arm and naked side of what he knew was Nisha.

Reaching across her stomach he felt for the floor and found instead thick grass. Slowly he moved the hand along her body, finding first her naked breasts, then her still, flat stomach and soaked panties as he slid the hand downward. Her legs were bare and he pulled the arm back onto his own side. His was also naked, except for a pair of soggy grey boxers.

With every ounce of strength he could muster, Marcus rolled onto his back and looked up into a dark sky that seemed to roll and shift in thick grey swirls about him. He felt across his body at the left arm and immediately knew that his shoulder was dislocated—an injury once inflicted on the same shoulder by a hard-hitting linebacker. He pressed against the wet grass with his right hand and pushed up, then dropped his weight back down onto the shoulder, grunting through clenched teeth as it popped back into place. He remained on his back for another few moments, letting the pain ease until he thought he could again move, then slid closer to Nisha. A fiery vice gripped his chest as he gasped for air.

"Nisha ... can you hear me?"

There was no response and he reached over and found the side of her head, the hair matted heavily against her temple. He pulled it back and touched her cheek, feeling it cold and damp against his fingers.

"Nisha ...." Marcus forced himself again onto his left side with his face against hers, feeling for the curve of her neck with the fingers of his right hand. He found no pulse and with his chest against her back, could feel no rise and fall from her breath. He pushed her onto her back and forced her chin upward and her mouth open, locking his lips over her mouth and nose as he forced air into her lungs. Then three sharp presses with the heel of his hand against her breast bone, and another series of breaths. As he held her chin with his hand, his fingers felt sticky warmth on the left side of her face and he reached upward, finding a swollen split above her ear that continued to seep blood into her hair.

For some reason, Marcus felt relief. She was still bleeding—which meant that a heart continued to beat faintly in that small body. As he lifted his face away to press again against her chest, he felt a faint breath and paused, searching again for a pulse. At first there was nothing and he pushed deeper and farther under her chin to where a faint beat answered his probe. He grasped her and rolled again onto his back, pulling her onto his body with her face against his own cheek, rhythmically rubbing her back with his good hand. Gradually he felt warmth begin to return to her body and as the sky began to glow with misty light, he stroked her back, neck and sides until he could no longer move his exhausted arm.

Overhead and behind him he could hear the patter of rain on leaves and knew they were in an opening among trees. As the light grew, the trees moved in close around them and he was transported to the small clearing on the bluff above the Mississippi River where he and his friend O'dell played as boys. Kudzu had blanketed the elms and sycamores, forming grotesque leafy giants that loomed over them on every side, leaving only a round patch of sky to offer any light. He closed his eyes and stroked Nisha's back, wondering how far from that Mississippi bluff this spot in the forest had taken him.

Marcus' last memory before coming to on this patch of grass was of sitting on a concrete floor, tied back-to-back with Nisha around a steel I-beam. They had been taken to a warehouse in what Nisha guessed from the length of the drive must be Coimbatore, then strapped to the beam and left through the rest of the night and following day without food or water. Their hands and feet were tightly taped and though they tried every way to break free, their captors had done their job well. Neither could move more than a few inches. They had yelled until they were hoarse and their mouths pasty dry, but no one came.

"I don't think they plan to let us live," Nisha said. "We're going to be left here until we die of dehydration." The declining sun in the high windows below the eaves indicated that the day was moving toward evening. "They would have made some effort to take care of us," she rasped, "... and you heard them say we had to disappear. They can't afford to let us go."

Marcus licked at his lips with a thickening tongue. "I don't think they can leave us here. They'll move us somewhere and when they do, we need to try to overpower them. If we're still taped, throw yourself at them and see if we can knock them to the floor. Maybe ...."

As he spoke, an overhead door to his left rolled upward and a vehicle entered the warehouse. Marcus strained to look over his shoulder as a sand-colored Land Rover rolled to a stop a few yards from the I-beam. Their two captors climbed out, still masked with the looped scarves about their faces. Each carried a heavy wooden club.

"What are you planning to ..." was all that Marcus could say before one of the clubs smashed into the side of his head, launching him into blackness.

As he looked now at what he could see of the clearing, he wondered why they had not been killed outright—why they had been moved to this place, stripped of most of their clothing and left in the rain. From the slowing patter on the leaves overhead he could tell the rain was letting up and the grey mist that hovered below treetop-level was slowly lifting. To his right, just beyond the screen of trees, he thought he heard movement and froze with eyes closed, wondering if he should pretend to be unconscious or should call out. The sound was faint—a muted rustling of wet branches—and he decided it was neither his attackers nor a rescuer, but some forest animal moving along the edge of the clearing. The thought was no more comforting.

As carefully as he could with his one good arm, he eased Nisha back onto the grass, rolled painfully onto his stomach and forced himself to his knees, watching the place where he had heard the sound. It stopped, as if whatever had made it was studying his movements and deciding what to do. He and Nisha had been dumped near one side of the clearing and the tracks of the Land Rover moved away from them across the open space to a break in the trees opposite where they lay, disappearing into the forest.

Nisha was on her back and he moved slowly around her until he could turn her head to the side and examine the gash above her left ear, still watching the place that seemed to be the source of the rustling. Her wound continued to weep blood and a clear thick liquid, clotting slowed by the constant wash of the shower. Sliding onto his back he slipped out of his shorts, tore one of the legs halfway up with his teeth and good hand, then ripped around the circumference, pulling off a grey strip of cotton. With one end of the cloth in his teeth, he pulled it under her head and up over the wound, tying it as tightly as he could with the good hand. Again he heard movement, this time slightly farther around the clearing to his right and he turned with the sound, expecting some creature to bolt from the forest. As soon as he looked in its direction, the rustling ceased.

Pulling the shorts back on, Marcus gingerly eased Nisha onto her stomach. He hooked his right arm under her waist and kneeling beside her, struggled her limp body upward until she was draped over his shoulder, her legs hanging down across his chest. Pain raced again along his sides and back, crushing the breath from his lungs, and he knelt back on his heels, breathing slowly until the pain was tolerable. Slowly he pushed to his feet, watching the edge of the clearing as he moved. Steadying himself on trembling legs, he leaned sideways to slip Nisha's waist closer against his neck, hooking his good arm about her hips and edging backward toward where the tire tracks met the forest.

The path the Land Rover had taken was wide enough that he was able to back along its center without brushing Nisha against the wet branches that arched overhead. He moved slowly, feeling backward with his feet with each step, sensing that he should face whatever created the occasional whisper in the trees. The morning sun lifted the mist and reduced the rain to a subdued drizzle, leaving the air thick and wet.

Marcus counted his steps and tried to create a mental map of where he was going, pausing every twenty paces to turn in a full circle and listen. Nisha was heavier than he expected—dead weight, and firm muscle in her legs and stomach. When he had first become aware of her lying beside him in the grass, he had glanced with guilty embarrassment at her supple body, thinking again what a beautiful woman she was. As he struggled backward with his arm about her thighs, he tried to walk in slow, even strides to keep her from bouncing against his back, but felt again the tautness of her firm body.

Two hundred paces from the clearing, the path opened onto a stretch of knee-high grassland with a well-worn dirt road running along its side. He paused again, wanting to lay Nisha in the grass beside the road as he tried to get his bearings, but fearing he would not be able to lift her again if he put her down. As he turned to survey the open expanse, the forest behind him again rustled so slightly that he feared his imagination was getting the better of him. But as he swung again to face the trees where he had emerged from the forest, the source of his concern stepped into the edge of the clearing. The tiger stood with its broad, striped head slightly lowered and golden eyes watching every move Marcus made, its tail swishing rhythmically behind like an aroused cobra.

Marcus' heart bolted in his aching chest and he froze in place with one of Nisha's arms bumping loosely against his leg. All he could think about was an article he had once read about meeting a bear in the woods. *Don't run.* Look as large as you can, and back away very slowly. He didn't know if big cats were like bears, but both were predators and he knew the worst thing he could do was turn and run. He had to be the largest man this cat had ever seen, but he knew tigers could bring down a guar buffalo and if this one chose to charge, there was nothing he could do to save them. As the tiger studied him with every muscle set to spring into motion, Marcus realized why he and Nisha had been left naked in the forest.

To his right at the edge of the grassy stretch where it again met the jungle, Marcus had seen a dark shape against the wall of trees. His first thought had been the Land Rover, but it was too large. Too high. For what seemed an eternity he stood without moving, the creature that faced him also frozen in place. As the drizzle stopped and the mist lifted, a small building emerged out of the haze at the edge of the grassland: a rough wooden square with steps climbing one side to a railed observation platform on its roof. Easing sideways as slowly as any motion allowed, Marcus stepped toward the building, keeping his eyes locked on the tiger's. It tensed and lowered its head even closer to the ground, the tail freezing in mid-sweep.

What would he do if it charged? Throw up his arms and bellow as loudly as he could, hoping to startle the cat into turning away? But as he eased toward the building, each step followed by the intense, yellow eyes of the tiger, he decided that the only way to save Nisha would be to drop her and return the charge. Rush the giant cat and meet it midway. The charge may be more distracting than an arm-waving shout and if the tiger killed him, it may lose interest in the smaller, lifeless woman.

The slow side-step to the small building seemed to take an eternity, the tiger slipping slowly along the edge of the trees as he advanced, tracing every movement. The structure was without windows on the bottom level, its single entrance a heavy wooden door secured only with the lock in its knob. Marcus stood beside the door for a long moment, eying the crouching cat that had also frozen in place. If he turned to try the knob with his good hand, his back would be to the tiger—and instinct told him he needed to continue to keep his eyes locked on the beast. He edged across the doorway to a point where he could reach back with his good hand and try the knob. It turned and released the latch. But now to get inside, he would need to pull it outward, slip inside with Nisha on his back, and pull the door closed. It would take three to five seconds— about the time it would take the cat to cross the distance between them. As he was considering whether the door would hold up against the cat's assault, the tiger charged.

. . .

In the first chamber behind the Disciple's small chapel near Coimbatore, the five elders faced a single Guardian across the stone room. The chamber was cool to the point of seeming cold and three of the elders sat with arms folded tightly across their chests. Each movement, each scraping against the stone floor, echoed in the bare stone chamber as if amplified by the palpable nervousness in the room.

"What we have most feared has happened," the senior elder said, his voice breaking with emotion. "The letter of Thomas has been stolen."

The woman straightened in her seat but said nothing, knowing he would tell her what she needed to know without being prompted.

"A woman who lives across the road—a widow who says she sleeps very little—called the police to tell them she saw a man leave the church early this morning, about 2:30. He was carrying what looked like a flat case. I was called and arrived here just after 5:00. Everything was locked and seemed in order, but when I opened the letter chamber, both the letter and the matting it sat on had been taken. The authorities examined the entire building and found nothing. It has simply disappeared."

"Were others questioned along the street?" Meera asked.

"Yes—every house, but no one saw anything."

The group sat silently for several moments, waiting on the old man. When he said nothing, Meera spoke again.

"What are your thoughts, Babaji?"

"My thoughts are thoughts I wish I did not have," the elder said. "But the American who was going to break his oath, Professor Dixon Bartlett, was the only one beyond our church family who knew of the letter and where it was kept. His colleague, this Doctor Lemay, has been here only a few weeks and the letter disappears. This seems too much to be coincidental."

Meera nodded, confirming thoughts she had already considered.

"Do you think he took it himself?" she asked.

"I think not. This was a professional theft, and he would not have the skills. If he is involved, he had someone do this for him."

"I will go immediately to this professor and let him know he does not want to acquire this letter," Meera said. "If he has it, he will give it to me. If it has not yet reached him, I will find it."

"Kanta is on her way from Mumbai," the old man said. "She will contact the professor when she arrives. You have other talents that will be more useful. We need to know if he is contacted in any way and by whom. Follow him until Kanta arrives and establish links to his phone and computer. We must move quickly if we are to recover the letter before it becomes public."

"Where is Manisha?" Meera asked. "Perhaps she could follow the professor while I work on his communications."

"We have not been able to contact Manisha," the elder said, his voice reflecting his concern. "She was not at work or at her home and when I contact her cell phone, I receive a message that it is not working. I will continue to try to reach her, but you must follow Lemay until we find her, or Kanta arrives. And we must act quickly."

Meera stood and bowed slightly to the elders. "I will do what needs to be done, *Babaji*," she said, and left the church.

CHAPTER ELEVEN

By the time Hem returned to Kochi, the price of the manuscript had doubled. He had no idea what he had, but did know that Lemay wanted it badly and suspected he had the money. Hem lived in a second floor apartment in the Panampilli Nagar district of the Kochi suburb of Eranakulam. He generally took the stairs, bounding up two at a time, but on this morning he used the elevator, holding his case as if it were a pizza delivery. He paused in his small living room only long enough to lock the apartment door before hurrying into the bedroom, then returned to the kitchen for a white dishtowel. With the towel stretched out on his bedspread, he gingerly lifted the folders containing the manuscript from his satchel, spread the mat and parchment on the white towel, and photographed them with his smart phone. A quick check of the photos showed the quality to be good enough that characters on the manuscript were clearly legible. He returned to the living room and called Lemay. When the professor answered, Hem tried to keep the conversation brief and general.

"This is Hem. We need to meet."

"Were you able to obtain the item?"

"We need to meet as soon as possible. You live near Refineries Park. Can you meet me there in one hour? The entrance on Shamugham Road?"

Lemay paused. "I can. Will you have it with you?"

"Let us meet and we will discuss it. In one hour."

The Professor was waiting as Hem reached the entrance to the park, pacing nervously along the walk that edged Shamugham Road. As Hem approached, Lemay hurried toward him, his anxiousness confirming Hem's suspicion that he was desperate to get the manuscript.

"Did you get it?"

"Let's walk," Hem said, directing Lemay into the park. He waited until they were alone on a tree-lined path that looked across Park Avenue at the Maritime Academy on the greenway's west side, then said casually, "I was able to get what you want, but it was much more difficult than I anticipated—and a much greater risk. Now that I have seen it, I realize it also is much more valuable than you indicated."

Lemay stopped walking and glared at Hem, his face flushed. "So this is how we're going to play it. Every step means more money."

Hem beckoned for him to keep walking. "No—we are just talking about fair value. Fifty thousand will be much less than it is worth and you will not have another request from me."

"I can't come up with fifty thousand," Lemay sputtered. "That's twice what we agreed."

"I am quite certain there are those who would pay fifty thousand," Hem suggested. "Why don't you think about it for a day and let me know. If you decide it is too much, I will begin to seek other buyers."

"I don't even know you really have it," Lemay objected. "I'm not going to try to round up that kind of money until I have proof."

"Oh, I have it." He pulled his phone from his pocket and tapped its face, holding the phone up for the professor to see the photo.

Lemay squinted at the tiny image. "I haven't seen the manuscript before and this could be any photo. I need to verify that this is the parchment from the Disciples' church."

"You don't see the manuscript until you have the money."

"Then text me this picture. And I will need more than a day to translate ...."

"If you have the photo, perhaps you will not need the manuscript," Hem ventured.

Lemay scoffed. "It's worth nothing without the parchment and a sample that can be dated. And that will be true for anyone you contact. They will want to examine its content before they will even talk to you— and will want it dated. You put some public announcement out about this and you identify yourself as the thief. Text me the photo and give me three or four days. Then we can talk."

"Texts and email can be traced. When the Disciples discover this loss and you announce you have the manuscript, a text could be traced back to me."

"You see my point," Lemay said. "I'm your only real buyer. Print the photo in a size I can examine and drop it by my apartment later today. If I can verify it's the manuscript, I'll give you the twenty-five thousand we agreed on. But both verifying the letter and collecting the money will take several days."

They had reached the north end of the walk near St. Theresa's Church and turned back toward Marine Drive that ran through the heart of the park. The two walked in silence for a moment while Hem considered the professor's response. If he made a copy of the photo and deleted it from his phone, he should be safe. But Lemay was right. Other buyers would want proof of age and authenticity and he wasn't in a position to provide either. The American was his only sale and it would be an easy twenty-five thousand dollars. Then he would disappear.

· · ·

Had Marcus not already been in motion when the cat charged, he and Nisha would have been tiger bait. The animal moved with astounding speed, crossing the distance that separated them in a dozen lightning-fast strides. In a single motion, Marcus swung through the door frame and into the building, pulling the door behind them with his free hand. As the latch clicked into place, he threw both of their bodies against the thick planks just as the tiger hit with such force that the door cracked, but didn't push through the frame. Marcus braced for another charge, pressing Nisha's bottom and his damaged left shoulder hard against the door, but there was no second attack. Instead, in what sounded to Marcus like a single spring, the cat vaulted onto the roof of the building and began to pace across its top, the rafters creaking beneath its weight.

Marcus turned and scanned the small room. The only furnishing was a wooden bench against the wall to his left and a trunk in one corner. When he heard the cat pause above him on the back edge of the building, he eased Nisha to the floor, hastily retrieved the bench, and planted it firmly across the doorway. The tiger dropped silently from the roof to the back of the building and began to circle, a low, rumbling purr the only indication of its movements. Marcus lifted Nisha's still form to the bench and stretched her on her back, then sat with his back against the seat and both feet planted solidly against the wooden floor.

The tiger paused outside the door and the purr stopped, replaced by the sound of the cat sniffing back and forth across the width of the entrance. Then it was on its hind legs, its wide paws against the top of the door and claws raking the rough planks. Marcus' heart leapt into his throat and he turned sideways against the bench and pulled Nisha toward him, expecting to see the wood shred under the cat's razor claws. But the dark aged wood was as hard as weathered oak and after clawing at it without success, the tiger dropped again to all-fours and made one last circuit of the building. Then there was silence.

Marcus sat without moving, letting his pulse return to normal and listening for the slightest whisper of movement. He realized that his arm was across Nisha's hips and he was clutching her to him, her own right arm hanging loosely down from the bench with her hand against the floor. Her firm breasts rose and fell with each long, slow breath and a troubled frown creased her sleeping face. He was suddenly seized with a feeling that he should not be seeing her like this—that she deserved some dignity that lying nearly naked on this bench denied her. He listened for another moment for any sign that the tiger was still lurking outside and, hearing nothing, rose and walked to what looked like a green footlocker in the corner of the room. The latch was unlocked and the top item in the trunk was a khaki wool blanket. He carried it to the sleeping woman and gently draped it from her chin to the end of the bench, then dropped to the floor beside her with his arm again across her hips and his head against her stomach.

"It's going to be alright," he said quietly, knowing that he had no idea where they were or how he was going to get them out of there.

Nisha's first conscious thought was that she must be dead. She was wrapped in a rough cloth but knew that otherwise she wore only her panties. The surface beneath her was hard and rough. A slab in a morgue? A casket? But if she were dead, why could she feel the heavy material and her nakedness? She had been taught all her life that at death her spirit flew skyward to heaven to be embraced by God who would greet her in such brilliant splendor that she would hardly be able to endure it. But she saw no light and felt no divine embrace. Either she had been misled about the afterlife, or she hadn't yet arrived.

The realization was confirmed by the feeling of an arm slipping under the back of her neck and shoulders, lifting her slowly upward into a sitting position. The arm remained propped behind her, holding her upright. She felt a cup pressed against her chin and mouth and a sip of water flow across her lips, moistening her tongue. She swallowed greedily, then lapped with her tongue to draw more into her mouth.

"Nisha?" The voice came from just beside her left ear and she recognized it as Marcus and felt his breath against the side of her face. Reluctantly she forced her eyes open, looking dizzily across a small, bare room at a plain board wall. She became aware again that she was nearly naked and that whatever covered her had dropped to her waist as she was lifted upward. Her hands fumbled for the drape and she pulled it tightly up across her chest.

"Nisha, can you hear me?"

She nodded painfully and reached again for the water with her tongue, indicating she wanted more. He tipped it farther and she drank slowly, feeling the tepid water moisten her dry mouth and throat as it went down.

"Where are we?" she asked when the cup was empty.

"I don't know. Somewhere in the jungle."

"How long have I been unconscious?"

"Don't know that either. At least a day. I woke up early this morning and it's evening now. Can you turn a little?"

The arm eased her around to her right and back against a rough wooden wall so that she faced across a room that appeared to be about four meters square. She held the blanket tight around her and turned her head painfully to look at Marcus who was now seated beside her on a bare plank bench. From what she could see of him, he was also naked.

'They left us with nothing but our underwear ... underpants," he corrected. "There was a blanket in a box in the corner—and some bottled water, a little first aid kit, and what look like military rations."

Her head throbbed violently and she reached up with her left hand and gingerly touched the cloth bandage wrapped about her head.

"You have a bad gash over your ear. I wrapped it as well as I could but it needs stitches. When they hit you, it split your skin open."

"What is in the first aid kit?"

"Some water purification pills, gauze pads and tape, and some kind of anti-bacterial ointment. I put some on your cut but I think it needs to be sewn up."

She studied him for a moment, trying to grasp what she had been told.

"Nothing here that tells us where we are?"

"This looks like some kind of observation station," he said. "There's a sign over the door that says 'Mavadappu.'"

"Mavadappu," she muttered, closing her eyes and reaching for a memory that seemed much more distant than she knew it should be. "I know Mavadappu."

"Where are we?" Marcus twisted one leg up onto the bench to face her. "Do you know where this is?"

She kept her eyes closed and fished around in a mind that felt like it had been ransacked, every item scattered about so that nothing was where it belonged.

"Mavadappu," she said again, mainly to herself. Gradually her brain picked through the rubble, finding pieces here and there and laying them beside each other.

"Anamalai," she said finally. "We're in Anamalai."

"Where's Anamalai?"

"The tiger reserve. It used to be Indira Gandhi Wildlife Reserve. Mavadappu is one of the observation stations—and I think maybe a native village. I have a camera near here."

Marcus sat silently for several moments as if what she had just said explained everything. "Do you want to try to eat something?" he said finally. "These bars are dry, but not too bad."

"More water," she said. "I need to drink more."

He set the cup on the bench and refilled it from a two litre bottle that sat beside it on the floor, using only his right hand. She leaned slightly forward and looked at his left. The arm hung loosely at his side.

"You've hurt your arm." She reached forward with one hand as she held the blanket with the other.

"They must have dislocated it when they beat us—or dumped us out of the van." He moved the arm gingerly away from her reach. "I popped it back into place, but it's still too sore to move much. Let's get you taken care of and we can worry about it later."

"You popped it back yourself?"

"It's happened before."

"Can you move your fingers?"

He slowly raised the arm and moved each finger one at a time. "Just dislocation. Very sore, but okay." He helped her drink, then knelt in front of her and looked at her with dark, serious eyes.

"The tiger reserve. What does that mean?"

Nisha glanced around the room that was empty except for the bench and chest that had held the few supplies. Just below the eaves, long narrow windows no higher than the width of her hand ran the full length of two sides, letting in the last muted light of early evening.

"Mavadappu is in the Tiger Reserve. I think this is one of the observation stations they've created for tourists."

He followed her gaze up to the high, narrow windows. "How can you observe anything?"

"From on top. There are stairs up the side."

"I don't think I'd want to be watching tigers from on top of this place," he said, glancing at the low ceiling. "They can jump as high as this roof."

"If it's the place I'm thinking of, visitors come here mainly to watch for other animals that graze in the open grassland. Tigers usually don't attack people and visitors rarely see them in the park."

"They're here," Marcus muttered.

"You've heard them?"

"One followed us out of the forest. He charged me just as I was carrying you in through the door. You notice anything about these walls?" he said with a wry smile.

She looked at the wall she was facing, then at the one on either side. "No door," she said in confusion.

He reached behind her and slapped the door. "The bench is pushed up against it. The thing hit the door just as I pulled it shut, then vaulted right up onto the roof. I had you over my shoulder with your bottom against the door." He laughed to himself. "I think the two of us weighed about as much as he did."

"Is it still around?"

"I haven't heard it for a long time. It walked around on the roof, then paced outside with this sort of rumbling purr. All I could think to do was push everything against the door—including us."

Nisha gazed again about the room, then clutched the blanket more closely about her. "You carried me here?"

Marcus stood and walked to the other side of the room, leaning with his back against the wall. She could see that he wore only a pair of torn grey shorts. "They dumped us about three hundred yards from here in a little clearing. We're lucky the door wasn't locked or we'd be tiger food—like they planned, I think."

"You carried me with that arm? I know I'm small but..."

Marcus smiled self-consciously. "Like a sack of potatoes—thrown over my shoulder. I was afraid I'd injure you more, but I heard the noise in the trees and knew we needed to get away from that clearing."

Nisha looked at the tall black man standing against the wall and noticed that what she had first taken as a large and awkward frame was actually lean and tough, with legs, arms and chest that rippled under his ebony skin. He was a man who could easily carry her.

"We can push the trunk against the door too," she said, diverting her eyes self-consciously. "If the tiger can't find other prey, it might be back."

Marcus retrieved the trunk and pushed it tightly against the edge of the bench. "You say tigers don't usually attack people, but this one did. And those guys must have left us here because they thought the tigers would find us."

Nisha nodded. "There was an attack on some villagers near here in March that received a lot of media attention. They closed the park to visitors for a few months. My guess is that is what gave them the idea."

"Did they catch the animal?" Marcus sat heavily on the trunk and pressed his back against the door. She judged from his expression that he didn't trust their little barricade to keep the door from being forced inward.

"I don't think so. There are only thirty to forty tigers in this reserve and that was the first reported death in years. Up north, in the reserves along the border with Bangladesh, they create more trouble. Maybe fifty deaths a year. Here, it's more likely you'll be attacked by leopards."

"You're not making me feel safer," Marcus said, looking up at the last light as it faded from the high slotted windows. "I suspect the men thought that if they left us bleeding and without clothes, one or the other would get us. We were there overnight—just lying in the open. I wonder why the one that followed us didn't attack until I got you here?"

Nisha stood unsteadily to wrap and tuck the blanket about her like a sarong. "How did you find this station?"

"When I woke up, it was raining pretty hard—and foggy. As it let up and got lighter, I could see where the Land Rover came into the clearing and followed its tracks back to the road." He laughed nervously. "To be honest, I backed all the way to the road. I didn't want something coming up behind me. I could see this place when I came out of the trees."

"The rain, perhaps ... and your backing up."

He looked at her quizzically.

"The rain may have made it more difficult to hear and smell us. It may also have kept us alive and probably woke you up. Once it becomes light, I think the animals are more cautious."

"I felt like it was tracking me ... as I carried you from the clearing."

Nisha smiled and sat back beside him on the bench. "Maybe the natives are right. They say tigers won't attack from the front, so villagers sometimes wear face masks on the back of their heads. And they carry poles or tools over their right shoulders because they believe tigers charge from that side. My dangling over your shoulder probably confused it."

Marcus' look was one of amusement and doubt. "Any idea which way we need to go to get out of here? Maybe I can strap you to my back so we're facing both ways."

"I should be able to walk this time," she said, tucking her legs under her. "But I think we should just wait until someone comes. This isn't the main part of the park near the Topslip entrance, but they have opened the reserve again to visitors and I would think someone comes by here every day or two. We have enough food and water to keep us until then. No sense tempting the tiger. Now, let me look at that shoulder ...."

CHAPTER TWELVE

As Meera sat a hundred meters down Eranakulam's Park Avenue from the Park View Apartments and waited for Kanta, her computer scanned the eight story apartment building for wi-fi activity. She had quickly learned that the complex had its own network, finding *ParkViewAp* as soon as she looked for signals in the area. Gaining access to the network was almost as simple and added to her conviction that most people paid little or no attention to computer security. She knew Nolan Lemay was in his apartment. He had arrived on foot from the north along Park Avenue about fifteen minutes after she began to watch the building, wearing the blue cap with the panther head logo she had been told would be a clear identifier. He looked agitated but unconcerned about whether he was being watched, moving briskly along the sidewalk to the entrance with eyes on the pavement and what appeared to be a scowl on his face. She knew he had never met her, so she hurried from her car and entered the building immediately behind him while the front entrance was still unlocked, joining him in the elevator. During the ride to the sixth floor he didn't acknowledge her and she exited behind him and turned in the opposite direction down the hall. She paused at one of the apartment doors as he fumbled with a key at his own. When the door closed behind him, Meera retraced her steps down the hall to his apartment, noted the number, and walked to the end of the hall where she stuck a camera the size of a thick thumb tack to the frame of a window that looked down over the wide street below. Her iPad displayed the camera's image and she adjusted the fish-eye lens slightly to center it on Lemay's door. Satisfied that she could see most of the activity in the hall and anyone who entered or exited the apartment, Meera returned to the main floor where she waited until another resident entered the building.

The man appeared to be in his early thirties and wore an expensive-looking suit. As he entered, Meera walked toward the door, smiling and nodding a 'good morning.' As he passed, she stopped suddenly and said, "Excuse me, but perhaps you could help me. I'm new to the apartments and was trying to log onto the wi-fi network. What I thought was the security code the manager gave me didn't work. You don't happen to remember what it is, do you?"

"I'm not surprised you didn't get it right," the man said with a smile. "It's 'WildBananas389,' all one word and case sensitive. The W and B on WildBananas are caps."

"That's where I made my mistake," Meera said, showing a touch of embarrassment. "I had the W in caps, but not the B. Thank you!"

"My pleasure," he said as the elevator opened. "Welcome to Park View."

Meera returned to her car, wrote WildBananas389 on a pad on the seat beside her and below it, Room 613. She logged into the network and initiated a scan of its activity, using a program called *SpiderEye* that watched the stream of information coming over the network for key words, tying them to the IP address from which they originated. The trick was to find words that would not show up in common conversation, but were likely to appear in transmissions she was looking for. She had chosen "university, manuscript, ancient, letter, Thomas, text, Disciples, church, possession, acquired, exchange" and variations on these terms.

For nearly an hour she watched activity on the street, monitored Lemay's apartment, and listened for a series of beeps that would indicate her computer had identified one of her word cues. As lunch traffic began to pick up along the Avenue, a slim man in jeans and a sports jacket with an open collar caught her attention as he hurried toward the apartments to enter behind a heavy woman carrying an armload of packages. He carried a large manila envelope in one hand but assisted the woman with the door and her parcels, slipping in behind her. Meera turned her attention to the camera image on her iPad. Moments later, the man emerged from the elevator onto the sixth floor and walked quickly to 613. Without hesitating, he slipped the manila envelope under the door and strode quickly to the lift. Two minutes later he exited the building, crossing Park Avenue to a grey Toyota Etios that was parked on Meera's side. Her instincts said that she should follow him and she switched on the ignition, just as her computer beeped and a line of text flashed on the screen. "... acquire a manuscript that may be of great value. Please wire $25,000 in additional funds to ...." She quickly clicked the cursor on "save" and pulled into traffic behind the Etios.

As the driver turned right onto Banerji Road, Meera tapped a "2" on the autodial on her phone and waited for Kanta to answer.

"Are you here?" she asked when she heard Kanta's voice.

"On my way from the airport to the Park View Apartments."

"The number is 613 and the doctor is in," Meera said. "He received an envelope under his door and I am following the courier. I may have some useful information for you, but will need to call again after I see where this man goes."

"I'll wait when I get there," Kanta said.

Meera ended the call and followed the Etios across the Market Canal and past St. Albert's College, south onto National Highway 47, then left on South Over Bridge Road. The man drove with the aggressive abandon characteristic of Kochi drivers and didn't appear to be worried about a tail. At Manorama Junction he turned again south onto Panampilly Nagar Road, then after 300 meters made a quick right into one of the narrow side streets. Almost immediately he turned again into a drive in front of the Panampilly Apartments and pulled to a stop.

Meera eased to the curb and watched him enter the apartment building, then followed him inside. He was no longer in the lobby but the elevator was stopped at the second floor. A staircase climbed between floors at the end of the hallway and she took it up a floor and pushed through the fire door into the corridor. Six apartments lined the hall on each side and no one was in the hallway. She walked its length looking for nameplates, but found none. Back in the lobby she studied the names on the collection of mail boxes, entered those on the second floor into her iPad, then drove back to meet Kanta.

The *SpiderEye* program Meera was using to scan the Park View Apartments captured all internet activity on the selected network for a five minute period, then purged each conversation if nothing triggered the key word scan. If a selected word, phrase or web address appeared, the program backed up to the beginning of the five minutes and recorded everything from that moment forward, unless the user deleted the thread. It also searched for identifying information for the sending computer, using the IP address from which the information originated; email log-in, addresses to which information was sent, web search data and any other activity that might identify the user. Meera resisted the temptation to check her screen until she again pulled against the curb on Park Avenue where Kanta stood, trying to look as inconspicuous as a woman who is stunningly beautiful can look on a public street.

Kanta slid quickly into the passenger seat of Meera's BMW sedan and gave her colleague a quick kiss on each cheek.

"Any news about Manisha?" she asked as Meera retrieved the message on her laptop.

"Not that I've heard. But we may not need her. Listen to this .... This message was sent about the time I called you, from a computer with the email address NLemay@amu.edu to a ReggieLemay@gmail. Looks like our professor. *'I have an opportunity to acquire a manuscript that may be of great value. Please wire $25,000 in additional funds to the account number I gave you earlier. This could be a career-maker. More later. NL.'*"

"It doesn't appear he has it yet," Kanta said. "But he must know who does and if that person is shopping it about, we may not have much time."

"What do you think was in the envelope?"

"Proof of some kind—but not the letter. He would not slip the actual letter under a door."

"Perhaps a photocopy ...."

"I think I will go introduce myself to Professor Lemay," Kanta said.

"And I will see who he has been communicating with."

As Kanta stepped back onto the walk, with a few keystrokes Meera entered Nolan Lemay's email account and rapidly scanned his Sent Mail, stopping on an item from four days earlier. The address was TVHem0426@TelIndia.com. She retrieved the iPad from her handbag and pulled up the list of names from the second floor of the Panampilly Apartments. The third on her list was Tiruchirappalli Vishwanathan Hem.

"I have found you," she murmured.

Kanta approached the main door of the Park View Apartments just as a distinguished older gentleman was removing his key. He stepped back and pulled the door open for her, bowing slightly as she smiled and moved past him, then hurried ahead of her to summon the elevator, standing admiringly as it descended from the fifth floor.

"Are we acquainted? You look very familiar."

"Some people tell me I look like the actress, Kanta."

"That's it! You look exactly like her! Do you live in the apartments?" The elevator doors slid open.

"Just visiting," she said, hoping he lived on a lower floor and wouldn't feel compelled to question her all the way to the sixth. He was going to one of the upper floors but chose to just look, and she stepped off on Lemay's floor with no more than a smile and a nod.

The doors had buzzers and a security peep hole and Kanta pressed the button and stood immediately in front of the viewer, looking as radiant as she could muster. She heard Lemay approach the door and knew he was looking at her, and she wondered with some amusement what he might be thinking. She heard the security chain slide across and the door opened, revealing a man of about her height with thin, dishevelled brown hair, a pleasant face, and a slight paunch that drooped over his belt. He wore a rumpled long-sleeved white shirt, open at the collar, and navy blue pants. He held the door with one hand as he looked her over with a curious smile.

"May I help you?"

"I hope so," she said, returning the smile. "I have some important information about the Thomas Letter. May I come in?"

The smile faded and he studied her cautiously for a moment, then pulled the door fully open and beckoned her in. She waited inside for him to lead her down the short hallway to a tastefully furnished living room, then paused again until he indicated a seat on a long mauve sofa. He remained standing beside an overstuffed chair to her left, his hands joined nervously in front of him.

"May I get you some tea?"

"No thank you. I have come to deliver a message and then I'll be leaving."

"About a letter ...?"

"Yes. The one you just sent an email to your wife about. It is very valuable to us and we want it back."

Lemay's face flushed and his eyes darted downward and to the side, telling her he had to consider his reply before he spoke.

"I ..." he stammered, "... I have been contacted about an old manuscript. But I haven't seen it. And I don't know where it is. I ... I wasn't aware that it had been taken from someone."

"I think you know from whom it was taken," she said. "Otherwise we would not have known who to watch. And I suspect you do know where it is."

Lemay lowered his head and thought for another long moment. His face was a mottled shade of pink and sweat was beginning to bead on his high forehead. "I received a call several days ago ... that a valuable manuscript might be available that would be of interest to a man of my profession. Today a messenger left an envelope under my door with a price offer ... telling me that I would be contacted in a few days to see if I was interested in buying. I don't know who has it, and I don't have any way to contact them."

"May I see the note?" Kanta asked.

Lemay swallowed and glanced toward a door that led into another room. "I destroyed it immediately. Flushed it down the toilet. It asked for twenty-five thousand dollars, so I sent a message to my wife to wire the money—a message you apparently intercepted."

"When you are contacted again about the purchase, arrange for the transfer and contact me please," Kanta said. "We will meet the seller and recover our manuscript. Will you do that?"

Lemay nodded immediately. "Of course ... although if you have been watching me, perhaps the seller has been as well. They may not get in touch with me again."

Kanta rose from the sofa as Lemay moved toward the door. "I think they will. And when they do, call me at this number." She handed the professor a card that had no more than a cell number on it, then paused until she knew she had all of the professor's nervous attention.

"And I need to stress that you do not want to mislead or betray us. Your friend Doctor Bartlett was about to betray us. I don't think you want to suffer the same fate."

The flush on Lemay's face drained to a pasty grey. "I don't have the manuscript, and don't know where it is," he stuttered.

"Then if I were you, I would do everything I can to help us recover it," she said. Kanta let herself out of the apartment, leaving the American standing mutely in front of his chair, staring at her cell number.

CHAPTER THIRTEEN

The police in Pollachi seemed more amused than concerned. They had never had a large black man and a nearly naked Indian woman delivered to the station. Though Nisha sat in the glassed Inspector's office completely wrapped in the blanket while a female officer was sent to find her clothes, every other officer in the building, male and female, passed by the windows three or four times as if expecting her cover to drop to the floor. Nisha decided the women may be coming to look at Marcus, who sat in all his sculpted glory in a chair opposite her in front of the inspector's desk, wearing another blanket wrapped about his waist and a white T-shirt that was clearly two sizes too small and only served to accentuate his physique. Finding something to fit the tall American was proving to be more difficult.

The inspector leaned back loosely in his chair and polished his glasses with a lens cloth from his center drawer.

"You were able to get through with your call?" he asked amiably.

"Yes, thank you. Someone is on the way to get us."

"So if I understand you correctly, you followed a van that had dumped dangerous chemicals in the forest to some place on the outskirts of the city where they rammed your car and took you hostage. Then they knocked you both unconscious and left you in the tiger reserve without your clothes. Is that a fair summation?"

"Yes, that is correct. They left us in a clearing, and Marcus found the observation station and carried me there."

"And why are the two of you together?" The inspector squinted without his glasses from one to the other.

"I am a doctor in a clinic in Sunkam—north of the Parambikulam Sanctuary. Marcus has been staying at the clinic while he studies languages of the tribes in the region."

The inspector nodded skeptically, replaced his glasses and looked at Nisha more directly. "Have you been staying together? Perhaps your father or brothers found you together and it was they who took you to the tiger reserve."

Marcus leaned forward in his chair. "Excuse me, sir, but ...."

"You may remain silent unless I speak to you," the inspector said evenly, not taking his eyes from Nisha. "This strikes me as an elaborate story to cover up what must be a great embarrassment to your family."

Nisha's dark eyes flashed and she pulled the blanket tighter about her shoulders, her voice dropping in pitch and volume, but becoming icy as she spoke. "Mr. Branscomb is a guest of my family and we both need medical attention. The call I made is to my father and he is a respected leader in Kochi. I suggest you call him yourself and we can get past this nonsense and you can start looking for these men. They are dumping poison in the forest that is getting into the water system. I have patients who are dying right now because of them. Surely you found my Honda...."

She saw his eyes glance at a sheet of paper on the corner of his desk and realized he had a report on the damaged automobile. "This could indeed be an embarrassment," she continued, her voice lowering another level, "... but for you, if you don't get us some assistance and begin to find these men."

The inspector sat upright and adjusted the cleaned glasses. "I will call your father and if he confirms that this man is a guest, you can take me to this place in the forest. But from your description, it is in Kerala and out of my jurisdiction."

"Then call the police in Kerala. But the poison is a solution used in manufacturing textiles and I'm certain it is coming from Tamil Nadu— probably Coimbatore. I think you will want to remain involved."

"I will decide on the level of our involvement," the inspector said dismissively, looking up as an assistant pushed open the door and leaned into the office.

"The district superintendent is calling for you," she said, then pulled back out of the office and closed the door. Nisha noticed that the crowd outside the window had suddenly disappeared.

The inspector's face paled visibly and his eyes darted from Nisha to Marcus as he picked up the receiver on his desk. "Inspector Battacharjee," he said as officially as his voice could muster. He listened without speaking for several minutes and Nisha could hear the commanding voice of the superintendent on the other end of the line.

"Yes, Sir," the inspector said finally. "I will see that everything is taken care of." He hung up and looked grimly at Nisha, his hands flat on the edge of his desk.

"It appears that the Kerala police are already involved—at the highest level. Your father will be here soon so let us get some clothes for you both and I will send for someone to look at your head and Mr. Branscomb's arm. Then we must see what we can do to find these polluters ...."

.   .   .

If Nolan Lemay had been asked to describe what he was feeling, panic would have been the first word to come to mind—but it didn't come close to describing the sensations. Terror? Desperation? Helplessness? *They had killed Dixon Bartlett*! The Disciples of Thomas had killed his closest associate because he was going to write about a manuscript that Nolan had just arranged to be stolen! He paced the room, dropped onto the sofa where the beautiful mystery woman had issued her warning, cradled his face in his hands while he tried to collect his thoughts, then jumped again to his feet and began to circle the room.

On the desk in the smaller of the apartment's two bedrooms, a page-sized photo of the manuscript sat on the envelope in which it had been delivered. Within a day—possibly a few hours—Hem would call or text to arrange payment. He couldn't call his guide to warn him. They seemed to know everything he was saying and doing. And he couldn't turn Hem over to the Disciples. The thief would immediately point the finger back at Nolan. He could sit tight and call the woman in a few days, saying he hadn't heard from the thieves—but Hem would make some sort of contact before then, and they would have them both.

He wondered fleetingly if the woman had just been trying to frighten him with the comment about Dixon. But he knew from looking into her black eyes that she was telling the truth. They had killed Dixon Bartlett.

Where was Marcus? He had hardly seen the graduate student since they arrived in Kochi and they had only talked by phone two or three times since he went up into the hills with Pillai's daughter. Nolan needed to talk to someone, and Marcus was the only person he could think of. But the assistant was so straight arrow. He'd tell him to go to the Disciples and fess up—turn Hem over to them and take his licks. But any group that had killed Bartlett just because he was going to *talk* about a manuscript wasn't going to turn the other cheek for someone who had actually stolen it.

He should go home. Escape back to Charlotte and leave the photo on the desk with a letter of apology. If they found Hem, they would know Nolan was involved but may not chase him to the U.S. But they had pursued Bartlett. And if Regina and her family thought he was bringing trouble—goodbye, Nolan Lemay! He was acceptable to her only as long as he didn't embarrass the family, and an academic scandal would not only shatter what was left of his fragile marriage, but ruin him at the university.

He plopped again onto the sofa, clenched his eyes shut, and massaged his forehead with both hands. The feeling of hopelessness transported him back to the living room of his family home in Huntersville, North Carolina, and the afternoon his Law School Admissions Test scores came in the mail. He had arrived home to find his father already pouring over the scores, though the letter had been addressed to Nolan. The senior Lemay was standing in the entryway when Nolan entered the house.

"You blew it," he said, waving the paper in his son's face. "We spent all that money on the prep course and you couldn't even get above the fiftieth percentile. But then, why am I not surprised?" The conversation that followed was a repeat of one Nolan had heard two or three times a year since he was old enough to understand what it meant to be a disappointment. He was never compared to an older brother or sister. There were no older brothers or sisters. It was always "Judge Fredrickson's son" or "Doctor Westcott's boy." The lecture always ended the same way. "Sometimes I wonder if you got any of my genes at all."

Entry into Religious Studies had been the final straw—the ultimate admission that he couldn't handle a real profession. No matter that he found it fascinating—a place he could finally search for some kind of personal meaning. And now he had messed that up too. He sat without moving until his cell phone buzzed, piercing a small hole in the cloud of despondency. He glanced at the text message.

"Money wired – but don't ask again."

He sniffed cynically. Not likely! But I'd better get ahold of myself. There's got to be some way out of this .... First, hide the photo. They might come back and it needed to be out of sight. He pushed from the sofa, checked the door to insure that he had locked it securely, then hurried into the bedroom he used as a study.

When the woman came to the door, he had just begun to examine the photograph and had confirmed that it was the Thomas letter Dixon wrote about in his journal. The beginning was just as Bartlett described. When he returned to the study, he scanned quickly again over the opening lines and began to slide it back into the envelope. Then he paused and dropped into the desk chair to gaze at it again. Beyond the Disciples, no living person knew what the letter said. The most important Christian text of the first century, and no one knew what was in it—or that it even existed.

He pulled it again from the envelope and looked quickly over the rest of the text. Perhaps he should read it before putting it away. If something happened to it, he would at least know what the letter said. So maybe he hadn't gone about this in just the right way. But at least for once in his less-than-stellar life, Nolan Lemay would know something that made him special.

He retrieved a pencil and legal pad from the drawer of the desk, placed a piece of paper over the photo to cover all but the first line, and systematically traced his left index finger beneath the line from right to left as he wrote.

From Thomas, twin of our Lord Jesus in the flesh and faithful servant in the spirit, to our brother James who ministers to the saints in Jerusalem. Peace be with you through the spirit of God and through our knowledge of the good news of our Lord, Jesus Christ. By his word I have been called to labor among the lost sheep of the house of Israel in Muziris from where I send you the prayers and blessings of many who have come to know the Christ. Before leaving you I told you that Jesus had spoken to me of mysteries that I could not share, knowing that you were not yet ready to understand them. I must share them now, for I am about to leave you and to leave the saints of Muziris. As Jesus walked with me he said, "Soon I must leave this world but you must remain. For as my twin, within you (missing word or words) light of God which will shine forth while you remain in the world, sparing it from utter darkness. And you must be part of the world until I return, for the Father has given you power over death. The powers of darkness cannot prevail against the light, and your light will preserve the world. And so, my brother James, though you will hear rumors of my death and believers will gather to worship at my tomb, I now leave this place to go forth into the world so that my presence will preserve it from the adversary until our Lord shall return in his glory. Peace be with you all who are in Christ. Amen

Nolan dropped the pencil onto the desk and again lowered his head into his hands, thoughts careening wildly about and striking one frayed nerve after another.

I have it and I can't do anything with it. They killed Dixon for knowing less than this. But my God! This does claim he is still out there somewhere! It could make me a household name—I must keep this and get away from here. But not home. They'll find me there. How much money do I have? Will they get to Hem? What will he tell them? I need to warn him—get him to give it back. They killed Dixon because he was about to speak .... Maybe I should give it back and ask forgiveness .... Perhaps this is the time to do something right ....

This final thought brought with it a surprising calm and Nolan sat upright in his chair. If he could get the letter back to the Disciples .... He needed to find a way to warn Hem and tell him to figure out how to return the manuscript. Nolan knew he was being watched, but could they have eyes on every door? There were four ways out of the apartment building—the main entrance, a back door onto the pool area, and doors at each end the of main floor hallway. He slipped the photo and translation back into the envelope and pushed it under the blue silk Persian carpet that spread under the coffee table, then walked to the window that looked down onto the back garden of the apartments. A gate exited onto Marine Drive Walkway that ran along the bay. He had Hem's address somewhere .... He would walk along the bay until he could cut between buildings over to Park Avenue and catch a cab to his guide's apartment.

. . .

Meera was already inside the apartment in Panampilly. As soon as Kanta entered the building on Park Avenue, Meera had returned to the building that housed Mr. TVHem to set up the same wi-fi scan that had picked up the message from Lemay to his wife. This apartment building did not have its own network and as her computer sorted through the dozen individual signals that emanated from the four-story building, the man she had identified as Tiruchirappalli Vishwanathan Hem emerged from the main entrance and walked briskly away from her toward Panampilly Nagar Road.

Without waiting for him to get out of sight, Meera pulled a small black case from a pouch beneath her seat, dropped it into her handbag, and crossed to the apartments. She glanced again at the mailboxes in the foyer and noted the number—202—then took the stairs to the second floor and stepped out into the corridor. Panampilly Apartments was several grades below those she had been watching on Park Avenue and the hall carpet was a threadbare maroon industrial grade with a geometric pattern that was almost dizzying. Room 202 was immediately on her left at the end of the empty hallway and she quickly examined the deadbolt, then stepped back into the stairwell where she selected a pick from another small case in her bag.

It took only seconds to enter the apartment. The deadbolt had not been locked and she was easily able to slide a card around the knob latch and slip it back. Meera stopped just inside the apartment and studied the living room. The air was heavy with the stale smell of cigarette smoke and she involuntarily brought her hand up over her nose. The room's furnishings were basic: an inexpensive fake leather sofa and matching chair, flat-screen TV in a veneered pressboard entertainment center against the wall to her left, a low glass-topped table that stretched in front of the sofa. Virtually everything in the room could be seen at a glance, as could the table, counters and white metal cabinets in an equally sparse kitchen that opened through an archway to her right. Few hiding places. Under the cushions on the chair and sofa, behind the television, or taped to the back of a cabinet or the bottom of a drawer. She guessed that if the manuscript was in this apartment, it wasn't in either of these rooms.

Beyond the entertainment center, a door entered what she guessed would be the bedroom and she quietly crossed the room and eased it open. The curtains were drawn but an overhead light had been left on and a goose-neck floor lamp pulled to the side of the bed to cast a brighter white arc across a plain beige bedspread. There was no need to study the room for hiding places. The manuscript and woven mat lay on a white dish towel on the edge of the bed closest to the door, centered in the halo of light. Meera paused, listening to the sounds of the apartment and the street below and wondering fleetingly if she had walked into a trap. The letter seemed to be on display—as if the thief were expecting someone to enter the room looking for it. Why had the dead bolt been unlocked and why would he leave with this lying out in plain sight? She slipped her hand into her bag and found the grip of a small Beretta, sliding sideways until her back was against the bedroom wall opposite the door.

The only sound in the apartment was a slow drip coming from what she guessed was the bathroom sink—a steady plop, plop that only added to the unsettling silence of the room. For a full minute she stood without moving, every sense probing the quiet apartment. A battered leather satchel was propped against one leg of the bedstead, its flap thrown back, suggesting the manuscript had just been pulled from the case and placed on the bed. She eased forward, keeping one eye on the doorway, and crouched beside the bag. From her own case she withdrew a white cotton glove, slipped it on and reached into the man's satchel, pulling out a small black kit almost identical to the one she had used to enter the apartment. Dropping it back into place, Meera stood and again surveyed the room, coming back to the manuscript displayed against the plain white background. Then she saw it. The letter was laid out to be photographed. He must have discovered he was missing something needed to complete the task and hurried out to get it, leaving the lights on and door latched only at the knob—meaning he would be back at any moment.

Meera left the manuscript where it was and moved quickly back into the living room, screwing a silencer onto the barrel of the Beretta as she positioned herself beside the door where it would open against her. She had only minutes to wait. The scrape of his key in the knob alerted her that he had returned and he opened and closed the door in a single motion, tossing a carton of cigarettes onto the glass table as he walked past it into the bedroom.

She walked silently across the room, raising the pistol as she stepped into the bedroom doorway. He was standing with his back to her, studying the manuscript.

"Turn around very slowly," she said in a soft, firm voice that she hoped would keep him from charging her as he turned. She had no interest in shooting the man in his apartment.

He reacted as she had hoped, freezing after an initial startled jerk, then slowly turning toward her with both hands raised to shoulder height, palms forward. He looked directly at the Beretta and swallowed hard, then raised his eyes slowly, but said nothing.

"You have something that belongs to us," she said in the same soft, firm voice. "I have come to collect it."

He shrugged his shoulders in surrender. "I just acquired it myself. I didn't know where it came from. I am only a middleman."

"What is your name?"

"I go by Hem."

"Well, Hem. For not knowing where it came from, it got to you very quickly. And I notice you have an interesting set of tools in your bag."

The thief glanced down involuntarily, then back at Meera, giving her a resigned nod. "I was going to return it. The person who was going to pay me for it can't come up with the money. I was getting it ready to return to the church. I didn't think it would have been missed so soon."

Meera looked again around the room for a camera. "Let me see your cell phone," she said, seeing the thin rectangle in his shirt pocket.

"My phone? What for?"

She raised the silencer menacingly. "Just put it on the bed and step over by the wall there."

He pulled the phone from his pocket and tossed it onto the bed beside the white cloth, then moved against the wall. She picked it up with the gloved hand and found the photo icon, thumbing quickly through four images of the manuscript.

"Who did you send these to?"

"No one. You can check my sent messages. None have been sent."

"Who were you planning to send them to?"

"No one. I had them on the phone so I could show my client I had the manuscript if he had the money. He couldn't get the money and I was getting ready to take the manuscript back."

"Who was the client?" Meera demanded.

"I don't know. I didn't have a name yet."

"You have been exchanging messages with the American professor Lemay. Was he the client?"

Hem flushed with surprise. He was silent for a long moment. "I have been working with him and learned about it from him. But the client was someone I found on the internet."

"I don't see a computer in the apartment."

"I use internet cafes."

"And your email comes to your phone?"

"Some does. I use several addresses."

"What did you deliver to Professor Lemay today?"

Again Hem flushed. "It had to do with the work I do for him."

"So you pushed it under the door."

Hem stood silently, seeming to realize Meera knew enough about him that additional lying might make things worse.

"Come into the living room," she ordered, backing through the door into the main room as he followed. "Now, turn and put your hands on the arms of the chair, pushing your feet back and apart. Look straight ahead at the back of the chair."

Hem hesitated and she thrust the Beretta a little farther forward. He turned and did as he was told.

"What are you going to do?"

"Look at your phone." But instead she pulled the black case from her handbag and opened it on the glass table. A capped syringe held 15 cc's of a clear liquid and she twisted off the red cover and replaced it with a needle.

"Keep your back to me. Straighten up and take down your pants."

He started to turn and she pushed the barrel of the Beretta into his back. "Do as I say or I will shoot you where you stand. Now, take down your pants ... and your underwear. Leave them around your ankles."

She stepped back as he lowered his clothes, then ordered him to again lean forward onto the chair's arms. Before he could settle, she thrust the needle deep between his buttocks along the edge of his rectum and depressed the plunger. Hem yelped and pushed away from the chair, whirling on his assailant, but Meera immediately thrust the barrel into his face. As she watched, his pupils began to dilate and he started to waver.

"Pull up your pants," she ordered and he hesitated, then in confusion stooped and fumbled his clothing back into place. Within seconds, he collapsed backward into the chair. Meera quickly pulled an elastic tube from her bag, stretched it tightly around his upper arm and thumped at a swelling vein. As Hem gazed at her in numb silence, she wiped the needle, poked it into his arm half a dozen places along the vein, then inserted it a final time, dispensing the last few cc's of the liquid. As his eyes began to glaze, she lifted his right arm and dropped it across his lap with the hand near the syringe.

Hem's head had dropped to the side but he still starred stupidly at the needle in his arm.

"You can return the manuscript," Meera said," but you can never forget that it was there to begin with. It is the secret that keeps it safe."

She tucked the Beretta and Hem's cell phone into her bag, returned to the bedroom and eased the manuscript and mat back into his makeshift folder. With the lamp back in a corner, she turned off the bedroom lights and took a final look at Hem to be certain the laced heroin was doing its job. The location of the apartment made the rest easy. She eased open the door and could see that the hallway was empty. Within seconds she was in the stairwell, carrying the folder carefully under her arm. Before she reached her car, she punched the first speed dial entry on her phone.

"I have it," she said simply when the man answered.

"Did you have any problems?"

"None that couldn't be dispensed with."

CHAPTER FOURTEEN

Nolan asked the driver to stop just as the cab turned off Panampilly Nagar into the side street that included Hem's address. As he left the cab, a slight woman with short black hair exited a drive fifty meters in front of him and crossed to a white BMW parked against the opposite curb. She made a U-turn in the street and as she passed, glanced over at him, then diverted her eyes so quickly he feared she had somehow recognized him. He hurried along the broken sidewalk, scanning the addresses as he went, and realized that the woman had emerged from a drive that connected Hem's apartment to the street. He turned to look after the retreating car, but it had already turned left onto the main avenue.

No one knows me here, he thought. It was probably a matter of her being surprised to see a foreigner walking in this part of the city.

Nolan walked past the apartments to an alley that ran between buildings, turned down it and into another that backed the apartments until he found the rear door to Hem's building. It took him into a short hallway that intersected the lobby near the elevators and he slipped into the lift and punched the button for the second floor.

Hem's apartment was at the end of the hall and he knocked softly, looking out the window at the end of the corridor so that anyone entering the hall could not see his face. No one answered. He rapped again and impatiently tried the knob. The door was unlocked and edged open under his touch. He pulled it back, but left it unlatched. After a long moment he eased it open enough to call inside and said in a loud whisper, "Hem? Hem?"

The apartment was silent and Nolan pushed the door the rest of the way open, recognizing immediately that something was wrong. He could see his guide's head resting loosely against the back of a brown chair that sat facing away from him. The man's feet were sticking out onto the carpet in front of him, the back of the chair hiding his face. But Hem didn't move. Nolan eased forward, closing the door behind him.

"Hem?" As Nolan reached the side of the chair he could see that the man's mouth was agape, his eyes open in a dull, blank stare. An empty syringe hung from his left arm that was still strapped in a rubber tourniquet. Hem was clearly dead.

Nolan stepped back instinctively, lifting his hands as if holding them lower would leave marks that could be traced. The door knob. He'd get it on the way out, but needed to hurry. Quickly he glanced around the living room and kitchen, then moved into the bedroom. A white dish towel was spread along the side of the bedspread and a brown leather case lay on the floor beside the bed. He eased it open with the back of his hand. It held two small black kits but no manuscript. The dish cloth must have been the backdrop he had seen in the photo and he wondered fleetingly if he should search the rest of the apartment for the letter, but knew immediately that it was gone. Hem had not overdosed and the manuscript wasn't in the apartment. And the woman in the white BMW did know who he was. Bartlett—now Hem. And Hem would have told the woman everything before he died. There were no second warnings. Nolan Lemay needed to disappear.

.　.　.

The three women faced the row of elders across the stone chamber and waited for their leader to speak, their scarves pulled forward to cover all but their faces. Manisha had rejoined them, offering her apologies for being beyond reach but promising she would do what was necessary to make up for the other's work.

"We have been fortunate," the senior elder said, nodding appreciatively at the Guardians. "The letter is back in its place and the thief will not be able to share its contents. Now we must learn what others might know."

"I fear the thief was told where it was by the American, Lemay," Kanta said. "He may not have known exactly what was here, but he knew from his colleague Professor Bartlett that the church contained a valuable record."

"Has he seen it?" the elder asked.

"I don't think so. Meera found the letter still with the thief."

"I fear he may have seen it anyway," Meera said soberly. "The letter was photographed on the man's iPhone and though it was not sent to Lemay, it was forwarded to Mr. Hem's email address. I suspect he may have printed a copy."

"And an envelope was delivered to Professor Lemay," Kanta added.

"We must assume he has a copy of the letter."

"Manisha, it must be your assignment to find out," the senior elder said. "See if you can draw him out of his apartment and Meera can search it and examine his computer."

"And if we fail to find it and he refuses to admit he has it—or has seen it ... what then?" Manisha asked.

The old man looked at the other elders, each of whom nodded solemnly. "We have conferred on that possibility," he said. "The thief worked for him and must have learned about the manuscript from the American. We suspect it was taken at the professor's request. We must assume he knows of its contents and must be silenced."

"Forgive me, *Babaji*," Manisha said, tenderly fingering the side of her scarf-covered head. "But the man may be innocent."

Her superior nodded. "He may be. But the evidence suggests otherwise. And it is better for even an innocent man to die than that the Second Son be revealed and the world thrown further into chaos. If it is believed that he lives, he will be hunted to the ends of the earth. We cannot take that risk."

"If we can determine that Lemay does not have the letter and is not aware of its contents ...?"

"What would serve as proof?" the elder asked. "His word?"

Manisha bowed slightly. "The irony could be that his word is all he has."

CHAPTER FIFTEEN

The door buzzer shattered the quiet of the apartment and Nolan jumped so violently he dropped the shoes he had in his hand and had to reach for the closet door to steady himself. He held his breath, thinking first that he should let it go unanswered and let the caller leave. But the person might enter anyway, and if he was pretending to know nothing, there would be immediate suspicion. He walked quietly to the apartment door as the buzzer sounded a second time and squinted through the security hole. Marcus stood in the hallway, his chin and neck visible through the viewer. Nolan quickly released the chain and ushered his assistant into the room.

"Sorry, you caught me in the ...," he began, then reached again for the door frame for balance. It looked like they had already gotten to Marcus. His head was bandaged and his left arm hung in a sling. "What in the world happened to you?" he sputtered.

Marcus shrugged it off. "Long story—and I guess you haven't seen the news. I let Nisha talk me into tracking some men who've been dumping solvents in the jungle near the national park and they caught us and beat us up. Left us in the tiger reserve to be eaten. Fortunately, the rangers found us before the tigers did."

"Is Nisha okay?" Nolan was more interested in finding a way to get Marcus out of the apartment than in Pillai's daughter's health, but knew he should ask.

"About like me. I thought I should check in with you though."

"I was just getting ready for a little day trip. Thomas supposedly started seven churches between here and Chennai. I thought I'd visit a couple of the other sites."

"Want company?"

"No. Hem's taking me and I want to be free to go where the spirit moves, so to speak. You look like you'd better take it easy for a few days. You going back out to the clinic?"

"I think so. I want to keep an eye on Nisha to make sure she's okay. She said she was going back to work, but I think she may be in worse shape than I am. And I know she won't give up on the people who are poisoning the streams up there."

"I'll give you a call when I get back," Nolan said, edging toward the door to encourage his assistant into the hallway. "Hem's on his way, so I'd better be pulling things together."

"Let me know what you learn. Sounds like an interesting trip." Marcus eased through the door and Nolan closed it without comment. He hurried back into the bedroom, stuffed the last few items of clothing into a duffle bag and tucked a small envelope with the folded photograph and translation into the zipped compartment in the side of the bag. He exited the building through the back gate onto the Marine Drive Walkway and this time turned south. After walking a quarter of a mile along the bay, he cut across a children's park toward the main boulevard to hail a cab as his cell phone rang. The ID showed ' Nisha Pillai' and he let it ring, then realized that as long as he had the phone with him, people with the technology to intercept his messages could figure out where he was. He turned it off, looked to see if anyone was nearby and seeing no one, dropped it onto the pavement and smashed it under his heel, tossing the broken remains into an elephant-shaped trash receptacle.

Nolan knew nothing about disappearing, but he did know he needed money. His plan, to the degree he had one, was to get to the Ernakulum branch of the Union Bank of India, withdraw the $120,000 he should have in his account, and get to the central bus station. He would pick a destination when he got there. If he didn't know where he was going, neither could anyone else.

. . .

Just as Marcus was thinking of calling her, Nisha called him. He was collecting enough clean clothing to make it through another week at the clinic and she had offered to pick him up later in the afternoon.

"How you feeling?" he asked.

"Much better. I was thinking I might come by early. There are some things I'd like to discuss with Professor Lemay. Do you know if he's in?"

"He may be gone. I talked to him about thirty minutes ago and he was about to leave on a trip to see some of the Thomas church locations. He said his driver was coming by within a few minutes to pick him up."

"His driver? That man named Hem?"

"I think so. He said he was on his way."

There was a long pause at the other end, then Nisha said, "Could you go down the hall and see if he's there? I really need to talk to him before he leaves. I'm on my way... ask him to wait until I get there. And could you stay on the phone while you go to his door?"

"Sure ...." Marcus' apartment was three doors down from 616 and he walked the few steps to Lemay's door, talking to Nisha as he pressed the buzzer and waited. "Anything I can tell him while you're getting here?"

"No. Just tell him I need to talk to him before he leaves the city."

"I don't think he's here ...."

"Is the door unlocked?"

Marcus tried the knob. "No. What's going on?"

"Do you have a key, by any chance?"

"No .... Nisha, what's this all about?"

"Go down and tell the superintendent you think something might be wrong with Professor Lemay and ask if he can let you in. If you can't find him, wait outside the door. I'll be there in a few minutes."

"Nisha ...."

"Please. Go now. I'm almost there."

Marcus found the superintendent in his office and talked him into opening Lemay's apartment on the pretext that he was concerned that something had happened to his sponsor. The landlord walked closely behind Marcus as he looked through each room, then ushered him back to the door when it was evident the professor was gone.

"It looks as though you have no need to ...," he began as they stepped back into the corridor, but was interrupted by Nisha rushing from the elevator, waving for him to leave the door open.

"Please .... Something may have happened to him," she panted as she reached the pair. "Can we check to see if some of his things are missing? I know you remember me from when I came with my father to arrange the leases. The apartments are leased in our name and you can stay with us as we search."

Marcus glanced at her curiously but hid his surprise from the superintendent.

"This is most irregular," the landlord said. "But I do recognize you. What are you looking for specifically?"

"I'm concerned he may have been taken," she said, "... and some of his valuables with him. If we can just look quickly ....”

The superintendent gave a resigned bow and beckoned her into the suite, with Marcus close behind. She moved quickly through the apartment, checking drawers and closets and surveying each room with a studied eye while Marcus watched her closely. Clothes still hung in the closet and Lemay's large suitcase stood empty in one corner.

“I can’t see that anything important is missing,” she said finally. “Forgive us for the inconvenience and thank you for your help.”

When the landlord was back in the elevator, Nisha stood with arms folded and back to Marcus, gazing down the hall. He turned her toward him and stooped until she had to look into his eyes.

“Are you going to tell me what that was all about? I told you he was headed somewhere with that driver of his, and might be gone by the time you got here.”

Nisha returned his gaze steadily but was silent for a long moment. “I believe Professor Lemay is gone,” she said finally. “But not with his driver. I think he won’t be back.”

Marcus smiled skeptically. “What’s gotten into you? If we’re going to worry about someone, it should probably be us. We were both on the news last night and this morning, and those men who took us will know we made it out of the park.”

“Let’s go to your apartment,” she said, turning toward his door. “There are some things I need to tell you.”

Nisha sat at the small kitchen table and fingered the bandage on her temple while Marcus made tea, watching her curiously as he moved from kettle to cupboard and pulled out two green ceramic mugs. It was a characteristic she had quickly learned to appreciate about the tall American—his lack of concern about gender roles and who should do what. When she was having a busy day at the clinic, she often looked up from a patient to find that he had prepared lunch for them both.

“My mother told me I could be anything I wanted to be in this world,” he told her with a broad grin when she asked about it. “Today I wanted to be a cook.”

She wondered now if the trust she had in this man—a trust that had developed as she watched him work with the villagers and as he fussed over her in the observation station prior to their rescue—was one she

114

could bet their lives on? She knew she owed hers to him, and had felt both strength and tenderness in him when she awoke with his hand against her cheek after their attack. Thoughts of those moments stirred something in her soul and told her she had to trust him now.

"Before I say too much, tell me what you know about the Disciples of Thomas," she began, watching him carefully as he filled the electric kettle and poured black tea leaves into a small mesh container.

Marcus gave her a faint smile and shrugged. "Probably not as much as I should. Only what Doctor Bartlett told me when we worked here last summer—and what I gathered from his book. And you've told me a few things when I've asked."

"And from Doctor Lemay?"

"Practically nothing from Doctor Lemay. He invited me to come with him mainly because I'd been here before and could provide some translation assistance in Tamil. He doesn't have any background in Pali or Tamil. But so far we've worked entirely on our own."

"Did either of the professors ever mention a manuscript that was particularly important to the Disciples?"

Marcus paused with a second tea ball poised above one of the green mugs and appeared to be thinking back over his conversations with his advisors. "No—I don't think so. What kind of manuscript?" He looked over at Nisha with an expression that showed only open curiosity, and she knew he was being truthful.

"One from the early centuries of Christian development in India. Concerning Thomas' work here."

"Did they know about it? The professors?" he asked.

"I know Doctor Bartlett did, and I'm quite certain Lemay knows about it. In fact he may be responsible for it having been taken several days ago from the church where it is kept."

Marcus walked to the table and slowly placed the steaming cups in front of Nisha.

"Taken? I'm hearing that to mean 'stolen.'"

"We don't think he took it himself," she said, continuing to watch his expression for any indication this might not be a surprise. "We suspect this guide of his—or driver, or whatever he was—took it and was delivering it to Professor Lemay."

Marcus eased himself slowly into the chair opposite her at the table.

"And you think this man Hem was bringing it to him—or they were going somewhere together to get it?"

Nisha took one of the cups and wrapped her hands around it. "Hem was not on his way here and Professor Lemay was lying to you," she said bluntly. "Mr. Hem died this morning of a drug overdose."

Marcus raised his left hand to the back of his head and rubbed his short black hair as he stared at her, his eyes a window to the collision of thoughts that was happening in his brain. He dropped the arm again to the table. "Where was Dr. Lemay going ... and how do you know all of this?"

"We are a small and close community," Nisha said, deciding as she spoke how much it was wise to share. "And my father is one of its more prominent members. We learned the manuscript might be with Hem from an anonymous source and he was found dead when they went to recover it."

"And it was there?" Marcus asked.

She nodded. "And there were indications he had been in touch with Professor Lemay."

Marcus leaned forward onto his elbow and propped his chin on his hand, wrapping his fingers across his mouth. His deep brown eyes looked at her with such intensity that she knew he was also trying to decide if she was being completely truthful. She wasn't, but his safety depended on him not knowing too much.

"What did you want to talk to Doctor Lemay about?" he asked through his fingers.

It was time to consider her answers more carefully—to decide what Marcus should know and how far she could extend the trust. She took several long sips of tea and reached across the table to touch the arm that stretched in front of him in the sling. He didn't pull away, but his jaw tightened and a trace of suspicion narrowed his eyes.

"He may be in danger," she said seriously. "To the Disciples, this manuscript is more than a sacred object. It is the foundation of our faith. There are those who will protect it and what it says at any cost. There is some fear that the professor may have a copy."

Marcus slowly pulled upright against the chair back, then stood suddenly and thrust a hand into his pants pocket.

"I'll call him. If he's not with Hem, he can't be far away. I'll get him back here and we can ....”

“He won’t answer,” she interrupted. “I tried on the way here. In fact, I’ll be surprised if he still has his phone with him.”

Marcus’ look was incredulous. “You think he’s running? Why would he run? He can’t know that he’s in danger ....”

“I suspect he knows about Hem,” Nisha said. “And about Professor Bartlett ....”

Marcus snorted his disbelief. “Oh, Nisha .... I don’t know what they’ve been telling you, but this is all way beyond belief!”

“Please sit,” she said, holding her hand out to him again. “I’m trying to save Professor Lemay. We need to find him before others do.”

He dropped back into the chair and stared questioningly at her across the table. “You’re serious about this, aren’t you. You think someone killed Doctor Bartlett because he was going to reveal something, and that they’re now after Lemay.”

“No,” she said solemnly. “I *know* they killed Doctor Bartlett and Hem—I *know* they are looking for Lemay. And I’m pretty certain he knows it too. Where do you think he would go?”

“So you think Bartlett knew about this manuscript?”

Nisha nodded.

“Was it the ‘proof’ he was going to offer to support his book?”

“Very likely.”

“And Lemay learned about it somehow and came here to get it?”

“That is the way it looks.”

Marcus threw up his free hand and leaned away from her. “Whoa!” he said, shaking his head. “This is getting way too heavy for me.”

“It may be heavy, but it very much involves you. For your safety, you must keep what we have discussed just between the two of us. Let’s go out to Sankum and we’ll pick up some of my things. I’ll get someone to look after the clinic. We can talk while we drive, but we need to find the professor. And you know nothing about the manuscript?”

“I don’t,” Marcus said honestly. “And if we find him—what then?”

“Perhaps we can get him to return the copy and convince them to let him go.”

“He may be trying to go home.”

“I don’t think so. He knows they got to Dr. Bartlett in the U.S.”

“And if they get to him before we find him?”

"Then ....," she said, taking his hand and refusing to let him pull it away, "... then we just have you to worry about."

. . .

Kuldip Singh had unwrapped his waist-long hair from the yards of turban cloth and was leaning forward, gripping the shiny black tresses in one hand as he brushed them with rhythmic, downward strokes with the other. The cell phone on the table beside him buzzed and he glanced quickly at the ID, then threw the hair back over his shoulder and snatched up the phone.

"Yes, sir."

The voice at the other end was low but edgy. "You said you had taken care of our problem with the doctor and her black friend."

Kuldip swallowed hard, knowing that what he was about to say must not be true. "We did, sir. They are gone."

"Do you ever read the newspaper or watch the news?"

"Of course, sir, but I have been very busy."

"They were found alive in the Tiger Sanctuary. It has been quite a story."

Kuldip closed his eyes and felt his mouth go dry. "But they were nearly dead when we left them. We wanted them still living so the tigers would smell live prey."

"They weren't dead enough," the voice said. "They are cleaning up the dump site but haven't traced it to us. But she won't give up. Take care of them—and do it right this time."

Kuldip started to say "Yes, sir," but the voice was already gone.

CHAPTER SIXTEEN

As what he thought was a purely random choice, Nolan bought a bus ticket to Pondicherry. But now that he was there and locked away in a cheap hotel in the heart of the city, he suspected he had chosen to come here for a reason.

Nolan had never really considered himself a man of faith. Though his adult life had been committed to studying the world's belief systems, on those rare occasions when he took the time to think about it very seriously he had decided he was probably agnostic—not completely discounting the existence of God, but unconvinced by evidence of his existence. He leaned toward a religious explanation based on cults of personality, systems that developed around the teachings of charismatic men who appeared at times of social crisis with messages of hope or liberation. Lao Tzu, Confucius, Mahavirah, the Buddha—any that he could think of right up to the time of Jesus, Muhammad and Nanak—had demonstrated that in times of uncertainty, human nature seeks answers in myth, heroes, ritual and symbols that bring meaning to an otherwise senselessly cruel or meaningless existence. These men offered a psychological release from the trials and challenges of their time and in most cases, after their deaths stories of supernatural origin and powers developed around them. The main exception was in the country where he now found himself a fugitive: India. Here, Hinduism's great myth-makers were long forgotten, leaving a tradition that was essentially agnostic in its theology, seeing God as a cosmic consciousness that drove an endless cycle of creation and destruction.

But for the first time in his life, Nolan felt the shadow of death hovering over him and could think of nowhere to turn. Its shroud squeezed at his heart and lungs and he found himself gasping for breath. The constant flush on his face and itching behind his eyes told him his blood pressure was running amuck, and he had to struggle to keep his thoughts from returning to the beautiful woman with the black, deadly eyes saying "I don't think you want to suffer the same fate."

But now as he sat in the dank, dimly lit room of the Shri Perumal Inn, with the constant clatter and honking of one of the city's main thoroughfares adding to the dissonance in his brain, he pulled the copy of the letter from his bag. Tracing a finger downward until he found the passages he was seeking, he looked again at the phrases that had been forcing themselves into his thoughts like a beacon on a mist-shrouded coast. They began with the line with the missing words. "... *within you* _____ *light of God which will shine forth while you remain in the world* ...." The space was only large enough for a word or two. "... is the?" "... shines the?" He could think of no combination that would negate a statement that within Thomas shone the light of God, and he read through the passage, inserting the simplest verb.

> ... *within you is the light of God which will shine forth while you remain in the world, sparing it from utter darkness. And you must be part of the world until I return, for the Father has given you power over death. The powers of darkness cannot prevail against the light, and your light will preserve the world.*

Dixon had believed the letter to be authentic—to have been written by Thomas. Not the wishful thinking of his followers three centuries later, and not a creation of a contemporary disciple who wanted to deify his teacher. It was a statement by the man himself that he had learned he possessed a divine spark that protected him from death, and that he was charged with preserving that spark until the return of his brother whom he acknowledged as the Messiah. And now, more than ever in his life, Nolan needed hope.

He had not even considered returning home. There was nothing for him there but a wife who viewed him as an embarrassment and a university that would be more than happy to end his employment. And there was the probability the Disciples would find him there as they had Bartlett. To face any of these realities was much more frightening to Nolan than facing complete uncertainty. He was not a fighter, but for years he had learned to be a survivor by attaching himself to someone who did the fighting for him. Now those people were beyond his reach or beyond his desire to seek their help—unless what he had read was more than a myth. "*Within you is the light of God,*" he kept thinking, "*and your light will preserve the world.*" Perhaps that light could save Nolan Lemay. He had to find Thomas—and by legend, Thomas had died a martyr near Chennai. So as Nolan had scanned the list of departures from the Ernakulam bus station, he had subconsciously chosen the first one that went in the general direction of India's eastern coast.

The Inn provided no internet service but Nolan learned from the desk clerk that a small café attached to a place called Unicom Computers offered free 24 hour wi-fi service if he had a laptop and could find a table. It was two blocks south on Anna Salai Street, not far from the hotel. He still feared that someone among the Disciples was tapped into his university email account, but his Gmail used an innocuous log-in name and they couldn't be monitoring every network in India. He waited until the late night traffic began to subside on Anna Salai and found the café, hurriedly laying claim to the one open spot at a corner table. He ordered coffee, plugged in his laptop, and scanned the area for accessible networks, finding the wi-fi signal for the café surprisingly strong and fast.

A quick Google search revealed that by tradition, Thomas was murdered on a small mount that stood in what was now the Guindy neighborhood of Chennai near the international airport. The Church of Our Lady of Expectation marked the spot and was now a national shrine. Three kilometers northeast, the Blessed Sacrament Chapel stood over a cave where the apostle was purported to have lived. Nolan scanned the articles and saved them to his computer, then checked morning train schedules to Chennai. If he caught a six forty-five he could be in the city within an hour and a spur of the Suburban Railway Network ran from the main terminus to the St. Thomas Mount station. Tomorrow, Nolan would begin his search for the Second Son.

.   .   .

It was a few minutes after midnight and Nisha was still awake, pulling together the clothes she thought she would need and trying to decide where they should begin the search for Professor Lemay. She had suggested that Marcus get a few hours' sleep at the clinic and she would pick him up shortly before 6:00 a.m. They would start with the train and bus stations, then check auto rental agencies. If nothing panned out, they would go to the docks and ask about westerners trying to get passage out of the country by sea.

She heard the car coming when it squealed around the turn at the end of her street. Sunkam was more a village than a town, and what few automobiles drove through the quiet streets never squealed. Instinctively she grabbed her small roller bag and ducked away from the bedroom window that faced the street. The car slowed in front of the house, then sped up again as her living room window shattered and she heard the whooshing explosion of a fireball as the front part of her three room cottage burst into flame.

Her bedroom opened directly into the inferno and the only doors to the outside were through the rapidly spreading flames. She grabbed her cell phone from the bed and forced the window open on the side of the house away from the door, throwing the roller bag into the bushes that bordered the cottage and scrambling after it. Neighbors ran from the homes next door and across the street, shouting and pointing, and fingering the buttons on their own phones.

"Call the fire department," she shouted, realizing as she reached the middle of the street and turned to watch flames engulf the cottage that it would only be to save neighboring buildings.

"I heard the car," a neighbor said beside her. "What happened?"

"A fire bomb of some kind," she gasped. "Someone was trying to ...." She stopped in mid-sentence, realizing that whoever was after her would want to get rid of someone else as well. She pulled the phone from her pocket and dialed the clinic.

Marcus had been asleep and his voice was thick and husky. "Is it six already?"

"Get out of there" she shouted into the phone. "They've bombed my house and will be there next." In the background she heard the squeal of tires on the gravel drive that led to the clinic.

"Get out the back! Now!" From the other end of the phone, the same shatter of glass and whooshing blast assaulted her ear.

She looked helplessly at the Honda parked beside the low wall that fronted her house, realizing the keys had been hanging on a hook inside her front door.

"Can you take me to the clinic?" she asked the man standing beside her. "The people who did this went there next. I heard the explosion on the phone."

He ran toward his home as sirens sounded in the distance, returning with his keys and pointing Nisha toward an aging Ford that stood opposite the Honda.

As soon as the car was beyond the glare of the fire that burned her home, Nisha could see the glow to the south where she knew the clinic was also burning. The small fire service in Sunkam could not respond to both and they were headed toward her cottage. Both buildings would be lost.

As the Ford turned up the gravel drive that led to the clinic, Nisha scanned the small cluster of on-lookers who had gathered along the edges of the parking area to watch the spectacle, and her heart sank. No tall black figure stood a head above the crowd, and otherwise the lot was empty. She signaled her driver to pull up beside the huddled group and was out the door before the car had fully stopped.

"Has anyone come out of the building?" she shouted above the rumble and crack of the flames.

"No, Doctor Nisha," a woman said. "Was your man in there?"

Nisha didn't answer but rushed toward the building, turned back immediately by searing heat. Tears streamed down her cheeks and she looked frantically around, moving toward one side of the flaming clinic, then the other.

"Doctor Nisha," the woman said, grasping her arm and pulling her away from the scorching heat. "There is nothing anyone can do."

Nisha collapsed onto her knees, dropped her face into her hands and sobbed. She had known she was beginning to care for the man, but she hadn't realized how much. The heat was beginning to singe her hair and she felt that she might also burst into flame, but she didn't move. The murmur of the crowd behind her quieted suddenly and she looked up, expecting to see his beautiful black body stride out of the flames toward her, but she saw only a shower of sparks as the roof collapsed into the skeleton of the building.

Then she felt a strong arm wrap around her waist and was lifted as if she were a child and carried away from the flames. Her face was pulled against his broad naked chest and she felt his cheek nestle into her hair.

"You're going to get burned if you stay up here," he whispered and she twisted against him and threw her free arm up across his shoulder, beginning again to cry.

"I thought you were in there," she sobbed, nuzzling her cheek against his chest. "I was so afraid I'd lost you."

"I went out the back just as they threw the bomb through the window," he said. "Your call saved me. But I didn't know if they would stay out front so I ran back into the trees and waited, then circled around and came back up the drive. I was afraid you were about to run into the building ...."

He set her down on the grassy verge of the road and she held him for a moment, then realized his chest was bare. She eased away and he stood smiling at her, wearing only the familiar grey boxer shorts.

"This is becoming your standard emergency outfit," she laughed through her tears.

"It's what I wear when I sleep and you didn't give me much time." He wiped tears from her cheeks with a long finger and chuckled. "But I was harder for them to see this way."

She caught the finger and pulled his hand against her face. "You look wonderful," she said, then looked around cautiously. "And I think we'd better both disappear. If the police talk to us, we'll be on the news again and they will know we are still alive."

He glanced around at the crowd. "These people know anyway. Someone will tell the police."

Nisha walked to the group standing a few yards away and waved for them to gather around her. "The men who bombed the clinic and my home are the ones who left us in the tiger reserve," she said. "They will continue to look for us as long as they think we are alive. If you are asked, would you say you don't know what happened to us? We need some time to get away somewhere."

The small crowd shuffled nervously, then the man who had driven Nisha from her home spoke. "You have been good to us all, Dr. Nisha. We can do this for you." The others nodded slowly.

"Will you come back to us, Dr. Nisha?" the woman who had pulled her away from the fire asked.

"I'll be back as soon as I know we are safe. Just help us until then."

"Can I take you somewhere?" the driver asked. "The police will be here soon."

"If you can drive us to Kochi and my parents' home. I'll be happy to pay you when we get there...."

"I would not be a good man if I allowed that," he said. "It is my gift."

.   .   .

The apartment Meera shared with her roommate Rasa could best be described as half artist's studio and half command post. It was located on Peterceli Street in old Fort Kochi, a few blocks from the parade grounds, and had once been a second floor storage area for a spice merchant. Now the front portion of the floor was a long spacious room with Rasa's studio area in the southwest corner against the windows and Meera's bank of computers and servers covering the walls on the north and east. A small kitchen filled the center of the back of the apartment with bedrooms on each side. When the room had been remodeled into living quarters, a balcony was added that stretched out over Peterceli Street. This was where Meera and Rasa spent their mornings, drinking tea and watching the ancient part of the city come to life.

Rasa's gallery filled the floor below and she did a brisk tourist business with her paintings of colorful street scenes of Fort Kochi and of the Chinese fishing nets on long tripod poles that lined the nearby shoreline. Her art had a quality that clearly separated it from the work of the street painters whose wares lined the walks along the beaches. She had earned a word-of-mouth reputation that brought visitors into the old city to buy more valuable reminders of their trip to the Malabar Coast.

Meera worked entirely in the apartment, her computers probing the security systems of her clients for back doors, breaks in firewalls, and passwords that could too easily be decoded. Her considerable skill and intuition allowed her to find and patch these weaknesses and to develop stronger and less permeable security solutions. She had developed a reputation of her own as one of India's most respected IT security analysts. These same talents made her an invaluable member of the Guardian team and had been at work since she learned that Nolan Lemay was missing from his apartment in Ernakulam. She was not surprised by the disappearance. He had been right behind her when she left the thief's apartment and must have known his death was not an accident.

One of Meera's most useful tools was a program that continuously scanned the major search engines, email sites, and social networks for access from a computer with a predetermined MAC address. It was a bit like watching for use by a specific cell phone, but notified her home computer when the machine with the desired MAC entered one of the systems, then determined its location. Meera awoke early on the morning following Lemay's disappearance and glanced at the screen that displayed tracking information as she headed for the balcony with her morning tea. A red bar across the bottom of the screen flashed an Alert message and she quickly slipped into the chair and placed her cup on the edge of a wide mouse pad that displayed a picture of her and Rasa standing arm-in-arm on the lawn in front of Delhi's Red Fort.

The message said: *"Target computer activated at Unicom Computers, 116 Anna Salai St., Pondicherry. Accessed sites concerning St. Thomas Mount, Chennai."*

Meera swiveled her chair to a second computer to her left and quickly typed in a password that opened one of her email accounts, selecting a group address from a list on the right side of the screen.

"Person of interest at Unicom Computers, 116 Anna Salai St., Pondicherry at 1:15 a.m." she typed. "Active for 27 minutes." She hit the send button and sat back, cupping the tea in both hands as Rasa emerged from the kitchen with her own drink.

"You are busy early," she smiled. "No big problem, I hope?"

"Not if we can act quickly enough," she said. "One of my clients has a potential breach and I've passed along the information. Now it's up to them to close it down."

CHAPTER SEVENTEEN

It seemed only minutes after he fell asleep that Marcus felt Nisha shaking his shoulder.

"Marcus, we need to be going. I think I know where Professor Lemay went and we need to find him before he moves."

Marcus stretched and sat up, reaching for her hand as she began to leave the room. She turned back toward him and stood for a moment, looking down at him with her gentle, dark eyes and he knew that his desire that she share his growing affection was not just wishful thinking. She squeezed his hand and said softly, "We need to hurry. We have a flight in two hours."

Their driver the night before had taken them by Marcus' apartment to pick up some clean clothes, then to the Pillai home. Nisha's parents listened to an abbreviated version of the attacks on her home and clinic, promised to follow up with the authorities in Sunkam, and found them beds for the night. Her father accepted Nisha's explanation that they would be leaving the next day to "stay out of sight" until the attacker could be apprehended and showed surprisingly little concern. Her mother looked from her husband, to Nisha, to Marcus with worried eyes but remained silent.

Marcus found Nisha in the kitchen putting fruit, a crepe-like bread called dosa, and a container of dal, the lentil stew that was the staple of South Indian meals, into a covered basket.

"Father will take us to the airport," she said as he entered. "He will arrange for us to pick up a car when we get there."

Marcus took a handful of cashews from a bowl on the table and grabbed a couple of bananas as she headed for the back door and the garage.

"Get where? Do I need more clothes?"

"We'll get what we need as we go," she said over her shoulder. "I don't know how long we will be gone, so there is really no way to prepare."

"I don't have any money with me," Marcus said. "I grabbed my passport as I ran from the clinic, but I didn't get my wallet."

"I have what we need." She led him into the garage where her father already had the door raised and car running. She took a seat in the back and Marcus slid into the front passenger seat of the black Mercedes, buckling his belt by habit. "You still didn't say where we're going," he repeated, half turning toward Nisha.

"Chennai. Our flight is at 9:00 and we should have tickets waiting."

As they maneuvered through the streets of Ernakulam toward the main highway out of the city that would take them north to the airport, Marcus watched the senior Dr. Pillai. He looked ahead without expression or comment, suggesting he knew exactly where they were going and why.

"Why Chennai?" Marcus asked.

"We're not only a small community, but a sophisticated one," she said simply. "Lemay's computer was used in Pondicherry late last night, making inquiries about a place called St. Thomas Mount in Chennai. By tradition, it is where Thomas was martyred. We think he may be going there."

Nisha's father continued to watch the road ahead as if oblivious to the conversation. Marcus again wondered who "we" referred to, but decided this wasn't the time to inquire. Instead he asked, "Is anyone else on their way there?"

"I'm sure of it," she said soberly.

The ease with which they moved through the domestic terminal at Cochin International Airport indicated that more than the Pillais were interested in the pursuit of Nolan Lemay. Dr. Pillai dropped them in front of the domestic terminal but didn't go in. As they entered the picturesque pink stucco building with its columned front and terra cotta roof, a middle-aged man in a crisp white shirt and dark trousers approached and handed Nisha two boarding passes, nodded pleasantly and disappeared into the crowded terminal. At security, one of the guards waved them to a separate screening conveyer and hardly looked at the few items they placed on the belt. They found themselves at the gate without Marcus having to show his passport to anyone. The flight was boarding and the young woman at the counter beckoned them forward and ran them through with the first class customers, even though their tickets were in economy class.

When they were seated, Marcus leaned over to within a few inches of Nisha's ear. "You're a small group, but connected everywhere," he whispered.

"In Kochi, yes. We consciously place people where they can be of service."

"And what is your role, Doctor Pillai?"

"I'm the physician—and sometime counselor and tour guide."

"Was I invited to the clinic to interview some of the tribal people or so you could keep an eye on me?"

She turned with what he judged to be mock surprise. "Why, you're starting to become suspicious of me, Mr. Branscomb. I'm not sure it becomes you. Perhaps I just wanted to have you close by."

"You're a dangerous woman to be close to. So far I've been kidnapped, beaten, dumped in a tiger reserve, and fire bombed. Now you have me flying across the country to find a man who may also be in danger. What should I expect next?"

"Never expect," she said, placing her hand on his arm. "Then you won't ever be surprised."

.   .   .

A broad paved road climbed the side of St. Thomas Mount and shortly after 8:00 a.m. when the shrine opened, the taxi was able to drop Nolan within a few yards of the entrance to the Church of Our Lady of Expectation. A guide was beginning an English tour and Nolan asked the driver to wait, then eased in among the group of assorted tourists as she led them into the long narrow chapel of the white stucco building. The church had been built in 1523 by the Portuguese, its altar marking the spot where by tradition, Thomas had been praying when speared by a Hindu antagonist of the growing Christian church. Nolan followed the tour through the guide's elaborate description of the many relics that adorned the shrine and of the miracles each had produced. As the tour concluded he waited until the crowd dispersed, then handed her a generous tip and asked if she had a moment for questions.

"Are you familiar with the tradition that Thomas traveled as far as China?" he asked, glancing nervously around as other groups assembled at the back of the sanctuary for the beginning of a new tour.

"It is my personal belief that he did," she said. "He went as far as Xian and his disciples there extended the church into Japan. There are congregations there that still trace their roots to St. Thomas."

"You say it is your personal belief. What leads you to believe that?"

"Thomas was a builder—a builder of churches. We find his work in many parts of Asia."

"His work? Perhaps they are simply churches built after the fashion of the churches Thomas built here ...."

"That is true of some," she said. "But on the ones he built himself he left his mark—the mark of the double Ichthus."

"The entwined fish. Some say this signifies that he was the twin of our Lord Jesus," Nolan offered, hoping that by sharing in her piety she might be more open with her thoughts.

"Some do. I am not among them. I think it simply signifies his commitment to being servant to the Lord."

"And where do these churches appear? Other than Xian?"

"There are two theories about how St. Thomas traveled to China. One that he went north from India through what is now Pakistan to join the Silk Road. The other is that he crossed by sea to Burma—what is now Myanmar—and made his way north from there. Perhaps he went one way and returned another. But the first church that I am aware of that bears the sign of the double Ichthus is across the Bay of Bengal—in Yangon, the old city of Rangoon in Burma. Then they create a chain that crosses East Asia into China. But we don't know if he built them while going to China, or while returning."

"That must have taken years," Nolan mused, looking again at the growing group of visitors flowing into the church.

"The saint lived a long and fruitful life before his martyrdom here," she said, but Nolan did not hear her. His eyes were on the young Indian beauty who had just entered the sanctuary. She had not yet seen him and he nodded his thanks to the guide and slipped quickly through an archway into a side chapel and out into the courtyard.

His heart pounded and he again felt his eyes burn and the flush rise in his face. How had they found him here so quickly? Even if someone at the bus station had remembered him buying a ticket to Pondicherry, they couldn't have known he would come here .... It had to be the computer search. They knew how to track his computer wherever he switched it on! He saw the driver leaning against the hood of his cab under a thick, ribbon-draped tree that stood along one side of the church compound and hurried to him.

"I'd like to go to the port where passenger ships leave," he said, sliding into the cab and leaning back into the seat, keeping one eye on the doors of the chapel.

"Are you sailing somewhere?" the cabbie asked, easing the car out of the lot and out of sight of Our Lady of Expectation.

"Meeting someone. You can drop me there and I will be going to their home when they arrive."

"Very good, sir. I will show you some of our beautiful city as we drive to the port."

Nolan glanced at his watch. It was 8:50. "I need to be there as quickly as possible. Give me a card and I'll call you about a city tour some other time."

The cabbie shrugged. "The port is north all the way across the city in George Town. We will see much of it anyway."

"As direct as possible," Nolan said, glancing back involuntarily and mopping his forehead.

. . .

It was just after 11:00 when Marcus and Nisha reached St. Thomas Mount. The shrine was only a few hundred yards off the end of Runway 25 at Chennai's International Airport and they could see it from the plane as they taxied to the terminal. But it had still taken half an hour to deplane, clear the terminal, and get to the Mount. The Disciples' influence spread beyond Kochi and as soon as they left the secure passenger area, someone was waiting to take them to a car. What Marcus hadn't expected was the stunning beauty of their greeter: a woman of about Nisha's age with a full, curvaceous figure, shoulder-length black hair and a perfection in her features that turned every head in the terminal. As she walked toward them, people nudged each other and whispered as if they recognized her, but she seemed unfazed by the attention. Like Nisha, she wore blue jeans and a loose long-sleeved shirt that was untucked and draped over her shapely hips.

"You got here quickly, Kanta," Nisha smiled.

"Six o'clock flight," she said, eying Marcus with what he took to be mild irritation. Nisha turned toward him.

"This is my friend Marcus. He is Doctor Lemay's assistant and is as anxious to find him as we are. I thought he may be able to help with the search."

Kanta nodded with a tight smile, continuing to look at him critically as if trying to decide how much he knew about the situation, then turned abruptly and led them from the terminal.

"I've already been up to the Shrine, Manisha," she said as they reached the car. "There is a guide there who might be helpful. She is waiting for us."

Marcus slid into the back seat, with Nisha joining Kanta in the front. "Manisha? Is that your full name?"

"My family and patients all call me Nisha," she said. "But it is really Manisha. Please stay with Nisha."

Marcus leaned back in the seat, wondering what else he didn't know about this woman he was beginning to care about so deeply. Before he could give it much thought, Kanta pulled the car into a lot beside a white Spanish-style church with a large cross above the door.

"She said she would wait for us at the gift shop," Kanta said, leading them across the lot to a small room crowded with booklets and religious trinkets. A distinguished white-haired woman in a dark navy suit who looked more European than Indian recognized Kanta and came to meet them.

"Mrs. Silcox, my associate Doctor Manisha Pillai and her friend Marcus," Kanta said. "Doctor Pillai is a physician and they are helping me in our search for our friend Doctor Lemay. I know they will be very interested in your conversation with him." She turned to Nisha and Marcus. "Mrs. Silcox' family is British and stayed in Madras after independence. She has been serving as a guide here for ... did you say twenty years? I explained that Doctor Lemay is a visiting professor from the U.S. and has been showing some signs of disorientation. We are quite worried about him."

"Very concerned," Nisha affirmed. "He is the responsibility of my family while in the country and Marcus is his assistant. We hate to say this is an onset of early dementia, but after going on for some time about wanting to see the places St. Thomas lived and worked, he suddenly disappeared without notifying anyone. We were able to trace him here."

"He did seem rather nervous and a bit disoriented," Mrs. Silcox said.

"He joined my tour but wasn't paying close attention. I think he mainly wanted to visit with me afterward."

Marcus listened to the exchange with lingering traces of the wonder he had felt during the drive from the airport, but decided to step into the conversation.

"What was he interested in knowing?"

The guide repeated her conversation with Nolan Lemay and finished by saying, "he ended the conversation very abruptly ... before I think he had asked all he wanted to know. It was as if he suddenly decided he needed to be somewhere else."

Kanta nodded knowingly. "Very consistent with what we have been seeing. Did you happen to notice where he went?"

"He ducked into the side chapel and beyond that, I'm not sure where he went. I certainly hope you find him."

They thanked the guide and excused themselves to the church's courtyard, stepping into the shade of a row of trees that bordered the shrine along the edge of the hill.

"It is possible that he saw me," Kanta said. "From my conversation with the guide, I think he disappeared about the time I arrived. But I looked about the grounds quite carefully and he was gone." The women looked at each other uncertainly, then Nisha turned to Marcus.

"You know him better than any of us. What do you think he is planning?"

Marcus shook his head. "He's a difficult person to know well. Since we arrived, we've hardly spoken a dozen times. He does his own thing and I do mine—and I've never been certain what his thing really is. You were clever with your talk about dementia ... but I was wondering if you may not be that far off. He's a strange fellow."

"What if he thought he were in danger?" Kanta asked. "Would he try to get home?"

"That depends on the danger, I think. And whether he thought it would follow him."

Kanta again studied him as if wondering what he knew.

"And if he thought the danger might follow him there?"

"I don't know a great deal about Doctor Lemay's personal life, but my impression is that he didn't have a very happy one. It wouldn't take much to convince him not to go back."

"In which case, where would he go?"

Marcus looked from the beautiful face of Kanta to the pretty and much less challenging face of Nisha. He replayed his earlier conversation with her in his head, trying to decide what might be helpful to Dr. Lemay and what threatening. She said someone would be after the professor. Was this Kanta one of those people? He decided that for now, all he could do was trust in Nisha's judgment.

"He's not a man with a lot of personal confidence and always seemed desperate to make a name for himself as a scholar. From the questions he asked the British lady, my guess is he may be trying to retrace the steps of Thomas as he went to China."

"Which way?" Kanta probed. "North to the Silk Road, or across the Bay of Bengal?"

"He's more a man of convenience than commitment," Marcus said. "Which way would be more comfortable?"

"If he's trying to get to Xian without going directly, neither of those routes would be easy," Nisha said. "One would take him into the Himalayas, the other through Burma. If he goes north, he'd go through Delhi, so would need to catch a flight from here or go by train. If he's headed for Burma, he could fly or go by sea."

"I'd suggest plane rather than train," Marcus offered. "He wanted to take the train to Kochi when we first arrived, but wasn't that happy about it after a day in that sleeper car."

"I'll call Meera and get her searching travel reservations," Kanta said, "then get a cab back to the airport and see if I can find any trace of him there. Why don't you two take the car and head for the harbor ...."

"And if we find him ..?" Marcus asked.

Kanta gave him the same dark, penetrating look. "The first thing we do is see what he has with him, what he knows, and why he is running. When we know that, we go from there."

CHAPTER EIGHTEEN

Marcus had been wrong about Nolan Lemay and comfort. Fear had taken over Nolan's natural inclinations and replaced them with a will to survive. And survival meant being where no one would expect him to be. But now he wasn't so certain survival was all that important. For the last two hours he had been leaning over the rail at the stern of a battered, rust-stained vessel named the *Swaraj Dweep* as it plowed through the Bay of Bengal toward the Andaman and Nicobar Islands. With one hand he gripped the peeling rail and with the other moved a large napkin from his forehead to his mouth, wiping away spittle as with each roll of the ship, he threw up into the ocean. They were twenty-five miles off the coast of the Port of Chennai, sailing in light swells that constantly pitched and rolled the ship. It reminded Nolan of the moving walkways in carnival fun houses that came to Huntersville when he was a boy. His sister had teased and chided him into going through one of the "Tunnels of Fun," and he had hated it then as much as he hated this now. Death, he decided, didn't seem like such a dismal alternative.

Other passengers moved silently past him—some sympathetic to his discomfort and some visibly disgusted that he was out in the open where everyone had to endure the sight. Though he was being careful to stay out of their way, he needed to be up in the fresh air and within a few feet of the rail. He couldn't imagine that there could be anything left inside him—then he would throw up again.

At the Port of Chennai he had gone into the first place that looked like a booking office and learned that the only passenger service out of the port was to some tiny Indian-owned islands he had never heard of. They were 1200 kilometers across the Bay of Bengal—much closer to Burma, Thailand and Indonesia. But if he wanted to get to Yangon by sea, he had to go through Port Blair in the Andaman and Nicobar Islands.

"You're in luck," the agent at the Chennai office told him. "These ships to Port Blair go out only three or four times a month and one sails early tomorrow morning. I can get you into a berth tonight, if you like. From there, Gati Shipping has opened commercial service into Yangon and though their ships move mainly cargo, they book a few passengers if space is available in the sleeping quarters." He called Gati while Nolan waited and found that a container ship leaving Port Blair three days after Nolan arrived could provide him passage.

"You know you can fly to Rangoon," the agent suggested, using the old name for the Myanmar capital.

"Do you know the expression 'mid-life crisis?'" Nolan asked. "Well, I'm in the middle of one and my solution is to do all the foolish things I didn't allow myself when I was being a responsible adult. One is to take a tramp steamer to Rangoon."

The agent smiled and nodded. "I grew up on the sea and that is not what I dream of when I think of things I have always wanted to do. And my dreams do not include Burma or Rangoon."

"To each his own," Nolan said and booked what was listed as a "luxury cabin" on the *Swaraj Dweep* for 8000 rupees.

He was grateful now that he had been able to get a room on one of the two decks that rose above the ship's hull. Two levels of cabins were below deck, some with small, weather-etched portholes that peered out just above water level. In addition to his motion sickness, Nolan was mildly claustrophobic and being down in the bowels of the ship would only have added to his misery. He managed to get a cabin on the upper level with a nice-sized window and a door that opened into the corridor within feet of the exit onto the aft balcony. They were 50 to 70 hours from Port Blair—as exact as the crew was willing to be about time—and Nolan was beginning to realize that he was in for three or four of the worst days of his life.

.   .   .

The Andaman and Nicobar Islands lie 120 miles west of the narrow peninsula that Myanmar shares with Thailand on the eastern side of the Bay of Bengal. The islands form a long tropical chain that parallels the Thai coast, extending south to within 100 miles of the Indonesian island of Sumatra, and have a long and infamous history of colonial occupation and exploitation. Though 750 miles off its eastern coast, India controlled the islands as a naval outpost from the 11th through the 17th century when Dutch explorers claimed the islands for Holland and tried unsuccessfully to establish colonies on these narrow strips of malaria-infested rock. In 1858 the British established a settlement at Port Blair with primary interest in developing a penal colony and a decade later purchased the islands from the Dutch, making them part of British India.

Until India's independence in 1947, the Cellular Jail at Port Blair housed hundreds of India's dissidents and freedom fighters, locked away in a massive three-story fortress whose seven arms radiated from a central tower like brick spokes of a bicycle wheel. In 7' by 14' cells designed to keep prisoners from seeing or communicating directly with each other, India's most notorious revolutionaries wasted away in complete isolation until they perished or were eventually freed by the government of liberated India.

As the Jet Airways Airbus banked steeply to its right over the northern tip of Great Andaman Island to begin its approach into Port Blair's International Airport, Marcus was glued against the window gazing down at the dark green canopy of rainforest that spread across the island to meet an emerald sea.

"This place is absolutely beautiful," he said, looking back at Nisha who sat beside him. "A little piece of paradise."

"Almost paradise lost," she replied, leaning across him to peer through the thick glass at the white sand beaches and stretches of volcanic rock that defined the coastline. "The prison here held some of our great heroes of the struggle for independence and the image we gain from school isn't one of paradise. Plus, these islands were almost washed away by the tsunami in 2004. Over two thousand people died and forty thousand were left homeless."

"Not much sign of it now," Marcus observed.

"Yes. In this climate the jungle grows back quickly, and the villages were so completely washed away that there is no sign they were once there. One of the ironies was that the few native people who are scattered through these islands all survived. Their legends told them that when the earth shakes, they must get to high ground. It was the immigrants who were caught in the low-lying areas."

Marcus nodded. "There's a lesson in that about what we can learn from myth and legend. There's almost always some kernel of truth in them somewhere."

Nisha settled back into her seat, thinking how true that statement was to their reason for being there. She and Marcus had had their first real disagreement when she announced they needed to fly to Port Blair. The traffic crossing Chennai had been horrible—cars inching along in mass rather than in lanes, horns blaring and helmeted motorbike riders weaving though the stalled traffic as if running an obstacle course. The air reeked of diesel fumes and Nisha's eyes stung as if they had been sprayed with fine dust. They had reached the harbor in Chennai after the shipping offices closed and could learn only from dock hands that the *Swaraj Dweep* sailed the next morning, two hours before the offices opened. There was no way to know if Nolan Lemay was on the ship.

"We need to be back here when they open tomorrow and find out," she told Marcus. "If he's on it, we fly to the Andamans and meet him when he arrives."

Marcus had looked at her with amused skepticism. "This is getting a little ridiculous. First of all, why would Doctor Lemay go to whatever islands you're talking about—and if he does, why would we follow him? I thought you wanted him out of whatever danger you think he's in, and going off to some tiny place in the Indian Ocean should about do the job."

"You don't understand the seriousness of this," Nisha said pointedly. "I can't really explain it to you without putting you in equal danger. Think of it as him having a virus that could contaminate much of the world if it were to get loose."

They were facing each other on the pier with the rusted white side of the *Swaraj Dweep* rising above them and Marcus frowning down at her as if she had just hauled him back into the warehouse in Coimbatore.

"I think we're having a little trust problem here," he said. "You tell me Lemay's in serious danger, but won't tell me why. You tell me I could be in equal danger but won't tell me how. You say he needs to get to safety, but if he's leaving India for places unknown, you think we need to chase after him. If you don't tell me what's really going on, I'm out of here."

"If we have a trust problem, it's that you can't trust me when I say your safety is in not knowing more than you do. I promise you—you can't know more. Not now."

"So we find out if he's on the boat and if he is, fly to Port Blake or Port Blair or wherever it is. Who's paying for all this?"

"You don't need to know that either. But you will be safest if you come with me. Please, Marcus, I really need to have you trust me on this. Let's find a place to stay near here and we can come back in the morning to see if Professor Lemay is on this ship. If he is, we have plenty of time to get to Port Blair."

"This is more than a matter of trust with me. I think you know I've started to care for you—very much. I was hoping it was mutual. But if we can't be honest with each other about something as important as this, I don't see this going anywhere."

Nisha knew they were going to have this discussion at some point - but not here and not now. She more than cared for him. She ached for him in ways she had never felt about any man. She didn't want to be away from him for a moment and knew that even without the danger, she wouldn't want him out of her sight.

"I want it to be more than a matter of trust for me as well," she said. "But right now, that's where we need to leave it. You are a man who studies religion. You know that faith and trust can be strong without having to know everything."

"That generally involves God," he said cynically.

"Or a savior," she said before she could stop herself. "Please ... can't you just trust me on this?"

"If you want more, this may be exactly the time to show me. We're finding a place to stay tonight. Stay with me."

Her look was of such utter disappointment that it shook Marcus to the very core and he wished immediately that he had said nothing. He had just violated the most important principle of mutual affection that his mother had taught him—that love should never demand submission of one human being to another.

"I'm sorry," he said immediately. "I didn't mean that."

Her expression softened and she took his hand in her own and pressed it against her heart. "If only it were that simple. I would give almost anything to stay with you. But I can't. Someday I will explain."

They learned from the shipping agent the next morning that Lemay was on the ship and Marcus agreed to go with her to the islands. But he had barely spoken again until looking down onto the Andamans from the air. He was silent again until they were inside the terminal. They purchased a thirty-day permit for him as a non-Indian visitor and found a driver waiting with a sign as they cleared the security area.

"I believe we are staying at the Hotel Sentinel," Nisha said as they loaded their luggage into the car. Their driver, a man who looked more Malaysian than Indian, nodded brightly.

"You have been here before?"

"No. But we had a text before we left Chennai. Is it nice?"

"Oh, very nice. You will like it very much. But you may be in for some bad weather. There is a tropical storm moving up from the south. It will probably be here day after tomorrow."

"How strong?" Nisha asked. "We're planning to meet a ship coming from Chennai that should be docking here in about three days."

"Very hard to say," the driver said, shaking his head. "Some are saying it will turn into a cyclone. Others that it will just be a heavy storm by the time it gets here. I am hoping for a light storm, *Inshallah*."

"If it becomes a cyclone, what happens to ships that are headed this way?"

"Very hard to say. They will go somewhere else."

"There is no standard port to which ships are diverted?"

"No. Very hard to say. How far is the ship when the storm comes? There are no standard storms. Some come from the south and keep moving north. Some move west. Others will just sit here. Very hard to say."

Nisha cast Marcus an irritated glance. "We may very well be in the wrong place and we won't know where the right place is until it is too late."

Marcus finally broke his moody silence. "What makes something a cyclone? Sounds bad."

"That's what we call hurricanes or typhoons in the Indian Ocean. Same thing. Just as bad."

"Resources don't seem to be a problem for you," Marcus said. "There can't be that many options for the ship. Cover them all."

His tone was laced with enough sarcasm that Nisha wanted to ignore him altogether, but he was right. If the ship diverted, it would either return to Chennai or move toward one of the few major ports along the northern coast of the Bay of Bengal. She pulled out her cell phone and was surprised to get a signal.

"There aren't any places beyond the reach of cell reception anymore," she muttered as she dialed Kanta's number. The phone was answered on the first ring.

"We're in Port Blair," Nisha said. "There's a storm headed this way and our ship may be diverted. We need to learn where it might go and have someone at each of those ports."

"It may come back here," Kanta said. "Perhaps I should just wait ...."

"If it's several days at sea, I don't think it will turn back. You can find someone to cover Chennai. The storm is a day or two away so I think if it diverts, it will be somewhere along the coast north of here. Call Meera, make your best guesses, and see if you can find someone who is in communication with the captain."

"What will you be doing?"

"By the time we know it has diverted, it may be too late to leave here. We need to stay put."

"You might find someone there who is in communication with the ship. Are we certain he's on it?"

"Quite certain. We will call if we learn anything." She poked the end button on her phone and looked up as they stopped in front of the Sentinel Hotel.

"Well," she said mainly to herself. "This looks like the kind of place to weather a storm."

.   .   .

Marcus was having just the opposite feeling. When he walked into the glass-fronted reception area and looked across the expanse of pink and grey marble flooring, his first thought was "they could put all of our house in Helena in here and have room for the house next door." The reception desk and stairways that rose to the second floor were teak and mahogany, the furniture upholstered with what looked to his unstudied eye like silk brocade. The service staff wore crisply-starched uniforms and were formally friendly, but looked at him with what he thought was resigned tolerance. When the bellboy reached for his bag, he waved him away and carried it himself down the wide hallway to his ground-floor room.

The bellboy followed and held the door, then hurried into the room and began to demonstrate all of its amenities; a key card that controlled the lights, a control set beside the silk-draped king-sized bed that allowed him to turn lights and television on and off from the bedside, a basket of tropical fruit and mini-bar stocked with drinks, snacks and dried fruit and nuts. He again waved the boy away and handed him a couple of the smaller rupee notes he had in his pocket.

The room opened out through lanai doors onto a short walk that led to a tiled patio, centered by a kidney-shaped swimming pool. Guests lounged beside it on wooden deck chairs, some in swimsuits and others in casual wear or bright saris. They glanced at him as he approached the patio, then returned to their conversations. He again thought the looks were critical. Was it because they didn't think he belonged, or simply a reflection of his knowing that he didn't?

Nisha joined him as he walked past the pool and down a walk fringed by perfectly pruned palms and lawn, and shrubs that looked almost artificial in their perfection.

"Isn't this an amazing place?" she gushed, taking his hand.

"I don't belong here," he said, allowing the hand to stay but not returning her light squeeze.

"What do you mean—here? On the island? At this hotel? Of course you do."

"Not on this island and especially not in this hotel. Look at this! This place cost more to build than the whole downtown area where I grew up."

"We can afford it," she said. "We have a couple of days to wait. Let's just enjoy ourselves."

"I'm sure you can afford it. But that's part of what's starting to trouble me. I know you've been upset by what you view as moodiness, but it's much more than that. Your group has made a decision that for whatever reason, Doctor Lemay shouldn't be allowed to live because he might reveal some deep secret—one I'm not even sure he knows he possesses. You spend money like it's water to get this done; like it's part of a grand vacation, with all your little contact people clearing the way for you as you go. It's as if the world should answer to you, and I'm not even sure you have any idea what the world is really all about. All you see is your own comfortable, carefully managed version of it."

Nisha released his hand. "You forget that I work to care for some of the least fortunate people in my country. I know what poverty is and what it means to live among it."

"I know that. And it's one of the things I love and appreciate about you. But that's not the same as living in it. And I'm not trying to play 'the little poor boy' on you here, but I come to a place like this and can't help but think about the good all this money could do elsewhere. It just doesn't feel right to me to be here when I know what it means to be part of that other half."

Nisha stopped them in a small circle of palms and flowering shrubs and looked at him with eyes that were both puzzled and admiring.

"You're right. I don't have any idea what that's like and I can't go back and change the way I was brought up. But I have done what I can to make life better for others ...."

He knew she had, and that he was probably being as insensitive as she appeared to him. She seemed convinced that if he knew more about what was going on with Lemay, he might also be in danger and this hotel was probably part of her effort to say 'I can't tell you everything, but will try to make the rest of this as nice as I can.' He wrapped his arm about her shoulders and continued along the paved pathway.

"Sorry—I was being a jerk. This whole thing is kind of surreal to me and walking into this place just ramped that up a notch. It reminds me that if these people could see the little three room house I grew up in—a place that could fit into that bedroom I just checked into—they would think even less of me."

They walked for a few moments without speaking, then Nisha squeezed his hand and let it drop to his side, pulling her phone from her pocket.

"You're right. There really is no good reason for us to stay here—even if we are not paying for it." Her fingers flew over the face of the smart phone, then she held it up to him. "Here are five other places to stay in Port Blair. Tell me what looks good to you and we'll check in there tomorrow. It's too late to cancel for tonight so you'll have to suffer in luxury until we can move." She smiled broadly and he knew she wasn't just playing with him.

"Lots of these end with 'resort,'" he said. "Those sound expensive. How about this Driftwood Hotel? I like the name and it looks a little more like my kind of place."

Nisha tapped again at her screen and held up a satellite view of the Driftwood. "Other side of the airport, but not far. And not too close to the beach. That might be good if we have a big storm."

"Are you okay with this?"

"I couldn't be more okay with it," she said. "Tonight, we are sentinels. Tomorrow, driftwood."

CHAPTER NINETEEN

From his window on the port side of the *Swaraj Dweep*, Nolan could see nothing but grey ocean and grey horizon. They blended so perfectly that he couldn't tell where one began and the other ended. He was beginning to get his sea legs, at least to the point that he could move around the ship without feeling constantly sick, but both nights at sea had been restless and plagued with fitful dreams. They weren't the nightmares he feared would come with being chased by a beautiful, raven-haired murderess, but the kind he had always had when feeling especially inadequate. Most were school dreams—tests he was not prepared for, classrooms he couldn't find, locker numbers or combinations he couldn't remember. He tried to convince himself that these things shouldn't matter, but he still awoke in a cold sweat and preferred staying awake to his dream world of incessant inadequacy.

His only real acquaintance on the voyage was an elegant middle-aged Indian woman named Kavitha who was a hospital administrator bound for Port Blair. He learned the hospital there was a wing of what had once been a British prison, but had been partially converted into a medical facility and partly into a memorial to those who had been incarcerated there.

"And are you going to work at the hospital?" he asked as they sat reading beside each other in deck chairs on the bow sundeck.

"Do you believe in destiny?" she asked, placing her book in her lap and giving him a friendly smile.

Do you mean 'fate'? That our lives are scripted in some inalterable way?"

"In a general sense, yes. That everything happens because it is intended that way?"

"I'm not sure I do," Nolan said. "I'm more inclined to think each of our decisions opens new options to us from which we can choose, and the next choice opens another set, and so on."

"I wouldn't disagree, if we were equally able to choose among those options. But I have come to understand that our cumulative experience predisposes us to one of the choices, so it really isn't a matter of the options being equal. For example, my husband died the first part of last year and it was important that I work again. I was educated as a psychologist and worked in hospital settings, but so do thousands of younger people and I was having trouble finding employment. Then at a family gathering one evening my cousin mentioned that his daughter was marrying a man who would be leaving a similar position at the hospital in Port Blair to move to Bangalore to be nearer her family. I called Port Blair and was almost hired over the phone. That is destiny."

"That's what I call serendipity," Nolan smiled. When a group of circumstances come together at the right moment to someone's good fortune."

"Life is a series of those sets of circumstances coming together," Kavitha said. "I was at the family gathering out of obligation. So was my cousin. Conversation inevitably turned to my employment needs and when I learned about the position in Port Blair, was calling really a matter of choice?"

"Many people would not have had the initiative."

"Only because life's circumstances robbed them of it," she said. "Destiny is that chain of circumstances."

"And destiny put us in these two deck chairs, side-by-side?"

"I have explained why I am in this one," she smiled. "Only you can know what circumstances brought you to yours."

He had decided that he thought of her as 'elegant' because everything about Kavitha seemed perfectly in place—or perfectly out of place. When a breeze blew across the afterdeck and lifted several strands of her dark hair, they floated as if they were meant to catch the breeze. When she kicked her sandals onto the deck, her feet, with perfectly painted nails, looked as if they were designed to be on display. Reggie had worked so hard to trim, pluck, spray and cinch everything in an effort to achieve that look, but the result always looked manufactured. Everything about Kavitha was perfectly natural.

They had managed to sit together at meals and he told her in only very general terms about his research tracing the journey of the Christian St. Thomas. She was bright and inquisitive with a subtle sense of humor that was announced before she said anything by a playful sparkle in her deep brown eyes. But inevitably her conversation turned to destiny.

"You are going to Rangoon because that is where you are intended to be," she said when she asked where he would be staying in Port Blair

146

and learned he would be traveling on to Myanmar.

"A week ago, I had never considered going to Rangoon—or—Yongon, or whatever they call it now."

She nodded. "My point exactly. This is a turning point for you. It may take your life in a completely different direction."

"I don't think I would find that disappointing," Nolan said and she turned to peer at him over her black, rectangular reading glasses.

"Are you trying to find something on this journey, or trying to leave something behind?"

"Maybe it's the same thing," he said.

"No, not really. One is a matter of moving away from. The other a matter of moving toward."

"When I left Chennai, I must admit that I was moving away from. But I also must admit that because of my brief time with you, you have convinced me that this is where I was intended to be."

"Then perhaps from this time on, you can think of it as a matter of moving toward," she said.

.   .   .

Kuldip Singh sat at the computer in his room in the Sentinel and indexed through a list of other Port Blair hotels, calling each, asking for Manisha Pillai, and crossing the hotel from his list when told she was not registered. His partner, who had been sitting silently on one of the matching double beds watching storm news on television, suddenly spoke without looking away from the set. The screen displayed a map of the Bay of Bengal and Andaman Sea, showing the storm moving up from Indonesia.

"Maybe they left already. This storm is coming in tonight and they may have gone back to Chennai."

"We've been at the airport for every departing flight and they haven't been on any of them. Nothing is coming in, and no ships are in port. They are here somewhere." The Sikh sat at the desk in a sleeveless undershirt and long khaki shorts and as he worked the computer with one hand, his other fingered a ceremonial dagger that hung from a strap across one shoulder.

"I wish if you were going to carry that thing, you would get one that is sharp," his partner prodded. "If you need it, that dull edge won't do us any good."

"You know why I carry it," Kuldip said, looking coldly at the stocky man. "And for your sake, it is good that it has no edge."

His partner scoffed but said nothing, turning back to the television as Kuldip dialed another number.

"Driftwood Hotel," the receptionist answered.

"May I speak to Ms. Manisha Pillai?"

There was a brief pause. "I'll ring that room for you sir. One moment."

Kuldip hung up. "I've found them!" he said, tapping the dagger against the desktop.

CHAPTER TWENTY

Nolan knew from talking to one of the waiters in the sparsely furnished dining area that they were sailing almost due east along the 14th parallel north of the equator—a bit of information that didn't make much difference, but explained why the sun remained so high and seemed always to track from bow to stern. The Lamoreaus had not been a yachting family and he was picking up a few of the nautical terms that had escaped his North Carolina upbringing. He knew bow and stern, but had never had reason to worry about which was port, and which starboard. But as he wandered around to the right side of the deck on their third morning at sea, he knew now that he was on the starboard side and that something had changed during the night.

The sea was almost dead calm aside from the billowing wake thrown up by the giant twin screws of the *Swaraj Dweep*. Nolan had been up for over an hour, pacing the deck to settle his stomach before breakfast and watching for the first glow of sunrise on the horizon in front of the ship. But the horizon was now beginning to glow, and it was straight off the starboard side.

The ship was surprisingly stable on the calm seas and Nolan walked confidently forward until he found a deckhand running through his morning chores. He pointed out at the brightening glow on the horizon to his right. "We're going the wrong way," he said, swinging his arm around to indicate that the sunrise should be in front of the bow.

The deckhand, who looked East Asian, smiled broadly and nodded, sweeping his own arm in a giant arc to the right. "Big storm. We go around."

"Port Blair?"

"Maybe. Maybe not. Depend on where storm go."

"How long?

The man shrugged, his smile widening. "Don't know. Depend on where storm go."

"Will we get into the storm?" Nolan's stomach was already beginning to churn.

"Don't know. Depend ...."

"I know .... Depends on where the storm goes."

"Just right!" the man said. "Maybe we know tonight."

By lunch time word had passed through the ship that they were headed north toward the coast. The seas were beginning to roll with waves pushed ahead of the storm as it moved northwest into the Bay of Bengal. Nolan huddled in his cabin, needing the open air of the deck, but made even queasier by the sight of grey swells that rose to eye-level, then lifted the ship until he was gazing down into a trough of water three stories deep. When time came for dinner, he struggled forward to the dining room where he drank a coke to settle his stomach and hovered near the door, belching sourly and hoping the captain would give them news. The ship's chief officer strolled into the dining room as the few who were eating were finishing their entrees, surveying the sparse number of diners with a self-assured good humor that made Nolan wonder if he was forcing a look of confidence.

"Good evening," he called out over the heads of the diners as the ship dove into a trough and several grabbed at their plates. "As you can see, we are encountering some rough seas. But we are on the front edge of the storm and it appears to be stalled, so we should sail out of it by morning. If it moves, it is expected to move west and will miss us." He paused and looked again about the dining room, his gaze falling upon Nolan.

"Unfortunately, the storm stalled right over our destination so we will be anchoring off the mouth of the Yangon River in Myanmar. Those of you who had plans to continue on to Myanmar from Port Blair will disembark there and will be transported upriver to Yangon. As soon as the storm clears Port Blair, we will take the rest of you down to the Andamans. For those whose destination is Yangon, we are saving you another trip."

Kavitha was the only person to whom Nolan had mentioned that he was bound for Burma and Rangoon. He wondered uneasily if the captain had just coincidently picked him out while making the announcement, or was aware that he was sailing beyond Port Blair. The captain nodded toward no one in particular, said good night, and left the diners hunched over their desserts, complaining to each other about what this would do to their travel plans. Kavitha moved carefully toward him through the maze of tables, holding to their edges as she inched across the room.

"Destiny," she said with a wry smile as she approached. "For some reason it has allowed you to bypass Port Blair."

Nolan clutched at his stomach. "This is a rougher destiny than I had in mind."

She laughed. "Perhaps it is purging you of something before you arrive."

"Almost everything," he muttered, stifling a belch. "But isn't this getting in the way of your own destiny?"

"My position will be waiting for me when I get there. Perhaps something needed to hurry your journey along."

"I wish it had been something a little less unsettling."

"If it isn't unsettling, it doesn't move us."

"I just wish I had a better idea what this is moving me toward—and what's waiting when I get there," Nolan said sourly.

"It will show itself," Kavitha said. "It always does."

CHAPTER TWENTY-ONE

The storm that hit Port Blair was like nothing Marcus had ever experienced. As a boy in Helena he had seen the spring thunderstorms of April and May rumble across the Mississippi Delta, announced by lightening displays in the western sky that exploded from purple, low-hanging clouds like rocket fire, charging the air until it sizzled. And he had been in Charlotte when the edge of Hurricane Sandy brushed the lower east coast before slamming into the Jersey Shore and New York City. It had battered the Outer Banks of North Carolina with waves that washed out sections of Highway 12 and dumped buckets of rain inland that flooded streets and snarled traffic. But he had never been in a storm that seemed bent on trying to wrest every building from its foundation and send everything that wasn't bolted down flying through the air to slam into whatever was.

The Driftwood had heavy shutters that could be pulled across the windows in anticipation of a storm such as this. Though they were locked shut, the wind grabbed them with both hands and shook them until Marcus was certain they would join the other projectiles he could hear slamming against the outer walls. The front of the Driftwood had been under repair when they checked in, with layers of metal scaffolding stacked against the building's side. As the wind rose, the metal frames first banged noisily against the stucco façade, then began to collapse as braces bent and the wind threw thick wooden planks into the side poles. Nisha came to his room shortly after the tempest hit, carrying two pillows from her bed and looking as frightened as he felt.

"If this building collapses, I don't want to be by myself,' she said, sitting cross-legged in her pajamas with her back against the headboard of his bed, clutching the pillows against her chest.

He tried to look reassuring. "I'm sure they build things here to weather storms like this. And we're on the second floor so the top one can't collapse on us."

"But the roof could blow off," she countered.

"At least that wouldn't crush us. And all that noise from the construction outside. That's pretty well ended."

"Well, aren't you Mr. 'Always look on the bright side of life!'"

"Monty Python—*Life of Brian,*" he chuckled, appreciating the diversion from the shrieking wind outside their window. "I'm surprised you know Monty Python."

"I haven't always been a stuffy old village doctor ... and we didn't reject *everything* British. Monty Python was worth keeping."

He plopped down beside her and pulled her against his shoulder. "You can't be completely stuffy and like Monty Python." A new torrent of rain thrown against the shutters drew his attention back to the storm. "Heard anything about how long this will last?"

"Apparently it's just sitting over us. I think they are hoping it will blow itself out. The clerk in the entryway had an emergency radio and he said maybe late tomorrow ...."

"What do you think is happening to our ship?"

"I haven't been able to reach anyone. Satellite service is out and that's about the only link."

"I hope it's okay. This thing is frightening enough locked inside four walls on dry land ...."

"You're worried about Professor Lemay, aren't you," she said, peering up at him over the top of her pillows.

He thought about it for a moment. "Yeah, I am. He's a funny little guy—not funny in a 'ha ha' way, but in a sad way. I don't think anyone's ever cared for him much."

"You're a good and kind man, Marcus Branscomb," she said, leaning into his shoulder.

"Not such a good man that I'm not happy this storm finally got you into my bed," he smiled.

"And I'm staying here tonight." She sat suddenly upright and turned fully toward him. "But no sex. Can we do that?"

"Is it me ... or something else?"

"I made a promise ...."

"To someone else?"

"To *something* else."

"Like you're a nun or something?"

"A little like that."

Marcus leaned back against the headboard. This was not an announcement he wanted to hear. "Is it forever?"

"Only if I wish it to be."

"My momma taught me to always respect a promise. But I hope you don't wish it to be forever."

"For tonight, what I wish is for you to hold me so I feel safe."

"We'll make each other feel safe," he said, and pulled her back against him, hoping beyond hope that he could someday help her change her mind.

.   .   .

The ferry lumbered away from the side of the *Swaraj Dweep* with twice the number of passengers Nolan guessed it was designed to carry. He had spent most of the night curled on the bed in his cabin as the storm lifted the ship and dropped it into one gut-wrenching trough after another. His misery led to superstitious thoughts and he had visions of being a Jonah—punished by an angry god for stealing the manuscript and bringing this tempest down upon the ship and its unsuspecting passengers. If they knew, they would storm his cabin and cast him into the sea as an offering—a sacrifice to Neptune or whatever being could calm the troubled seas.

In the early hours before dawn as the ship approached the mainland, the storm broke and the Captain announced over the intercom that they would not be going upriver to the terminal. Too many ships had moved into the port to avoid the storm and there were no berths. They would anchor out in the Bay and when a ferry was available, taxi passengers ashore who had planned to go on to Burma from Port Blair.

He joined Kavitha for an early breakfast of a savory cake she called *idli* and a thick vegetable stew. He ate sparingly, picking at the spicy cake and spooning some of the broth from around the carrots and potatoes. As they finished, she slipped a card across the table.

"Nolan, you are a good man," she said, reaching across to touch his hand. "Better than you are willing to admit. This is my email address. When you discover what has brought you here, please send me a note. I want to know how this journey ends."

He stood now on the deck of the ferry, waving up to her on the deck two stories above and hugging the railing of the overloaded tub. Somehow being on this floating accident-waiting-to-happen didn't seem to him like destiny, unless his destiny was to end up at the bottom of the sea. He looked down at the muddy plume flowing out of the distant river and wondered if he could plunge overboard and swim to shore if the ferry capsized. Probably not. He hadn't been swimming in any serious way since before college, and he'd been twenty pounds lighter.

Ahead, the mouth of the Yangon River emptied into the Gulf of Martaban, bringing with it a fleet of small fishing boats that fanned out on both sides of the laboring ferry as it entered the bay.

"At least they'll come to our aid if this thing turns over," Nolan muttered, but the fishing boats would have to get here in a hurry—and there would have to be a lot of them. The ferry had been diverted to the ship from an outlying port and teemed with people taking animals and produce to market. Women with cheeks caked with a chalky white paste carried baskets of fruit, bread, and flowers on their heads as they edged through the packed crowd. Others balanced bundles wrapped in faded sheets or cellophane, and men held goats on short tethers or pushed heavy carts covered with meat or produce. Two young girls supported the ends of a long pole along one of the railings, strung with trussed-up chickens that dangled by their feet over the thick water. Here and there a monk with shaved head and saffron robe stood quietly, clutching a round metal bowl. Though Nolan was not a tall man, everyone was shorter. Men and women alike wore ankle-length printed skirts, topped by long-sleeved white shirts for the men and fitted tops in solid colors for the women. Though the morning air felt like a hot locker-room shower, no one seemed particularly troubled by the packed-together conditions, seemingly accustomed to moving about shoulder-to-shoulder in the humid air.

They entered the mouth of the river without capsizing and Nolan began to relax as the terminal came into view. The ferry pier was a floating platform, attached to the main dock by a long covered gangway, and the captain eased the heavy vessel in as if it were a small skiff, nestling it gently against a row of tires that hung against the side of the bobbing dock. Crewmen jumped onto the pier and quickly lashed the ferry in place. Within seconds, a passenger bridge joined the ferry to the platform and people, animals and pushcarts began streaming onto the extended gangway.

Nolan stood back against the wall of the enclosed passenger seating area and scanned the main dock as people pushed past him toward the exit ramp. At the end of the gangway, a shoulder-high chain link fence separated it from the main dock, its gate pushed outward as the passengers surged along the covered bridge. Just outside the gate a low concrete building served as what looked like a customs or ticket office and beyond the building, hundreds of return passengers sat on boxes or leaned against bicycles waiting to board.

He saw her before she noticed him. She was standing partly concealed by the corner of the building, studying the passengers as they pressed through the gate. Like Nolan, she was half a head taller than the locals and either due to vanity or haste, was dressed smartly in a white silk blouse and tailored black pants. Her long black hair was plaited into a single braid that hung over her right shoulder, and large designed sunglasses hid much of her face. But even from where he stood in the shadows of the upper deck, she was stunning. Somehow the angel of death had known where he was going. He pulled off his blue Carolina Panthers cap and ducked below the level of the departing masses, slipping back into the ferry's seating lounge and exiting on the far side of the boat. So much for destiny, he thought.

CHAPTER TWENTY-TWO

When Marcus awoke, his first impression was of the warmth and softness of Nisha's body curled against him on the low bed. They had stayed awake until the early hours of morning, assuring each other that the roof would stay on the Driftwood, that the shutters would hold, and that nothing lethal would come blasting through walls or windows. She had succumbed to sleep first and he had struggled to stay awake a little longer, just to listen to her soft breathing and enjoy the feeling of her head against his chest.

His second impression was of quiet. The room was dark from both the shutters and heavy drapes that were pulled tightly across the windows, and he tried a bedside lamp to check his watch. No power. As his eyes adjusted to the dim light, he eased Nisha gently from his side and leaned forward, squinting at the dial. One fifteen. That couldn't be right. It had been after two when they fell asleep. Marcus moved Nisha's head to a pillow and she stretched as he twisted off the bed and pulled aside the drapes.

"The storm has passed," she murmured, still half asleep.

He unlatched the shutters and pushed them outward, stepping back as a bright shaft of light stabbed across the room.

"Ouch!" he winced, throwing an arm across his eyes. "It's after one o'clock! We slept half the day."

She scooted from the bed and came up beside him, slipping an arm about his waist and pulling him tightly against her.

"It doesn't look like we will be going anywhere soon. Look at this mess!"

The construction scaffolding was now a tangle of planks, pipes, cross-braces and tree limbs of various sizes and varieties. Marcus gave her a light squeeze and stepped back to the bed, sitting to pull on his shoes.

"I'm going out to have a look. Stay here in the window so I know which unit is ours."

The foyer was empty and he carefully picked his way to the street, looking back at the scarred face of the four-story building. The shutters had done their job and no windows were broken, but the facade showed the effects of hundreds of wind-borne missiles battering the stucco. In both directions the street was littered with branches and palm fronds, shredded paper and white plastic bags. People moved silently through the clutter as if not wanting to break the silence of the storm's aftermath, haphazardly picking up something they recognized as having come from their own shop or home.

Nisha pushed the shutters of the second story room open wide and leaned over the sill.

"I tried the water in the bathroom. No showers today."

He looked up at her and raised both hands to say "what do you do with a mess like this?"

"I suspect they are used to this," she said. "And this was just a bad tropical storm. No real damage to buildings."

"I wouldn't want to have to repair this one," he called up to her. "It's pretty beat up." She held up her cell phone and he could hear her musical ring.

"Cell service is back in operation. The towers must have stayed up and have backup generators."

She spoke a "hello" into the phone and listened intently while Marcus watched from below. He could see her answer with a few words that he couldn't hear from the street.

"Kanta," she shouted down to him as she ended the call, holding up the phone. "I guess this is back on us now. He didn't get off in Yangon and should be coming in with the ship when it gets here this afternoon."

Marcus frowned and moved closer in below the window. "That doesn't make sense to me. Didn't we think he was headed to Yangon?"

"That's just what I said, but she insists he wasn't on the ferry that brought passengers in from the ship. It sailed immediately and should be only an hour or two out of Port Blair. If he suspected he's being followed, he may think the guide in Chennai told us about his interest in Burma. Perhaps he thought this would be a safer place to spend a few days."

Marcus shook his head. "I don't think so. He's a smart man and would have realized you either flew to Yangon or came by sea. And if you came by boat, you came through here. My guess is he suspects by now that we know he was on the ship."

"If he does, he might expect us to go directly to Yangon to wait for him."

"Possibly. If we have to, we can probably walk to the harbor from here. Do you think he booked passage on the ship and didn't use it? He might be back in Chennai or on his way somewhere else altogether."

"No. Kanta talked to some passengers who got off in Yangon. They remembered him being onboard."

"But they didn't remember him getting off the ship?"

"I guess they had to climb down ladders to the ferry and the ferry was crowded. The people she spoke to weren't sure who got off." Nisha glanced up and down the rubble-filled street. "Come back up here. I don't like to shout like this."

Marcus headed back toward the front of the Driftwood. "Better get on your walking shoes. We've got some work to do if we're going to get to the harbor."

He picked his way through the tangled scaffolding back to the entrance and up the stairs to the second floor. The door to the room was ajar and he pushed it open and stepped inside, wondering how they would get through the storm damage to the harbor. Nisha stood against the wall to his left, the tall turbaned man from the dump site behind her with one arm around her chest and the other hand holding a short dagger tight against her throat. Her eyes burned like two gold embers and her mouth cut a hard straight line across her face. The man grinned at Marcus and he heard the door push closed behind him.

Marcus stepped right and turned to face the shorter, stocky member of the team. He held a large caliber pistol pointed at the center of Marcus' chest with a long silencer screwed onto the barrel. For a moment the four stood glaring at each other as if the attackers had planned only to this point, but now weren't certain what to do.

Marcus took a long deep breath to slow his racing heart. "I don't think you want to shoot us with that thing," he said, not sure where he was going with this. "Too many people saw you come in here, and you can't exactly hop in a car and race away."

"We are all leaving," the turbaned man said. "We will shoot you if we have to, but I think you would prefer to quietly walk out of here with us."

Marcus cast the Sikh a quick glance then turned to look more closely at the man. He could be mistaken, but from across the room the dagger appeared to have a dull edge. The man held it tight against Nisha's neck but without the point against her skin. Marcus knew from their previous encounter with the pair that they must be in mortal danger, but there was something strangely comical about the whole scene.

"Out!" the shorter man ordered, swinging the pistol toward the door. Marcus' mind raced through the possibilities. If he were in their shoes, he would get them out into an area of high damage but few people, bludgeon them with a board or tree limb, and leave them as casualties of the storm. If he started from the room ahead of Nisha, he couldn't try anything without her captor seeing him and using the point of the knife on her neck. He stepped toward the door and to within a few feet of the man with the gun.

"After you," he said, indicating the door. The man scowled and swung the weapon toward the doorway, gesturing that Marcus should go first. As Marcus stepped forward, he surged into the man, sweeping the gun hand farther toward the door and slamming his right knee up into the man's groin with all the force he could muster. The knee lifted his assailant a foot off the floor and the pistol fired a muted shot through the doorway and into the wall on the other side of the hall. A long gasping grunt erupted from the man's throat and the gun clattered to the floor. As he settled back on quivering feet, Marcus grabbed his right shoulder with his left hand, cupped his right around the back of the man's lolling head, and again slammed the leg upward, pulling the man's nose and forehead down hard onto the top of his knee. The cartilage of the nose crunched loudly and there was a muffled scream, smothered by vomit as the man retched onto the front of Marcus' pants. Blood gushed from the smashed nose and the stocky man struggled to stay on his feet, but his eyes rolled upward and he began to pitch forward. Marcus caught him halfway to the floor with a windmill swing of both fists clutched tightly together. The blow caught the man on the side of the head just in front of his ear and drove his head sideways into the edge of the door. He dropped motionless to the floor.

The last thing Nisha had expected was for Marcus to rush the pistol. The Sikh was also taken by surprise and for a brief second, neither moved. The second was long enough for Nisha's trained instincts to fire into action and in a single motion, she turned hard into her own assailant, sweeping her arm up to force the blade away from her head and neck and blasting her own knee up into the man's crotch. As he buckled, she grasped the wrist holding the knife with both hands and swung the man's arm down and behind him, forcing it up his back until she heard the shoulder begin to give and the man scream. She dropped backward onto her hands and swept his feet with a swift kick of her right leg, springing back to her feet before he slammed onto his back on the bare floor. Before he could move, she dropped her knee hard onto the center of his chest, driving the sternum into the man's lungs and heart. He could not scream again, but threw his head back, gasping for air and life.

She felt Marcus grasp her arm and pull her toward the door.

"Our bags and passports," she said, and while Marcus stood over their fallen assailants, gathered their few possessions into her roller bag and sprinted ahead of him down the stairs and out into the rubble-filled street.

The hotel stood near one corner of a four-way intersection, with one of the streets the Greater Andaman Trunk Road that joined Port Blair to the south part of the island. Vir Savakar International Airport was less than a mile north, separated from the Trunk Road by narrow city streets and compact subdivisions. They dashed toward the intersection where crews working the main highway were beginning to gather up broken terra cotta shingles and downed branches. A battered van with "Airport Shuttle" stenciled on the side was winding its way through the clean-up crews and Nisha waved it to a stop. They squeezed in among eight passengers who appeared to be airport employees trying to make their way to work, chattering and gesturing in animated descriptions of what had happened to their homes.

"Where did *that* come from?" Nisha asked, glancing back to see if either attacker had been able to follow them from the building.

"They must have learned we survived the tiger sanctuary and come here .... Your Disciples must not be the only people with a network."

"I don't mean that. Your Kung-Fu Panda."

Marcus shrugged. "I couldn't think of anything else to do. I'd thought about it sometimes ... how you might disarm someone like that. I didn't know if it would work but I couldn't let them get us out of the building—and I don't think they were very good."

Nisha chuckled nervously. "You never cease to amaze me. But no. I don't think they were very good."

"But how did you get free? By the time I had the guy down, you were on top of the big man."

"What did you think I was going to do when you initiated your little plan?"

He smiled over at her. "Somehow I thought you could probably handle this better than I could. And the guy's knife wasn't even sharp."

Nisha's chuckle grew into a soft laugh. "It was a Kirpan. A ceremonial dagger the Sikhs carry all the time. It was never intended for that kind of use. Sometimes they are sharp. Sometimes not." She paused for a long moment. "They are a very brave and noble people. They would be ashamed of this man."

"I don't think they were very good," Marcus repeated and found that he was also laughing, but had started to shiver uncontrollably. She wrapped her arms about him and rubbed his shoulders while the other passengers watched them curiously. The storm had done strange things to people.

A mile along the Trunk Road they turned right onto VIP Boulevard that ran parallel to the airport's single runway, then right again down the drive to the main terminal. A blue awning ran the full length of the long two-story building, matching its blue tiled roof, and much of the fabric had been torn away and scattered across the lawn and parking areas, exposing the building's faded façade. As the storm approached, planes had been shuttled to other airports and the familiar scream of taxiing jet engines was now replaced by the rumble of heavy equipment as clean-up crews piled debris along the sides of the parking lots. The curb-side area reserved for taxis was empty and when asked if he could take them farther toward the harbor, the van driver said he had to return south for another load of workers.

Nisha led Marcus to a man who appeared to be overseeing the cleanup operation.

"Do you have anything going up toward the harbor that might give us a lift?"

The man frowned and looked around at the array of equipment moving back and forth in front of the terminal. "We're dumping what we pick up along the north side of the park, near Dithaman Tank. One of the lorries can give you a lift up to the tourism office and from there, you might be able to catch something moving up Foreshore Road toward the harbor."

"We'll take it," Nisha said and when the next truck moved out of the airport drive toward the dump site, she and Marcus were squeezed into the cab beside the driver. He dropped them at the vacant tourism office and they walked north to the intersection of the Trunk Road and Foreshore, the major road that ran north to the harbor. It was approaching four in the afternoon.

"If the ship sailed early from Yangon, it might arrive before we do," Nisha said, looking up and down the highway where nothing moved but a few curious children on bicycles. North along Foreshore Road, thick black smoke billowed into the afternoon sky. "Something major must be blocking this road," she said.

Marcus nodded. "Not too far up there. I think we might be on foot."

A half mile along the road, a car had overturned and as its fuel spilled across the highway, a downed power line sent a tongue of flame sprinting back to the automobile, torching it into a funeral pyre. Nervous bystanders ringed the fire at a safe distance as emergency personnel still worked to smother the last flames and get to the charred vehicle.

"Anyone inside?" Nisha asked a young boy who leaned nearby against his bicycle.

"A mother and two children," he said. "They couldn't get out. I saw it all and they couldn't get out. That old woman tried to help them, but she couldn't open the doors." He nodded toward an elderly woman in a blue sarong who squatted beside the road, hands pressed tightly across her mouth and tears streaming down her aged face. As they watched, she extended her arms toward the burning vehicle, shaking her head and mumbling incoherently.

Nisha walked to the woman and knelt beside her, putting her arm about the old woman's shaking shoulders.

"Where do you live, Grandmother?" she asked. The woman again clasped her head in her hands, then looked helplessly up at Nisha and pointed toward a small white bungalow that stood behind a stone wall a hundred meters beyond the wreck site.

"Come, let me make you some tea," Nisha said. "It will be alright. There is nothing you could have done." She lifted the woman to her feet and Marcus followed as she walked the old woman to her home. He sat beside her and held her withered hand as Nisha made tea and, for the next hour, tried to assuage the guilt of the only person who had tried to be heroic. When the woman's neighbors began to gather and surround her with their support, Nisha eased Marcus from the woman's side and out of the little bungalow.

They reached the harbor just as the long shadows of evening were stretching east across the bay, pushed by the sun as it dropped below the hills to the west. At anchor off one of the damaged piers, the *Swaraj Dweep* rode high on the evening tide. As they reached a spot several hundred meters from the sea-stained side of the ship, a small launch pushed away from its bow and churned toward them. When it reached the pier, two men climbed onto the dockside, both clearly officers of the ship.

Nisha intercepted them as they headed toward the buildings that lined the harbor.

"Excuse me ... we were to meet a friend here who was a passenger on your ship, but the storm delayed us. An American. Mr. Nolan Lemay."

The two officers glanced at each other.

"You were meeting him here?" one asked. "He must have expected you to be in Yangon. He disembarked there."

"You're quite certain that he didn't return to the ship?"

"I helped him onto the ferry," the officer said. "And it didn't come back—nor any other boat. Your Mister Lemay is in Yangon."

CHAPTER TWENTY-THREE

That one brief sighting of Kanta, half-concealed by the corner of the reservation office, was the most transformative moment in Nolan's life. As he stepped backward against the wall of the inner seating area, he felt a surge of adrenaline kick his mind into high gear. But he felt no fear— and for the briefest of moments, it thrilled him. He was not a competitive man by nature and had spent his life avoiding competitive games, so tired and embarrassed by the age of ten of being the last chosen for every team sport that he just stayed away from them. He had been as quick-witted as the next person, but found that having the best grade on a test or being first in class meant so much more to his classmates than it did to him, he simply didn't worry about it. But it was as if a new Nolan Lemay emerged from his soft, acquiescent body when he saw the bewitching face behind the expensive sunglasses. The new Nolan stood more erect, was suddenly fully aware of every sound and smell around him, and found in them an excitement that replaced what he had expected to be panic with a strange exhilaration.

He eased back into the enclosed seating area and made his way to the other side of the ferry, watching orange banana boats zip back and forth across the harbor. They were shallow skiffs with high pointed prows and raised square tails divided in the middle to allow a long motor shaft to drop into the murky bay where the propellers churned a white frothy trail as they sped through the water. Other than the boatman some were empty, but most carried baskets of fruits and vegetables or stacks of dry goods headed for market. He thought fleetingly of trying to signal one to the side, but there were no ladders down to the water and he could see no way to get from the deck without jumping - something that would hardly go unnoticed.

The line of disembarking passengers stretched around the outside of the seating area almost to where he stood: walking passengers in front, then those carrying parcels, followed by men and women pushing bicycles. To the rear were the vendors with carts—open two-wheeled carts carrying produce, meat, woven hats and bolts of cloth, and boxed cooking carts with inset fryers and enclosed bottoms carrying propane bottles and utensils. Nolan pulled a roll of bills from his pocket, peeled a

$100 bill from the stack, and approached a small man at the rear of the pack with a stout four-wheeled cooking cart. The man wore the traditional striped, ankle-length skirt and white shirt and looked to be about forty. Beneath the shirt, Nolan could see that he was lean and sinewy, tough as seasoned rope. Nolan held the bill up to the man, then through a series of gestures tried to convey that the money would be his if Nolan could curl up within the enclosed bottom and be carted off the ferry. The man's skeptical smile and shaking head indicated he understood, but wanted no part of the scheme. Nolan pulled another hundred from his roll and waved the bills in front of the vendor who obviously recognized their value. The man again shook his head but seemed less adamant, opening the doors of the lower cart to display his pans, cooking utensils and bottle of gas. Nolan nodded, drew a third bill from his pocket and gestured for the man to unload the supplies onto the deck. The third bill, he gestured, could more than replace the man's equipment once he got ashore.

The small nut-colored man studied Nolan for a long moment with an amused smile, then bent into the cart and unfastened the connectors on the propane tank, lifting the bottle onto the deck. The rest of the crowd had moved on around the corner of the inner seating area and Nolan and the vendor were alone on the far side of the ferry. With little noise, the man emptied the pans and cooking instruments beside the tank of gas, then held out one hand for the money and with the other, gestured for Nolan to climb into the enclosed box. Nolan handed him two of the bills and waved the other one toward the exit gates that separated the main dock from the street beyond the chain fence.

"This is yours when I'm safely off the dock," he said, knowing the man understood nothing he said but everything he meant. The man nodded and Nolan dropped to his knees and hunched sideways into the cramped space, pulling his duffle beneath him. He tucked his chin tightly against the bag and his knees and the man closed the doors, leaving a wide flat pan and two sets of tongs still hanging on the inside of the cart and pressed uncomfortably into Nolan's side.

They moved quickly forward then stopped, inching along again bit by bit as the passengers disembarked. The boxed cart smelled of burned grease and fish oil and Nolan took only quick, shallow breaths and held them as long as he could. He heard other carts beside and behind him and realized the man was moving forward into the departing mass of vendors. Smart little fellow. He didn't want to be first off the ferry with a cart, or the last.

The box closed in around him, straining every tendon and muscle, and his legs began to cramp and scream for relief. The sound below him changed and he felt the strain of the vendor as he struggled onto the upward slope of the gangway. It hadn't occurred to Nolan that he might be too heavy for the small man, but the cart seemed to gain momentum as he pushed upward. Nolan tried to force his shrieking muscles to relax but they knotted more tightly and he slid his hands back from his chin and squeezed his thighs, gritting his teeth as one cramped into a charley horse. Beads of sweat erupted along his hairline and ran into his eyes, and he pushed his forehead hard against the floor, intentionally creating a new locus of pain that diverted attention from the knotted muscle. Below, the hum of the wheels changed again in pitch as they rolled out onto the rough timbers of the pier, turning right and gaining speed as they approached the exit gates. Then the cart stopped abruptly.

Nolan heard voices above him to his left—an authoritative male voice and the vendor's. The authority barked some request and thumped heavily against the side of the box next to Nolan's ear. He sucked in a quick breath and trapped it as he heard someone shuffle around to the door-side of the cart. The doors opened wide enough for the vender to reach inside and remove the flat pan, holding it up briefly for inspection. There was another terse comment from the authority, then the pan reappeared and was slipped back onto its hook. The doors closed and the cart rolled forward for several minutes, then stopped again. The doors spread wide and the vendor rapped sharply with his hand on the top of the cart.

Nolan eased his head out of the space and looked in both directions. They were wedged between two vans parked against a railing that separated the street from the harbor and stood only a few feet from the drop-off into the bay. Nolan rolled out onto the pavement, stretched the cramp out of his left leg, and forced himself to his feet. He bent forward, extending one taut hamstring, then the other, and finally his back. He drew a fourth hundred from his roll and handed two bills to the vendor, giving him a deep bow.

"Thank you," he said.

The man nodded and tucked the bills into the pocket of his shirt, then turned without a word and maneuvered his cart back onto the street.

Nolan stood between the parked vehicles for a full five minutes looking in the direction of the port, watching the passing traffic, and getting some sense for the city around him. The side of the street opposite the harbor was lined with low metal buildings, each fronted by crates and barrels of assorted sizes and colors. Just to his right, away from the ferry terminal, the road turned away from the water and both sides of the street were crowded with small open-fronted shops. Some were eateries with two or three tables surrounded by plastic chairs, but most seemed to be repair shops piled with automobile and machinery parts of every description. The street bustled with constant traffic: men and women on bicycles and motorbikes weaving in and out of a stalled, single line of vehicles that seemed to be moving in both directions at once. The air was sticky warm and heavy with the smell of polluted sea water, diesel fumes and axle grease. Nolan sucked it in and it filled his lungs like tonic, flowing down through his chest, hips and legs and infusing them with new life. When his left thigh had seized in the cart, the pain had been as excruciating as anything Nolan had ever experienced and he had wanted to cry out through the clench in his jaw. But he hadn't, and he had never felt such a sense of accomplishment. It was a small victory, but it was *his* victory.

A taxi paused beside him, waiting its turn to ease back into the flow. The driver rolled down the passenger window and leaned toward Nolan.

"Taxi?"

Nolan glanced back toward the pier, pulled open the rear door and threw in his bag.

"You speak English?" he asked, sliding in beside it.

"Very good English," the driver smiled. The smile showed a mouth of broken, brown-stained teeth in a creased, leathery face that matched the teeth in color, topped by a thatch of wild grey hair protruding from beneath a camouflaged bucket cap.

"You go Yangon hotel?"

"I need to exchange money. At the hotel?

"You have U.S. dollar?" The cab had nosed its way in front of a square panel truck and was making gradual headway along the street.

Nolan nodded. "U.S. dollars."

"No hotel. I get better rate."

"What is the money here?" Nolan asked, checking back over his shoulder to see if the small truck behind them blocked the view of any following vehicles.

"Kyat," the driver said, pronouncing it "chat." "I get you maybe 860 kyat for one dollar. Hotel give you maybe 800. You have hotel?"

"No hotel. What's your name? You have suggestion?"

"You call me Myo. You want Parkroyal Hotel. Very good hotel. Maybe number one."

Nolan pictured the stylishly dressed Kanta with her designer sunglasses, peering around the edge of the terminal building.

"How about number three hotel, Myo," he said, falling into the patter of the driver's English.

"Don't like Parkroyal? Maybe you want Sedona Hotel. Also number one. Number three not so good."

"Good enough for me," Nolan said. "Don't want to be with all the other Americans and Japanese."

"Ah...okay. I know good place. We go change-money now."

Ten blocks away near the middle of a narrow side street, Myo pulled to the curb in front of an open air café with three round tables clustered under a sagging awning. "You come," he ordered, hopping out of the cab and heading into the empty café.

"What is this place?"

"Change money. Better rate here."

Nolan pushed back more deeply into the seat and rolled the window down a few inches. "I'd rather go to a bank or the hotel. Maybe an ATM."

Myo shuffled back to the car and pressed his creased forehead against the opening in the window, grinning at his American fare.

"No ATM in Burma. Only money. No credit card. Only money. Myo take care of you. Get good rate. You be okay. Come now."

Nolan touched the belt pouch he had hidden beneath the front of his pants where he held most of his cash, then fingered the roll in his pocket. The roll had about $600 in hundreds, fifties, and twenties. If this was a trap of some kind, he didn't know how carefully they would check him over. But if Myo was right and this was a cash society, there probably was an active black market.

Across the street a man as wrinkled and brown as Myo sat on a bench in front of a shop that sold what looked like jars of pickles, and a young couple walked hand-in-hand toward him down the street. No one seemed at all alarmed to see him in front of the café and he decided he wasn't being set up to be mugged. He opened the door and followed Myo to the back of the small eatery where a bare wooden counter separated the cooking area from the front of the shop. Myo slapped his hand loudly on the counter and Nolan heard voices in a back room, then a green curtain slid aside and a younger man stepped up to the back of the counter.

Rather than wearing the traditional skirt, the man had on dark pants and a white shirt and smiled broadly at Myo, exchanging greetings that Nolan couldn't understand.

"You would like to exchange money," the man said, maintaining the bright smile. His English was much clearer than the driver's and touched with a slight British accent. "How much would you like?"

"I would like to know the exchange rate first. Can you handle six hundred dollars?"

"Today I'm giving eight-fifty kyat to the dollar. That's about fifty more than you will get at a hotel. And yes, I can exchange six hundred."

Nolan pulled the roll from his pocket and laid it on the counter. The man opened the roll and separated the bills, placing the twenties in one pile, six fifties in another, and the two hundreds by themselves.

"I do not exchange twenties," he said. "Too many are bad and they are too hard for me to trade." He held each fifty to the light, then stroked them with a marking pen. One was a little worn and he set it aside. "Only new bills. I can exchange three-fifty. Maybe the hotel will take these others if you say they are all you have."

Nolan rolled the fifty with the twenties and slipped them back into his pocket. "I'll take what I can get," he said.

"One moment please." The man disappeared back though the curtain, returning moments later with a metal money box. Carefully he counted out 382,500 kyat in multi-colored 10,000 K notes bearing the state seal of Myanmar, and blue-pink 5,000 K notes displaying a white, orange-draped elephant.

Nolan studied the pile in his hand. "A man could easily become a millionaire here," he grinned.

"A millionaire one day, a pauper the next. I would not exchange more at a time than you need," the man cautioned.

"Good advice," Nolan said and followed Myo back to the taxi.

"I take good care of you, right? Now we go to Number Three Hotel."

"Are there any Christian churches in the city?"

Myo nodded. "Big one. We pass right by."

"Could you stop there for a few minutes and wait for me?"

The driver shrugged. "Sure. Okay."

They pulled onto a wide, tree-lined thoroughfare and three blocks later Myo eased to the curb beside a soaring, red brick church, its main square tower topped with a white, ornately carved steeple that rose high above the surrounding buildings. The main spire was guarded on each corner by smaller steeples, but above the arched entry the brickwork gave the church a distinctly central Asian look. Nolan walked to the head-high lattice fence that separated the church from a brick walkway and pushed through a gate into a neatly groomed courtyard. A sign beside the gate identified the church as the Holy Trinity Cathedral.

The huge carved doors opened into a high, arched sanctuary that echoed with his footsteps as he made his way through the nave toward the altar. The cathedral was completely empty with the exception of a tall white-haired man in church vestments who stood with his back to Nolan, gazing up into the nave. He turned as Nolan approached, showing a long, distinguished, and definitely western face.

"Good afternoon." The accent was educated British.

"Good afternoon. What a stunning building!"

"Dates to the late nineteenth century—at least most of it. Those windows above ...." He pointed at a row of arched, stained-glass windows high in the nave wall. "... they were repaired or replaced a decade ago and are now showing some loosening of the leading. I was just considering whether to get the people who initially did the work to come back to repair them, or try someone completely new."

"I wouldn't think your choices would be that great here," Nolan smiled.

"Precisely," the man said, then offered his hand. "Reginald Greenwood. I'm the vicar."

Nolan hesitated, then introduced himself by name. Those who were looking for him wouldn't be fooled by a false name when they learned what he was inquiring about.

"I'm a professor of religious studies from the United States with a particular interest in what the apocryphal records say about the journeys of St. Thomas, disciple of Jesus of Nazareth."

Vicar Greenwood smiled broadly. "Ah ... and that record has brought you here—or should I say, some of the legends that surround the record."

"Exactly. I was told there was an ancient church here that by tradition was built by Thomas himself."

"A few remnants of a church," the vicar corrected. "Or the remnants of *some* ancient building. There is so little left of it that no one is really certain what it was originally. Now it is little more than a pile of stone."

"I take it you don't give much credence to the legend."

"I can't discount it completely and there is a caretaker there who claims his ancestors have been protecting the site since the time of Thomas. But I met the man's father and he was hardly lucid about what was happening around him at the moment, let alone for the last two millennia."

"Where is the church? Is what's left of it accessible to the public?"

The vicar's smile widened. "It can be. Come into the office. I have a city map and will show you where it is. How are you getting around?"

"A cab driver has adopted me."

"Definitely the best way to see Yangon. And you are going to see some of its most interesting parts. I hope you like glass."

CHAPTER TWENTY-FOUR

The TSG Emerald View Hotel was a fifteen minute walk from where Foreshore Road joined the drive into the Port Blair harbor. Nisha had called Kanta and asked her to make the reservation by phone, guaranteeing it with her credit card. She had a pretty good idea how the Sikh and his friend had found her at the Driftwood and didn't want another registration under her name. While Marcus stood in the street behind a huge transformer that bristled with cone-shaped insulators and bare cables, Nisha convinced the desk clerk to leave the room under Kanta's name by booking for three nights, though she and Marcus had already arranged for a morning flight back to Chennai, and from there to Yangon.

"Kanta will be here tomorrow," she lied. "She has guaranteed the room with her card and wants the listing in her name for business reasons."

The clerk shrugged and handed her the key. "Third floor in back. It is all we have open for three days."

She carried her bag up the narrow stairwell and along a dark, claustrophobic hallway lined with plain, numbered doors. A king-sized bed with a blue, block-patterned quilt filled most of the room and she pushed past it and dropped the roller on a straight-backed chair that sat below a window with matching block-quilted drapes. Beside the window, a weathered brown door opened onto a small balcony that looked down into an alley. The narrow lane below was strewn with the remnants of a demolished building: large concrete slabs, wooden construction poles and sheets of corrugated metal, scattered haphazardly around the dead-end alley.

"Some Emerald View!" she muttered and checked the balcony to see if a fire escape made it accessible from the back. None did. She descended the stairs and found Marcus leaning against the transformer, watching two boys kick a soccer ball at a goal made from an old crate.

"It's going to be hard to get you inside unnoticed and there is no back entry."

"Give me the key. I'll just go in. Come up in a few minutes."

"You're not exactly inconspicuous...."

"That's just it. I don't look like someone who is trying to sneak in."

"What if he asks where you are going?"

"What's our number?"

"318."

"I'm going to visit the Holdens in 218."

"You might be sleeping out here tonight."

He disappeared through the front entrance and five minutes later she followed. He was stretched out on the bed in the third floor room and smiled as she came in.

"When you look like you know what you're doing, people assume you do. He didn't say anything. And look at this ...."

Enough power had returned to the city that television stations were airing evening news. An attractive female announcer described two men who had been found severely beaten in a hotel south of the airport. According to the man who was conscious, he and his partner had interrupted looters while trying to insure that visiting friends had survived the storm. The man's partner was in a coma and he was also listed as critical, with a broken sternum and multiple broken ribs.

"I don't think they will come looking for us tonight," he said. "I'm still surprised they were able to follow us to the island."

"I'm sure someone sent them," she said. "They weren't the type who would go to that much trouble on their own—or be able to track us."

"Whoever was doing the dumping ... they're that worried about you?"

"The authorities must not have been able to trace the mordant. We were the only people who saw the van and the two men. I suspect whoever owns the plant knows that after going to the trouble to find and follow the van, we're not likely to give up on this."

"But we've pretty well taken out his little hit squad."

"As you said," she frowned. "They weren't very good. I suspect that whoever they send next will be much better."

. . .

From his seventh floor room in the Panda Hotel, Nolan could see the gilded spire of the Shwedagon Pagoda rising across the top of the city against a cloudless blue sky. He felt a momentary calm that bordered on tranquility and his thoughts flew back to Kavitha on the ship and her suggestion that this was where destiny intended him to be. He remembered vaguely reading about this pagoda during his undergraduate studies of Theravada Buddhism. If he remembered correctly, tradition said it was one of the oldest stupas in Buddhist history and contained relics of four Buddhas, including hair from Siddhartha Gautama himself. After finding the Thomas church, perhaps he would have time to visit the shrine and soak in a little more of the sense of peace its glittering dome inspired.

But thoughts of the Indian beauty at the port office pushed aside his blanket of tranquility and drew his eye to the city that surrounded the temple. If the pagoda symbolized peace and hope, the rest of Yangon served as a counterpoint of ruin and despair. It was a city rebuilt by the British as a colonial capital during the nineteenth century and since they abandoned it when independence came in 1948, no one seemed to have painted or repaired anything. As Myo drove him though the city, Nolan noted that although official government buildings seemed well cared for and others were not completely crumbling, the city had an air of being tired and worn.

The phone buzzed on the small desk in the room and he knew Myo was waiting for him in the lobby. Nolan had arranged to pay a daily rate of $30 plus gas expenses for exclusive access to the taxi, but had sent the driver off for lunch while Nolan settled into the Panda. The little man stood beaming under his camouflaged bucket hat and bowed slightly as Nolan entered the hotel's spacious lobby. He also wore the long Burmese skirt—a green and red stripe that fell to the tops of his sandaled feet.

"You ready, Mr. Nolan?"

"Ready. Do you know where we're going?"

"Yes, I know. I already call."

"I like your outfit. What do you call this skirt the men wear? It looks comfortable."

"Lungi," Myo said. "Very nice. You want one?"

"Maybe later," Nolan smiled. "But I like yours."

Myo ushered him to the curb and opened the rear door of the taxi.

"May I ride in front? I will be able to see better."

Myo shrugged and smiled. "You want to drive? Then I can see good."

"If I drive, you won't see good for too long," Nolan laughed and slid into the passenger seat. They headed east for about five minutes then turned north onto a major thoroughfare that signs in both Burmese and English identified as Insein Road.

"You have spray for bugs?" Myo asked.

Nolan shook his head.

"Better get some. Many mosquitoes. Very bad." They passed a large university on their left and the highway divided. Myo stayed to the left and swung into the parking lot of a large market.

"You wait. I get bug lotion." Five minutes later Myo returned with a squeeze bottle of liquid that smelled like a combination of bath oil and kerosene. "This work pretty good," he said and encouraged Nolan to smear it on his arms, hands and neck as they continued north on Insein. A lively Burmese song blared from the radio and Myo's head bobbed and swayed with the twang of the strings and flutes.

They passed a mosque on the left and two minutes later, Myo swung the taxi right onto a side street. Though they were still in the city, the buildings to their left gave way immediately to closely-bunched tropical trees, bamboo thickets and heavy undergrowth. The taxi slowed, turning down a narrow dirt lane that wound through what looked to Nolan like heavy jungle. As the road disappeared behind them, he felt the hair bristle on his arms and the back of his neck.

"What is this place?" he asked, slipping his hand onto the door handle and bracing to jump from the car if he decided they were driving into a trap.

"Nagar. Be here pretty soon." The little man was smiling to himself and bobbing with the music and with the bouncing movement of the rutted road. Could the woman at the pier have located Myo and bribed the driver into bringing him here? This looked like a perfect place to disappear .... Then Nolan noticed the glass.

On both sides of the lane the ground was piled with broken bottles, vases, glass balls, and pieces of figurines of all colors and descriptions. Bamboo sprouted through the glass mounds, and tangled vines spread across them like a giant web, cradling handfuls of broken crystal. Side paths left the lane, each bordered by similar piles of brown or green bottles, dusty orange or blue balls, pieces of pink and green vases. Arbors overhung some of the paths with broad-leafed plants hanging like heavy drapes down over the trails.

"Glass factory," Myo announced as they rounded a bend in the narrow track and pulled up in front of a rough, single story wooden structure with a long, covered porch running across its front. The roof was a thick thatch of brown leaves, and bamboo as high as telephone poles bent over the structure from three sides, swaying with a light breeze that caught only its feathered tops. As the taxi came to a halt, a man of about Nolan's age in a long-sleeved white shirt, purple lungi and plain sandals stepped out onto the porch.

"Mr. Arun," Myo announced. "He can tell you about church."

"Please. Just call me Arun," the man said, stepping forward to shake Nolan's hand as he climbed from the car. His English was distinctly American and spoken as if it were a first language.

"Myo tells me you are interested in the Church of St. Thomas." He gestured toward a collection of wooden chairs that surrounded a small table under the awning. "Might I ask how you know about it?" His tone was curious without being suspicious.

Nolan recounted his conversation with the guide in Chennai and her mention of a legend that Thomas had established a church in what eventually became Rangoon in Burma.

"The city was once called Dagon and was little more than a fishing village near the Shwedagon stupa until the mid-seventeen hundreds," Arun said. "Many scholars don't believe the village existed before the eleventh century but by tradition, of course, the stupa is several millennia old...as is the church of St. Thomas."

"Then there is a church..?" Nolan inquired.

"More a pile of stones that was once a church, if the legends are correct."

"You aren't sure ...." It was more a statement from Nolan than a question.

"Not certain—but not entirely skeptical. My family acquired this property during the British period and the remains of the church were on it. There is a Mon caretaker whose family claims they have been caretakers since the church was built, but who can know?"

"Mon?"

"The Mon were the people of lower Burma in ancient times."

"And you have preserved what was left of the church?"

"My family kept the land mainly as gardens for several generations and then we started a glass factory here about forty years ago. You can still see the remnants of some of the garden paths, but most of it is overgrown. We were badly damaged by the cyclone Nargis in 2008 and with the costs of repairs and rising prices for natural gas, we are now only able to operate the glass works a few days a week. But we let the caretaker remain on the property and somehow he seems to manage. Money comes to him from his family and from Thomas Christians in India, I believe."

"May I see the church?"

"Of course. And you may speak to him. I told him you were coming and think he is delighted that someone has an interest in the old ruin." Arun stood and gestured for Nolan and Myo to follow. "Better stay close. You could get lost back in these pathways."

As soon as they stepped away from the covered porch, Nolan knew why Myo had stopped for insect repellent. Clouds of mosquitoes, bred in the bottoms of millions of broken, rain-filled bottles, swarmed to the three men and moved with them into the shadows of the covered pathways, filling the air with a low, incessant hum. Myo's repellant worked where it had been applied, but the insects found the thin material of Nolan's shirt where it was tight across his shoulders and before he could retrieve the bottle from his pocket, half a dozen bites pierced his upper back. He stopped and spread the smelly liquid across his shirt and the upper legs of his pants, adding another dose to his face and the top of his head.

"Vicious little creatures, aren't they," Arun chuckled. "One of the hazards of all this standing water." Nolan noticed that the insects didn't seem interested in either of the Burmese men and wondered if some evolutionary trait or staple in the diet made the natives unappetizing.

Under the arch of thick, overhanging branches, the piles of glass that lined the path were covered with a dull coating of brown dust. Here and there, a shining piece of bright blue or green appeared to have recently been thrown onto the heap. A hundred paces into the tangle of trees and vines the path opened onto a knee-high earthen platform covered by a similar thatched roof, supported by parallel rows of wooden poles. Beside the platform, two brick ovens thrust their chimneys up through the canopy.

"Glass ovens," Arun explained, pausing to point out features of the open-air workspace. "We draw a ball of glass from the furnaces with those long pipes, then hold it against one of these benches while the glassmaker blows and shapes the piece." He pointed at what looked to Nolan like worn sawhorses with blackened grooves burned into the cross-pieces by the turn of the hot pipes. Beside each bench a fifty gallon drum of brackish water served to cool the pipes between uses and bred more mosquitoes.

Arun lifted a carved wooden block from beside a work bench. "If we are making something like a bottle, we use forms. But most of these bottles you see lying around are factory-made. We just melt them down and use them to create more artistic objects. Most of our work is free-form."

Nolan nodded and thought of a dozen questions he would like to ask, but didn't want to delay reaching the church. Perhaps on the way back ....

The path that left the work platform had almost disappeared under the aggressive tangle of vines. Arun forced them aside as he led farther into the maze, dead-ending against a tall wooden fence framed from rough wood slats, nailed to three round cross-pieces that had been split along their length. As Nolan studied the jungle on either side to decide which direction the path turned along the fence, Arun stripped vines from the weathered boards and tugged open a crude gate, hinged with thick strips of cracked leather. The path on the other side showed even less wear and Arun had to kick at the undergrowth to open a track.

The caretaker's single room shack stood only thirty feet from the fence but wasn't visible until the men stood almost beside it. As they moved around to the front, Nolan saw that two other well-worn paths led away in other directions, one straight out from the rough plank door and one into the trees on the other side of the shanty. Arun rapped firmly on the door but the response came from down the path to their left. The man who appeared through the trees was much younger than Nolan expected—possibly mid-twenties—and bowed respectfully to Arun, addressing him in Burmese.

After a moment of conversation, Arun turned to Nolan and introduced the young man as Zaw. Zaw bowed and gestured for Nolan to follow, turning back down the same path.

The ruins were only a few steps into the trees and were no more than a square of piled, moss-covered stones, about twenty-by-thirty feet on the sides. Around the foundation and within the rectangle of the ancient walls, the grass was carefully clipped and groomed and a gap in one of the short ends indicated the site of an ancient doorway. As they entered the clearing, the swarm of mosquitoes disappeared, discouraged by the breeze that managed to penetrate the surrounding wall of green. The caretaker led them to the center of the old structure and turned to Nolan, speaking rapidly and gesturing about him.

"He says this is the Church of St. Thomas," Arun said. "St. Thomas built this church with his own hands when he stayed here for a year as he traveled to China."

"And Zaw's ancestors have been caring for the church since that time?" Nolan asked as Arun translated.

Zaw nodded vigorously and spoke for several minutes.

"He doesn't know how many there have been. Some of the caretakers have been men and some women. The oldest child has always become the caretaker and other children help support that person. He has two sisters who work in the city and bring him food and money."

"And does he have a wife?"

Zaw smiled and answered without waiting for Arun.

"Zaw says he will marry and have a son who will take his place."

"What if something were to happen to him before he has a son?"

"His sisters would care for the church. It is the most important duty of his family."

Nolan walked slowly around the perimeter of the old building. "What has destroyed the church over time?" he asked, wishing as soon as he posed the question that he had phrased it more delicately.

Zaw's face reflected the embarrassment the question implied and his jaw tightened as he spoke to Arun.

"Our history has been one of continuous strife and conflict," Arun said and Nolan suspected he was elaborating on the young man's explanation as he translated. "What hasn't been done by invaders or our severe weather, our own people have done. The stones have been used to build roads and for other buildings. Some are beneath the stadium that is just beyond these fences. His family has done its best to preserve the church, but what can one person do?"

"It's something of a miracle that anything remains at all," Nolan said, trying to reassure the caretaker. "The family has done a wonderful job of caring for the site."

Zaw's smile returned as Arun translated and he bowed slightly to his guest.

"I'm wondering, though," Nolan said cautiously, worried that he again might be risking an offense, "if after all these centuries there is any way to know if Thomas actually built the church himself—or if some of his disciples from India may have constructed it?"

Arun hesitated, then presented Zaw with the question. Rather than look offended, the young man smiled broadly and again gestured for the men to follow. He led them back to his small shanty and ushered them inside. Muted light filtered through one small window in the back of the hut and the room smelled of strong spices and cooked greens. Zaw signaled for them to stand beside a bare table in the center of the room while he knelt beside the narrow cot that pressed against the wall under the window. He reached under the draped blanket and dragged an object across the plank floor, then stood and held the stone at arm's length for Nolan's inspection. The flat rectangle of rock was book-sized and about two inches thick, and had carefully been scraped of dirt and moss. Carved deep into its slate-grey surface was a double ichthus, with one fish smoothly finished and the other roughly hewn—the symbol of the Second Son.

"May I?" Nolan asked, and Zaw nodded. He took the stone and ran his fingers slowly along the outline of the rough fish. It could, of course, have been carved by a disciple as easily as by the apostle himself, but as he handled the stone he felt again the moment of tranquility that seemed to emanate from the golden pagoda. With what he could only describe as reverence, Nolan handed the stone back to the caretaker.

"Thank you," he said. "And what do you know about Thomas' travels from here?"

Again Zaw replied without benefit of translation and Nolan realized he had probably understood everything that was being said. But he again answered through Arun.

"Xian in China. There is a church built by St. Thomas in Xian and a group of Thomas Christians still celebrate his ministry in that city."

"How do you know this?" Nolan asked, hoping his voice reflected the sincerity of his interest.

"The community of Thomas Christians is small," Zaw said, "but we are very close."

"Then I guess I go next to Xian."

Zaw's dark eyes studied the American's face. "What are you seeking?"

Nolan decided there was nothing to be lost by being honest with the man. "The legends tell us that Thomas returned to India and died either there or in Syria. My own research suggests that this may not be true— that he may have stayed in East Asia. I would like to learn where his journey ended."

Again Zaw looked at him seriously for a long moment. "And that is all you seek?"

A flush rose in Nolan's cheeks as he looked into the dark, inquiring eyes of the caretaker and something stirred deep within him, swelling and filling his chest as if warm, gentle hands were massaging his heart. The sensation was new to him—frightening—and as he struggled to understand it, he felt his eyes begin to well with tears.

"I think ...," he began, choking on the emotion that rose in his throat. "... I think I am seeking redemption."

Zaw took Nolan's hands in both of his own and held them without speaking. His face softened and he turned to Arun and looked directly into his interpreter's eyes as he spoke.

Arun hesitated, seemingly surprised by what he was hearing. "He says you do not need to go to Xian," he said finally. "He will tell you where you need to go."

CHAPTER TWENTY-FIVE

Once she learned Nolan Lemay was in Yangon, Kanta located the professor the same way Kuldip Singh had located Nisha at the Driftwood. She called hotels until a receptionist said he was registered there. Checking into a hotel under an assumed name in a foreign country, especially one like Myanmar, is a virtual impossibility without a false passport. Hotels always ask to see documentation and in a country as centrally controlled as Burma, the desk clerk wants to be certain who is staying there. And Kanta felt reasonably certain Professor Lemay wasn't sophisticated enough as a fugitive to know how to acquire forged documents.

She reasoned that he might pick a hotel below the five-star level, suspecting that if someone were looking for him, they might begin at places frequented by American visitors. When Kanta arrived in the Burmese city she had also thought briefly about staying in a lesser hotel—but only briefly. There was no reason this assignment shouldn't be carried out in complete comfort. The Savoy was a small boutique hotel, personal, centrally located on Dhamma Zedi Road overlooking the Peoples' Park, and careful to protect the privacy of its guests. Her ground-floor room looked out onto the pool and tropical garden and she felt quite removed from the oppressive drabness of the city beyond her lodgings.

Nisha's call late the evening before had both disturbed and irritated her. Lemay had been on the ferry. He was somewhere in Yangon and had slipped past her at the dock. Perhaps he was more sophisticated than she had given him credit for. But Kanta was a woman accustomed to getting what she wanted, and she would again in this case. She had slept soundly until seven, had a leisurely breakfast at a table beside the pool, and started her search for Lemay.

The professor, she decided, would pick a place that was clean, comfortable, central to the city, and reasonably priced. Burma under the Junta that had turned it into Myanmar had been closed to the outside world for so long that even in a city of over four million people, there weren't that many nice hotel choices. Thirty or forty at the most. The Panda had been fourteenth on her list and her approach was simple.

"Good morning. I'm calling to see if my associate Doctor Nolan Lemay has checked in yet. I believe he arrived yesterday ...."

The first thirteen inquiries ended the same way. "I'm sorry. We have no Doctor Lemay registered here." But the receptionist at the Panda acknowledged that he had checked in—then ruined Kanta's otherwise comfortable morning. "... but he checked out again an hour ago."

Kanta steadied her voice to hide the shiver of panic that crept up from her chest.

"Already? I thought he was going to stay in the city for several days. Did he say where he was going?"

"No. He had a small bag and a taxi was waiting. I think he was going to the airport."

Kanta dropped the receiver of the desk phone into its cradle, selected the icon for Viber, the international web-based calling service on her smart phone, and punched a selection on her contact list. The voice that answered sounded rusted and worn.

"This is Kanta. Our person of interest may already have left Yangon. I think he is still in the country since he appears to have entered without a visa. Perhaps you can guess where he might go next." She listened intently for several moments.

"Yes. That would be my assumption. I believe he is tracing the footsteps of St. Thomas."

Again she listened.

"I don't know if he is trying to visit each place or just find him," she said. "Nisha and her friend arrive here this afternoon by air. While I wait for them, I will find the caretaker and see what he can tell me. And no, I don't know if he still has the manuscript with him."

She hung up and rang the concierge. "Could you arrange for a car and driver as soon as possible? One is available now? I'll be there in five minutes."

The driver knew how to get to the Nagar Glass factory without directions and was well enough acquainted with Mr. Arun from tourist visits to provide Kanta with an introduction.

"For more than three years no one has come here asking about the Church of St. Thomas, and now I have two in two days. Can this be coincidence?" Arun asked, casting a curious eye over the beautiful woman in what was obviously a professionally tailored navy jacket and pants.

"Not a coincidence at all," Kanta said, deciding that she might make the most progress by being candid. "I represent a group known as the Disciples of St. Thomas in Kochi, India. The man who came yesterday, Professor Lemay, took something that belongs to us—something very sacred to our group, and irreplaceable. I am trying to recover it before he damages or destroys it."

Arun's eyes lingered on her perfect features and the long twist of glistening black hair that fell forward over one shoulder. "He seemed a very kind and sincere man," he said. "It is hard to know what one should believe. But you must visit with the caretaker of the church and he is not here this morning. You probably passed him on the way. He is visiting his sisters in the city."

"I believe the professor has already left the city," Kanta said. "Time is of some importance. Do you happen to know where the Professor was going?"

"I do. But again, I don't believe it is my place to become involved in what appears to be a matter among the Thomas Christians."

"I understand completely," she said with her most disarming smile. "But could you tell me this. Was he planning to go to Xian or travel north?"

Arun thought for a long moment, then gestured with a nod of his head. "If I were trying to find him, I would go north."

. . .

Two hours separated the arrival in Kolkata of Air India's Flight 0788 from Port Blair and the departure of Flight 0766 for Yangon.

"I was hoping to see Kolkata," Marcus muttered when Nisha showed him the reservation. "But I don't think two hours is going to do it."

"On the way back I'll show you the city," she said, leading him from the domestic terminal into the shining new interior of International Departures. "But we're already late getting into Burma. Kanta says Professor Lemay has left Yangon."

Marcus shook his head with a wry smile. "This isn't the Lemay I know. He seems like a man on a mission."

"I've been wondering about that. If he has been trying to follow the route of St. Thomas, he's jumping a step—or maybe several."

"But is staying in Myanmar?"

"At least for now. Kanta will meet us with a car and we'll be driving."

"Don't we need visas?"

"We have visas. I visited Burma several years ago and you could get one on arrival, but that changed in 2010. There is a new e-visa application process and our applications were submitted when we left Kochi. Visas will be waiting for us on arrival in Yangon."

Marcus stopped in the middle of the high, cream-colored terminal and frowned. Above him, the ceiling was covered with ancient cryptic symbols, adding to a disconcerting sense that though the space about him was flooded with light, he was feeling his way through a dark room and wasn't certain what he would bump into. "Why were they working on Burmese visas for us before we knew we were going to Burma?"

Nisha grabbed his hand and pulled him toward security. Just before entering the roped walkways that directed them to the agents, a young woman with short-cropped hair and an acne-scarred face approached them, handed Nisha an envelope and exchanged a few words, then with a slight bow, disappeared into the crowd.

Nisha opened the envelope and pulled out their boarding passes, checking them against the schedule on the giant digital board above the security gates.

"We knew where he was going," she said without looking up. "Port Blair was just a stop along the way if he went by sea."

"And you waited this long to tell me?"

"We thought we might intercept him in Port Blair. But when he left the ship at Yangon, we missed our chance. Ordering the visas anticipated that possibility."

"What are we anticipating beyond Myanmar? I'd like to be prepared for that ...."

"Possibly nothing ... if we catch this flight!"

'Possibly' didn't feel nearly definite enough for Marcus. The dark room was rustling with unfamiliar noises that made him nervous.

They passed smoothly through the security screening and headed for Gate 11.

"I know you've told me there are things I can't know about all of this right now," Marcus said as they wound their way through the crowds that gathered in disorderly masses around each gate. "But there doesn't seem to be much you *are* telling me."

"I can tell you now," Nisha said, "that Professor Lemay is getting himself into deeper and deeper trouble. I don't think he had time to get a visa and he seems to have slipped into Myanmar without going through customs. Sooner or later he's going to have to get out—and without a visa or an entry stamp, he'll be arrested when he tries. This is assuming those who are trying to find him don't get to him first."

Marcus pulled her against one of the cream-colored walls and turned her to face him. "Are we some of those who are trying to stop him?"

Nisha considered the question, holding his gaze directly enough that he knew she wasn't trying to lie. "Yes—we are trying to stop him. But not like the others."

"Is Kanta one of the others?"

This time she did look away. "We'll deal with Kanta when we have to."

The man who passed through security three positions behind them was also concerned about his visa. He had been called only four hours before and offered a sum of money large enough to justify considerable risk, but he was a man who liked to minimize risk and time was working against him. The caller had been referred by a regular client and knew exactly what he did for a living. The caller had offered a quarter of a million U.S. dollars, one hundred thousand in advance and the remainder when the job was done. All he had to do was follow a couple to Myanmar and insure they didn't return. That part was clear enough. How he would get into Burma and out again on such short notice was much less certain.

The caller assured him that a visa in his name would be waiting. It was an open business visa, issued in the name of the company that sold hundreds of thousands of dollars-worth of cotton cloth to Burmese merchants. Not just merchants, but buyers closely related to key members of the ruling junta who insured that, for a fee, company representatives could move in and out of the country unmolested. His name had been added to the list and when he reached customs, a visa would be waiting and he would be stamped through without question.

Or so he was told.

The couple would be easy to identify. She was an attractive, high caste Indian woman in her mid-twenties and he a tall, black American – traveling together. They were flying into Kolkata, his home city, from Port Blair and would be transferring to a flight to Yangon. He didn't ask how the new client knew all this, but assumed someone had been watching the couple in the Andamans and was either unable to follow them or had been identified. He didn't care. All he had been asked to do was insure that the couple disappeared while in Myanmar.

Until two years ago he had been a member of the Elite 9 Para Commando unit of the Indian Army, the best-of-the-best of India's Special Forces. For five years he had worked in counter insurgency in the disputed northern provinces of Jammu and Kashmir, infiltrating Pakistani units in what India considered its occupied territories, gathering intelligence, and eliminating men who were identified as doing the same work for the enemy. He was accustomed to killing without question, but had decided after five years that he deserved better compensation for his talents. He now worked as an independent contractor but in honor of his former unit, simply went by the name Nau, the Hindi word for the number 9.

The black man was massive—a good fifteen or sixteen centimeters taller than himself—and looked to be in fighting condition. But his eyes lacked the fierceness and intensity of a fighter and Nau had killed larger men before. The woman—her eyes had the intensity. But she was slight of build and had a fresh innocence about her pretty face that suggested she might be difficult to kill for different reasons. He didn't like assignments that included women, but this one paid too well to decline.

Aside from his finely-muscled body hidden beneath a moderately priced dark business suit, Nau's appearance could best be described as "average." He was of average height. Average looks: not handsome and not homely. Hair of average length—not too finely barbered but not unkempt. Non-descript tie and shoes. All were designed to attract no attention whatsoever. He stood away from the couple at the gate, watching them casually as they engaged in what he determined to be a mild disagreement. The black man was overly differential to the woman, and she overly patient with the man. They hardly looked dangerous, which led him to believe they were to be eliminated not for what they could do, but for what they knew. Though Nau never cared to know what the offenses of his victims were, he liked to guess. This couple knew too much.

Nau had only a small carry-on and had insisted that he be seated in first class. He wanted to get on the plane when he wished and disembark before the other passengers—and he wanted to be out and waiting when the couple cleared customs. Ah—that customs thing again. That's what made him nervous. But then, what was an assignment without a little uncertainty?

.　.　.

Kanta had a car and driver waiting when they exited the airport.

"He is a full day ahead of us so we may need to drive through the night," she said without further greeting. Nisha dropped her bag into the trunk and stood behind the car.

"I wonder if rather than driving, we should fly to Bangkok and then to Mae Hong Son. We can be at the village before he arrives. If we go overland, there are any number of ways he could take to get to the village. How will we find him?"

Kanta's reply in Malayalam indicated that the conversation was now to exclude Marcus. "There really are very few ways he can go and you have been to the village. It is a place of peace. They will not want any trouble coming there with us."

Nisha remained standing behind the car. "Perhaps there doesn't need to be trouble. To this point, the professor doesn't appear to be doing anything with the manuscript but using it as inspiration. That is exactly as we all do."

Kanta glanced at Marcus, then back to Nisha with dark eyes that spoke to why she was not a person to be trifled with. "I wonder if you aren't thinking more about your new friend here than your responsibility. Remember your vows."

"My vow ..." Nisha said in Malayalam, trying to keep her tone from revealing to Marcus the tension that was building in the conversation. "My vow was to guard the secret of the Second Son so that he could minister to the world unmolested. I see nothing in what has happened so far that compromises that vow. We are hunting this man on assumptions, not facts. First, that he has a copy of the manuscript. Second, that he plans to expose it. And third that he hasn't become as we are—committed to preserving this secret himself."

"This black man has stolen both your reason and your honor," Kanta said, making no effort to disguise the edge in her voice.

"My honor is very much intact. And as for my reason, perhaps we have not applied enough of it in the past. We are Christians as well as Guardians. We should be executing our responsibilities with some semblance of Christian charity. Doesn't it ever concern you that we are protecting a man of peace by destroying others?"

Kanta's face reflected open disdain. "You can fly to Bangkok if you wish, but I plan to stop this man before he reaches the village." She nodded to the driver who opened the rear door for her to slide into the seat.

Nisha gave Marcus a resigned shrug and closed the trunk. "Why don't you get in front where there is more leg room," she said in English. "I think we are in for a long night."

CHAPTER TWENTY-SIX

Myo sat on a bamboo mat across a low table from Nolan in what was more a lean-to than a restaurant. He poked nervously at a plate of yellow curried chicken and rice.

"I think this a very bad plan, Mister Nolan," he said, looking furtively at the two men who sat at one of the other tables, eating from three common dishes and paying little attention to the American and his driver. "You want to go with men to cross Thai border with no visa. No good reason to do that. Lots of bad reason. I think you make big mistake."

The day before, they had driven north out of Yangon on national Highway 1, passing through Bago and stopping briefly for lunch in Toungoo. For some reason that the American chose not to explain, he had also asked to be taken to a barber in Toungoo, where he had the young woman cut off all of his hair to within a few centimeters of his head. Perhaps it was the heat—or he wished to change his appearance. But when Mr. Nolan emerged from the shop, he still looked very much the same, but with no hair.

From Toungoo, they had taken Highway 5 east out of the central river valley and into heavily forested hills, thick with bamboo, drooping broad-leafed trees, thorn-covered bushes with bright red flowers, scattered palms and long-needled pines. A sign announced that they were passing into the State of Kayah and villages became scattered and showed less of the colonial influence of the central plain. Myo had never been into this part of the country and it seemed wild and unsettled.

Eighty kilometers from Toungoo, Highway 5 turned again north and briefly followed the Thanlyin River. Where the main road veered away from the river valley, Myo turned off onto a narrow crumbling strip of pavement that stayed along the river to the town of Ywathit where a small, three-room inn had rooms for the night. Myo spent the first part of the next day finding a way for Mr. Nolan to get into Thailand.

When they met near noon at the small eatery, the American leaned cautiously across the paper-covered table. "Why are these men going into Thailand? Drugs?"

"Maybe drugs. Maybe rubies. No good reason."

"But they will take me for five hundred U.S. dollars?"

"Five hundred dollars for one man. Five hundred dollars for other man."

"Five hundred dollars each, then?"

Myo nodded. "But they know you have more. They get you in jungle and say 'you give us more or stay here.'"

"Do you have a better idea, Myo? I came in with no visa and need to get across the border."

Myo did not have a better idea but cautioned, "Then you are in Thailand with no visa. No better."

"Better in that I'm in Thailand and that's where I want to be," Mr. Nolan said with a smile.

Myo did not smile back. "I think you a crazy man. But you a good crazy man and give me good money, and these men will take you. I tell you one thing, then you go." He leaned close and whispered across the table. Mr. Nolan first looked puzzled, then nodded slightly.

"I'll remember that," he said. He stood and shook Myo's hand, then pulled off the cap with the black panther head and handed it to Myo. Myo removed his camouflage bucket hat and replaced it with the blue cap. His hair splayed out beneath it like a thick grey mop.

"What you think? Look pretty good?" He handed Mr. Nolan his bucket hat.

The American laughed and pulled the hat down over his newly-shaved head, gave Myo an embarrassing embrace, and signaled to the two men at the other table that he was heading out back to the bathroom, then would be ready to go. Myo waited until he returned and watched as Mr. Nolan left the café with his escorts.

"One very bad plan," he muttered, pulling the panther cap more tightly over his grey thatch.

The vehicle was a battered Series I Land Rover that looked like it was a castoff from the British departure from Burma in 1948. Its canvas top was ripped along both sides and fastened back together with what looked like grey duct tape, causing it to flap and pop as the Rover rolled north up the paved road from Twathit. The spare tire strapped to the boxed hood was bare to the cord, and rusty splotches turned the military green paint into a perfect camouflage when they left the pavement fifteen kilometers from the village and disappeared into the jungle.

Nolan sat in the back, his case pulled tightly against his hip, and tried to roll with the Rover as it jarred along what was no more than a wide rutted path and splashed through shallow mountain streams. Overhead, birds of every color shrieked and chattered an alarm as the rumble of the poorly tuned engine announced their coming. A ferret-looking creature with a sleek weasel body and long fluffy tail perched upright on a moss-covered stump as they lurched by, then dived back into the cover of trailing vines.

They drove for over two hours without stopping or speaking, winding up narrow valleys and crossing ridges where brief breaks in the tree line offered glimpses of more forest, stretching to the horizon. As they rounded a turn near the crest of a high overlook, the driver pulled onto an open spot beside the dirt track and turned off the engine. The three climbed from the Land Rover and stretched their cramped backs and legs.

"Thailand," the driver said, pointing off across the canopy that stretched below into a late afternoon haze. "We just cross into Thailand." Nolan nodded in acknowledgement.

"Money, please," the second man said.

Nolan reached into his pocket and retrieved the two wads of bills he had prepared in the bathroom before leaving the restaurant, handing one to each man.

"Take off clothes," the driver said.

Nolan's heart skipped a beat and the blood drained from his face. He shook his head as if he didn't understand.

The second man pulled an old black Luger pistol from the back of his waistband and waved it in Nolan's face, grinning darkly at their passenger. "Clothes off," he repeated.

Slowly Nolan stripped off his shirt and undershirt, revealing two packets of cash strapped under his arms with self-adhesive cloth tape. The man with the pistol used its barrel to indicate he should unwrap the band and drop the money to the ground in front of them. Nolan knew that each packet held five thousand dollars.

With the bundles on the ground, the armed man motioned for him to remove his pants and shoes. Two more packets were wrapped on the inside of his thighs and he dropped them on top of the others—three thousand dollars in each. As the man with the pistol sorted through the packets, the driver picked up Nolan's shoes and examined the insoles, then patted around the bottom and groin of his blue boxers. Finding nothing, he pulled Nolan's bag from the seat and dumped its contents onto the ground, then stuffed the few clothes roughly back into the duffle when he found no more cash.

"Where is passport?" he demanded.

"I don't have a passport."

"How you come to Burma?"

Nolan nodded toward the Land Rover and jungle path they had just driven. "From India—this same way."

The driver looked at him skeptically. "Why no passport?"

"I had to leave India quickly and didn't have time to go back to my apartment. No visa—no passport."

The men spoke to each other in animated Burmese for several minutes, the Luger carrier holding up the money and smiling broadly as he announced how much was in the packets. The driver finally turned back to Nolan.

"We say we take you to Thailand. You in Thailand." He nodded for the armed man to climb back into the Rover and backed slowly toward it himself.

"Wait!" Nolan shouted. "I can't do you any harm. How could I report you to anyone? I'm in the country illegally. At least take me to a village."

"We take you to Thailand. You in Thailand," the driver repeated.

Nolan stepped past him to the driver's door and pulled back the seat before the man could object. "I need my rain jacket and hat." He lifted the jacket from the rear seat and Myo's canvas bucket hat from the floor beneath the seat.

The driver grabbed the jacket and quickly ran his hands over it, feeling for cash or the missing passport, then tossed it over onto Nolan's pile of clothes. He slid into his seat and slammed the door, lifting his hand in mock salute.

"Welcome to Thailand," he said, and the Rover surged forward and disappeared down the hill into the trees.

. . .

At the intersection of the road to Mandalay and Highway 5 in Toungoo, Kanta ordered the driver into an MMTM Fuel Station and while he waited for the car to be filled, the three entered the sparsely-supplied red and blue shop, looking for bottled water.

"I think we should go east from here," Nisha said, searching the travel map she had picked up at the airport. "Highway 5 takes us toward the Thai border south of Mae Hong Son."

"He has to cross somewhere in the jungle," Kanta said. "All the road crossings are closed except for day passes that require you to leave your passport. He will try to cross somewhere in the mountains."

"That still means going east," Nisha said. "And the chances we will find the right place are practically nil. We should have flown into Thailand and up to Mae Hong Son. Then we could be watching the road to the village."

"He might cross north of Mae Hong Son and go directly to the village," Kanta countered.

"As I said earlier," Nisha retorted, "if we go to the village and wait, he will come to us—or we won't find him at all. He may not even be going there. This is what the Americans call a 'wild goose chase.'"

She felt Marcus grip her arm and lean in toward her. "May I speak to you privately for just a moment?" He pulled her to the front of the shop where the glass front looked out on the fuel pumps. "Look at the little man standing beside the taxi."

"I see him. What about him?

"The hat. That's Professor Lemay's Panthers cap."

Nisha headed for the door without waiting to hear more. The man was beginning to get back into his taxi when she reached him and she slid quickly around the driver's door and leaned down to him before he could pull it closed.

"Pardon me," she said in English, "but could you tell me where you got that hat?" Marcus had stepped out of the front of the shop and stood watching her across the row of pumps and automobiles.

The small man frowned and pulled at the door handle. "From a friend," he said.

"I need to find your friend," Nisha said. "He is in great danger."

The driver looked at her suspiciously. "Who are you?"

Nisha improvised as she talked. "I am also a friend of Professor

Lemay. He is trying to get to Mae Hong Son in Thailand and some very dangerous people are trying to stop him. They are waiting for him there and we need to warn him before they find him."

"We?"

Nisha nodded toward Marcus and Kanta, who had joined him under the large block-letter MMTM sign. "His friend from America, my sister, and me. Can you tell us where he went?"

The little man sat upright and peered at the tall black man and the beautiful Indian woman, then looked back at Nisha and shook his head. "You can't go there. Too hard for car."

"How did he go?"

"Men take him," the taxi driver said.

"They could take us ...."

"No!" He shook his head adamantly. "Mr. Nolan crazy to go. But you? No!"

"Will you take us to where he left with the men? I will pay you."

Again the little man looked at Marcus and Kanta. "I will take you, but not them. They stay here, then I bring you back."

"Why not all of us?"

"If you go and they stay, then you come back."

"Wait here," she said and joined Kanta and Marcus.

"This man knows where the professor tried to cross," she said, looking back at the cab driver who watched her intently. "He will take me there, but not all of us."

Kanta sniffed. "What difference would it make if one goes or three? We all need to go."

"He says it is too dangerous to follow and if only one person goes, I will have to come back."

"Coming back doesn't do the job," Kanta said. "Go with him and we will follow."

"He says a car can't make the trip over the border. It's too rough. Even if we find where it starts, we won't be able to follow."

Marcus inserted himself into the conversation. "And if you go by yourself, what do we gain if you can't follow him?"

Nisha looked intently at the little cab driver. "I have an idea. Both of you go back to Yangon and get to Mae Hong Son by air as quickly as you can. There was an afternoon flight to Bangkok and I think flights go to Chang Mai from there every hour. You may need to drive to Mae Hong Son from there or wait until tomorrow."

"No way," Marcus said. "I'm not letting you go up there by yourself. And how do you get across if the three of us can't?"

Nisha felt her jaw tighten and tried not to sound as irritated as she felt.

"I don't think you decide what I'm allowed to do and what I'm not. And I'm not sure how I will get across, if I do at all. I may just come back to Yangon with the driver and join you in Chiang Mai. Now I'm going. You should hurry or you won't make the flight to Bangkok."

She turned and walked back to the man wearing the Panthers ball cap.

"I'm ready to go," she said to the cab driver, "but I need to make a stop first."

When the couple separated, Nau made the split-second decision to follow the woman they called Nisha. As his driver fell in behind the taxi that was headed into the city of Toungoo, he made a call on his satellite phone.

"The woman and the black man have separated. I am following the woman but can go back and pick up the man if he is of greater importance. They met another woman in Yangon and he is with her." He listened intently and nodded into the phone. "I thought so. She appears to be making the decisions. I will try to pick him up again when the woman is out of the way."

The taxi carrying Nisha drove north on Highway 1, then turned left onto what appeared to be the main road into the heart of the city. It stopped briefly while the driver spoke to a shopkeeper, then continued for three blocks and turned again north. At the next major intersection, it pulled to the side in front of an open air shop with an array of used motorcycles parked along the sidewalk. The shop was an open, dark cavern with motorcycle exhaust systems, fenders and handlebars hanging from the rafters like metal stalactites, reaching down toward stacks of tires that littered the floor. The woman exited the taxi and quickly looked over the row of bikes, then disappeared into the cavern as Nau directed his driver to the side of the road.

The woman Nisha emerged again from the shop, followed by a grease-covered young man in tattered coveralls. She pointed to a black Yamaha 135LC and spoke to the mechanic. He nodded and went back into the shop while she gave the bike a more thorough examination, feeling the tread on the tires and checking the amount of fuel in the tank. When the owner returned with the keys, she mounted the bike like an experienced rider and kicked it to life, revving it up in neutral and leaning forward to listen to the rhythmic rumble of the 4-stroke engine. She nodded approvingly, dismounted, and followed the man back into the shop.

As he watched the scene unfold, Nau drew a black box, half the size of a package of cigarettes, out of his bag. When she disappeared again into the back of the shop, he jumped from the car, walked quickly to the row of motorcycles and began his own inspection, paying particular attention to a late model Suzuki 150 that stood beside the Yamaha. As he bent to inspect its engine and tires, he slipped the magnetized box under the cowling of the Yamaha, then proceeded down the row, examining other bikes. Five minutes later the woman returned to the Yamaha with an inexpensive black helmet with tinted visor, climbed aboard, and rocked the bike off its stand. She started it again and eased it out onto the street, pulling up beside the taxi she had taken into the city.

Nau waved to the young mechanic. "Do you speak English?"

The boy shrugged. "A little."

"Is this Suzuki a good bike? Run good?"

"Very good," the young man said.

"What are you selling it for? How much?"

"Good price for you."

"How much?"

The man gave him a figure.

"I'll buy it," Nau said and led him into the shop. Five minutes later he had retrieved his own bag from the car, paid off his driver, and strapped the bag behind the seat of the Suzuki. He fixed a small magnetic screen to the top of the fuel tank in front of him, activated the switch, and swung the bike into the street. The screen beeped and a red dot flashed on the green grid, showing that she was still within range and somewhere behind him. He drove to the intersection, turned right until he hit the Mandalay highway, and raced back toward the intersection with Highway 5. As he turned east, the red dot centered in front of him and within ten minutes he had her in sight. The taxi was still directly in front of her and didn't seem to be in a great hurry. He stayed three cars behind and relaxed into the seat. She appeared to be headed into the mountains. This might not be too difficult after all.

· · ·

Marcus moved into the back seat beside Kanta. During the ride back to Yangon International Airport he sat in silence, worrying about Nisha and watching the Burmese countryside go by as Kanta talked on the phone. Her conversations were mostly in English, occasionally switching to Malayalam when she wanted privacy. He understood enough Tamil to know that she was both arranging tickets and explaining that Professor Lemay was turning out to be more elusive than anticipated. She warned the listener that Lemay might reach 'the village' before he could be stopped.

Marcus was both troubled and amused by how a woman who was so physically beautiful could be so unappealing. Nisha was pretty, but Kanta was drop dead gorgeous—like Halle Berry and Catherine Zeta Jones. You couldn't look at the woman without taking a second glance, and then had trouble pulling your eyes away. There was nothing about her appearance that wasn't perfect. Eyes, lips, nose, mouth, hair, body, clothes—the whole package. But underneath, as his grandmother used to say, Kanta was as cold as a dead possum in winter. Nisha, by contrast, was kind, thoughtful, loving, tender when she needed to be, tough when it was necessary. He knew that she would try to follow Lemay. He had known since she said "I have an idea." With her heading off somewhere behind them trying to intercept the professor in the mountains before he self-destructed, Marcus realized how deeply he loved the woman.

Kanta punched the "end call" button on her phone and slipped it into her handbag, an irritated scowl creasing her flawless lips.

"We can get to Bangkok tonight, but probably not Chiang Mai until tomorrow morning—and Mae Hong Son no sooner than noon."

"And what will we do with Dr. Lemay if we find him?" Marcus asked.

The scowl shifted to her eyes and she turned to look at him with what he could only read as contempt.

"We will do whatever is necessary. And this is no concern of yours."

Marcus returned her glare with a cool smile. "It is every concern of mine. Doctor Lemay is my sponsor and I have some responsibility for his safety."

"He has gotten himself into some business he should not have become involved with, and you would have been wise to stay out of it as well."

"I didn't ask to be involved. I wasn't aware Nisha had any part in this...."

Kanta sniffed. "She shouldn't have involved you. She is forgetting who she is."

"You don't care much for me, do you, Kanta." It was more a statement than a question.

Kanta's lips curled into a caustic smile. "Let me think where I should begin .... I don't like Americans. I especially don't like American men. As a nation, you are so full of your own importance that you are rapidly becoming a second-rate country and don't have any idea it is happening. At least your women have been subjugated for so long that they have an appreciation for the values and struggles of others." She paused and looked directly at him with that same look of disdain. "And I don't like pariahs."

Marcus felt the Arkansas Delta boy bristle within him and he returned her look with equal feeling.

"Well, aren't you the conflicted woman! So full of yourself about gender, but still so frightened about race. And what do you know about struggle? My guess is that your biggest fear is that some of that Pariah blood might show up in the family if you looked back a few generations."

Kanta threw off the idea with a toss of her head. "We are Kshatrias. Descended from some of India's most noble families."

"If you were Hindu, I might understand some of this attitude," Marcus said. "But you present yourself as Christian. Whatever happened to all of us being created in God's image?' Do you think it was the image of some Brahmin or Kshatria?"

"And you think American Christians see all people as equal?" she retorted. "You make me laugh!"

"Laughing would be a pleasant change," he said. "Something or someone has made you a very angry woman."

"It makes me angry that Nisha has fallen for you."

"She's said something to you?"

Again Kanta sniffed dismissively and turned to look sullenly out her side window.

Marcus turned to his own window. He wondered how much Nisha cared for him—and what was happening to her in the mountains of central Burma.

CHAPTER TWENTY-SEVEN

Nisha braked the bike to a stop at the edge of a shallow stream and inspected the bottom. It was the third streambed she had encountered and as she crossed the last one, the tires had slid from beneath her on the mossy stones and dropped her on her side in the ankle-deep water, bruising her shoulder and stalling the engine. It had taken nearly ten minutes to get the Yamaha started again—time she couldn't afford. She was a little more than an hour into the mountains and judging from the position of the sun, didn't have more than another hour before dark. The man who had given her directions to the road—the one Myo had driven her to meet, and whom she had persuaded with a $100 bill—told her it was a three-hour trip to the nearest Thai village, but he had never seen her on a bike. She had run the road like a motocross competitor, vaulting over ridges in the jungle path and spraying dirt as she spun around blind corners, confident that no one would be coming in the other direction. But she would still not make the Thai village before dark and she had no desire to spend the night in the jungle.

The stream tumbled down a shallow ravine partway up a heavily wooded slope and as she studied the bottom of the streambed through the clear water, looking for a path that would keep her off the bare bedrock, she heard in the distance behind her a sound that chilled her blood and caused her to trap her breath. She lifted her head and stripped off the helmet to listen more clearly. Another motorcycle was making its way up the valley she had just crossed. The thick screen of jungle muted the sound, but it couldn't be too far behind and was moving under another experienced rider.

Her first thought was that Kanta and Marcus had decided to follow her, but she knew immediately that neither could ride like that. Drug runners or border patrol? Either would mean trouble. She wondered if the other rider had stopped long enough to hear her bike ahead, knowing the sound would travel better down the mountain than from below. She needed to get moving, and quickly, if she wanted to stay ahead of the other bike.

She picked a path through the stream that kept her on looser gravel and slipped the bike into gear, edging slowly through the water, then accelerating up the hill and over the ridge. It was just possible that the man who had given her directions sent someone after her, suspecting she was carrying more money and seeing her as easy prey. The taxi driver, Myo, had initially found the man for Professor Lemay, working his way through the seedy underbelly of the town of Twathit until he discovered those who directed trafficking across the border. When Nisha met the man in the back of a ramshackle Quonset hut on the edge of the city, he had looked more like the images she had seen in Japanese shops of the happy Buddha—bald, over-stuffed, and sitting contentedly on a small couch that barely contained his girth. The building smelled of oil and lathed metal and to reach the small office where the man held court, she and Myo had navigated an obstacle course of old earth-moving equipment—small dozers, road graders, and backhoes.

The fat man inspected her with mild amusement. "Why do you want to cross into Thailand?" he asked in clear English.

"I am part of a television travel race. The contest is to see who can get around the world most quickly without a passport."

A deep laugh began in the man's belly and worked its way outward until his entire body shook. "And the American who went earlier today? He is one of the contestants?"

"Yes. Myo said the American is ahead of me."

"I like this story," the fat man said, continuing to jiggle. "But the American did not look like a person who would be in a television race. I don't care why you want to go. I am only a business man. For a fee, I can tell you how to get there. For a larger fee, someone will take you."

"Just tell me how to get there," she said. "But I might caution you. I have a back-up crew who follows my progress. If I don't make it, they will be here to visit you."

The fat man's laugh stopped as quickly as it had started. "We are doing business. Not threatening each other."

"It is not a threat. You have my assurance."

As Nisha now felt the other rider gaining on her, she wondered if this was a continuing part of the fat man's business transaction. Whoever was on the other bike also knew it would be dark before he could reach a Thai village, which probably meant that wasn't the intent. He was coming after her.

The jungle path crested a ridge and widened where the trees parted, providing a clear view down across kilometers of tropical forest that were already darkening as the sun dropped behind her in the west. Her eye caught a strip of light brown that looked out of place against the green of the grassy verge and she stopped abruptly and leaned from the bike to pick it up. She heard the other bike's engine shift down as it began the ascent toward the ridge. Nisha started down the slope, inspecting the strip of cloth bandage in the dim light as she drove and imagining why it had been left. It wasn't stained or soiled in any way, so hadn't covered a wound or been on the ground for very long. Not more than a day. So it must have been used to stabilize a sprain or strap something to the body ... something that had been removed at that overlook. The hillside to her left dropped off steeply for fifteen or twenty meters and if someone were to tumble down into that tangle of trees and brush, they might never be found. She tossed the strip behind her onto the road, hoping it might cause the rider who followed her to stop for even a few moments. She needed every second to stay ahead.

At the bottom of the downgrade she raced forward along the floor of a long narrow valley, trees arching over a fairly straight stretch of path that continued for nearly five kilometers. The sun had dropped below the horizon and she flipped on her headlamp, adding to the impression of breakneck speed as trees flashed behind her into the growing darkness. The tinted visor of her helmet added to the shadows and buffered the sound of the pursuing bike and she pulled it off, wedging it onto the seat behind her. As the valley ended, the dark expanse ahead suggested that the terrain opened into what looked like a wide bowl where several other small valleys came together. The trail again crossed a stream, then swung out around the edge of the basin. She slowed as she approached the stream, shifting down and easing the bike into the ford, her light glaring off the glassy stretch of water. As the rear wheel entered the stream, she again felt the bike slide from beneath her, slipping so quickly she barely had time to tuck her left leg in against the side and draw her arms tight against her chest. As her shoulder hit the water, she felt a jarring blow to the side of her head, then nothing.

When she awoke, she was lying on the near bank, the bike on its side a few meters farther up the gradual slope. Her head throbbed and her first thought was that she had been a fool to take off the helmet. Her second thought was that aside from the murmur of the stream, the jungle was completely quiet. Too quiet. She could not hear the engine of the trailing bike and there was no chatter of birds or monkeys. The forest usually quieted just after sundown and before the night animals came to life, but not like this. Something had startled the jungle into complete silence. As she lifted her head and began to push up onto an elbow, he came toward her along the trail as a dark shadow emerging out of the deepening night. She could barely distinguish the features of his face but she had seen him before—just a brief glimpse when she was buying the bike. The face was expressionless and he made no attempt to shield the long knife he carried in his right hand. She knew that he was not going to say anything or explain why he was going to kill her. And there was nothing to be gained by screaming. No one would hear.

Nisha pushed onto her knees to prepare for the attack and felt a wave of dizziness and nausea swell up from her stomach. The shadows became deeper and she feared she would again slip into unconsciousness. Perhaps it would be best. Then she would feel nothing. He was no more than ten meters from her, fading into a shapeless apparition that drifted toward her. But she couldn't just let it happen. She tried to force one leg forward, staggering upward, but the shadows around the figure only seemed to expand and sway. As she fell forward again onto her knees, she heard a swooshing crunch, and the man pitched forward onto the path in front of her.

CHAPTER TWENTY-EIGHT

After standing in his boxers for what must have been ten minutes listening to the Land Rover retreat into the jungle below, Nolan had dressed quickly and stood for a much longer time looking out over the endless expanse of rainforest. He turned slowly in each direction, trying not to let the panic that hovered on the edges of his mind get the best of him. The sun slanted into the opening along the ridge top, heating the air and baking his newly exposed scalp. He stepped back under the trees, finding that the cool of the shadows calmed his thoughts. For a moment he had been certain that the men would kill him, and just being alive kept the panic at bay. If he could keep his wits about him, he could stay alive and find some way out of here.

He wondered if the men had been telling the truth—that they had crossed into Thailand. For some reason he thought they had. Honor among thieves. He had crossed the Thai border, so the wise thing to do was continue along the road until he found a village or ran into someone. Judging from the sun, it was mid-afternoon and he should be able to walk for two or three hours before it became dark. If he hadn't found anyone as dusk approached, he would worry about spending the night in the jungle when he had to.

Myo's camouflaged bucket hat lay on the ground at his feet beside the strips of cloth bandage that had strapped the money to his body when he made the change at the restaurant. His passport and the rest of his cash were wrapped in the hat. His driver's advice, that he keep enough on him to convince a thief they had discovered his stash, but separate most of it and hide it in the Rover until safely among other people, had saved most of his supply. He had wrapped it in the hat and tucked it along the side of the rear seat, leaving it in the Rover when they stopped to search him. He had almost let them drive away with it, but they didn't seem to mind him grabbing the hat and rain jacket before leaving him on the hilltop.

When confident that the Rover was not going to return to leave no witnesses, Nolan searched around in his duffle for the repellant Myo had purchased, covered himself with the smelly liquid, and started down the mountain road. Not far below the ridge crest the track slipped again beneath the arched canopy of trees and vines and he realized that dusk would come much sooner than he had anticipated. Birds whistled, chirped and fluttered above him and despite himself, Nolan began to laugh. It was mainly out of sheer relief at being alive, but there was something eerily exciting about finding himself—Nolan Lemay— trudging down a mountain road in the jungles of Southeast Asia. He wished Regina could see him now! Wouldn't that just crack her Botox!

At the bottom of the hill he paused beside a stream where someone days before had set up a campsite. The framework of a low lean-to had been lashed together out of bamboo and hemp rope and he thought for a moment about stopping until morning. But he had nothing to stretch over the frame for shelter and the approaching evening was beginning to smell of rain. He would move on down the valley until dark and hope to find another suitable place to spend the night. A stout bamboo pole, about four feet long and two inches in diameter, lay beside the frame and he picked it up to use as a walking staff. The first hours of evening quieted the birds and cast long grey shadows onto the jungle path, bringing a dampening dose of reality to the excitement of being the happy wanderer. He gripped the staff and used it to steady himself across the stream, then walked for another hour into the deepening evening.

At the next stream crossing he knew he would not find a rescuer before nightfall and needed to figure out how to spend the night in the jungle. For the first time it occurred to him that there would be dangers other than smugglers moving through the forest in the dark, and he could be easy prey. A giant banyan tree, thick as a Volkswagen beetle, stood beside the path, its dangling aerial roots hacked off above the track as high as a man could reach, but forming a loose screen beside the road. Nolan parted the hanging roots and pushed back to the trunk, inspecting its base for a safe place to bed down. Nothing would protect him from snakes, but he vaguely remembered once hearing that mosquitoes stayed lower to the ground. If he could get up into the branches .... A limb as thick as his waist branched from the trunk at shoulder height, with another the same thickness four feet above it and a quarter around the tree. He left his duffle on the ground and struggled onto the first branch, pulling the bamboo pole up with him. Then to the second, and a third, gripping the hanging roots to pull himself upward. The third branch flattened out where it met the trunk and bowed slightly, creating a natural seat. He stretched out with his back against the trunk and looked for a way to secure himself to the tree. Large cats could get to him here—and large snakes. Weren't some pythons called Burmese pythons? But they could get to him just as easily on the ground and there was something comforting about being up off the jungle floor. If he had a knife, he could cut some of the thinner hanging roots and lash himself to the heavier ones ....

Back along the road in the direction from which he had come, Nolan heard the faint hum of an engine. He sat erect and listened, hearing it grow as it raced toward him along the floor of the narrow valley. He dropped the bamboo pole to the ground and scrambled back down the tree, moving to the edge of the veil of roots to a point where he could see the path in the failing light but remain hidden in the shadows. Nolan's heart quickened with the growing sound of the engine—what he determined to be a motorcycle or an ATV of some variety. Another smuggler making a night run? Could he risk showing himself or .... The thought that came to Nolan was so alien that it was as if it had emerged from another man's mind. When the rider slowed for the stream, he could step from the shadows of the trees and knock him from the bike with his bamboo staff. He had ridden a motorcycle a few times ... prodded by Regina when they were dating to do what other guys were doing. He didn't remember how to shift, or how the clutch worked, but he could figure it out ....

The dark tunnel of trees that arched over the path began to glow and the engine noise took on a low-pitched scream as the bike approached, then slowed, paused, and slowed again as the driver shifted down. Nolan pressed against a thick rope of hanging roots and squinted into the approaching lamp, closing his eyes to regain what night vision he could. The bike slowed beside him as the rider looked at the stream. When he peered again through the veil of vines, the bike was no more than twenty feet away, slowing to a crawl as it approached the water. He eased forward, clutching the staff, and could begin to make out the rider ....

For an instant the sight of Nisha Pillai froze him in place as his mind struggled to fit her into what was already a surreal world, and in that instant, she drove the bike into the stream. Before he could react—step forward and shout to get her attention—the bike slid onto its side, dropping her heavily into the water.

Nolan jumped from his hiding place to help her back to her feet but she didn't move, lying motionless with one leg beneath the bike. He grabbed an arm and pulled her around until he could reach beneath her shoulders, then slid her up the bank and onto her back on a grassy spot beside the path. As he leaned over her, he felt strong, even breaths and realized she was not drowning but had struck her head on a rock in the streambed as she fell. To his right, the bike began to shift and slide in the current and he instinctively splashed back into the water, grabbed it by its rear tire, and pulled it to the bank. As he returned to Nisha, he heard again the scream of an engine accelerating up the flat of the valley.

Nolan's mind raced. A second night rider this close behind was too coincidental to be unrelated. If Nisha had been traveling with someone, they would have stayed together in the dark. She was being followed. There was no good place to hide the bike and if he pulled Nisha into the thicket of trees, her pursuer would immediately become alert, staying back until certain what had happened. As the light of the second bike began to spread the darkness of the covered trail with its faint glow, Nolan grabbed his staff and slipped back into the heavy shadows of the banyan.

Nisha began to stir as the second bike rolled to a stop fifty paces from where she lay. The rider doused the light and dismounted. The night was now no more than shadows—the woman struggling to stand, the rider approaching her with slow, even strides. As Nolan's eyes adjusted to the loss of light from the headlamp, he saw that the pursuer was male and that he carried a long thick-bladed knife. Nisha was on her knees and her face showed first recognition, then resigned determination. As she struggled to get to her feet, the man passed Nolan's hiding place among the dangling roots and the knife came forward. Nolan raised the bamboo staff as he stepped into the open, his steps muted by the grass but enough of a whisper to be heard. As he swung with both hands, uncoiling every ounce of strength into the blow, the man turned in surprise and the bamboo shaft caught him squarely above his left ear, crunching into the skull with the sound of a ripe melon dropping from a countertop. The man pitched forward without a gasp, his face and knife hitting the earth a few feet from Nisha's trembling knees.

For a long moment, neither of them moved. Then Nolan dropped the club to the ground and stepped toward Nisha, reaching to pull her to her feet. She fell into him as she stood, wrapping her arms around him for comfort and support and crying softly against his neck. They stood silently in the darkness until her tears were gone, then she eased away and smiled at him.

"I don't know if I found you, or you found me. But I think it happened for both of us at just the right moment."

Destiny, Nolan thought, as she dropped back to one knee and felt at the side of her fallen assailant's neck.

"This man's not going anywhere," she said quietly.

"Do you know who he is?"

"Not specifically. But I think I know who sent him."

"So you were chasing me, and he was chasing you."

"More or less. Let's say I was trying to find you."

"Am I safe with you then?"

Nisha stood, but again began to lose her balance. Nolan grasped her arm and steadied her until she nodded that she was okay.

"I think I'm pretty much at your mercy. But yes, for now you are safe with me. Do you know how to ride a bike?"

"I might need a quick lesson, but I think I can get the hang of it pretty quickly."

She looked down at the body on the road. "We need to get him out of sight and keep going. I think we will be safest if we are on the move. The engine noise will scare anything away that might be a threat."

They felt their way through the man's clothing, finding only the bill of sale for the Suzuki, then pulled him back though the dark tangle of draping roots to the other side of the banyan and propped the body against the trunk.

"This seems a little inhumane," Nisha said, "but I'm not feeling very humane right now."

"I wonder how often this road is traveled?" Nolan asked.

"It looks pretty worn. And I would guess the men who took you will be coming back. That's why we need to keep going tonight."

As they dried off the Yamaha, Nisha pulled the small black box from beneath the cowling and held it up for Nolan to inspect in the light of the Suzuki's headlamp.

"This is how he knew where I was," she muttered, pulling the directional indicator from the top of the Suzuki's fuel tank and tossing both into the trees. "I doubt anyone else is following us, but let's get moving." She gave Nolan a lesson on the Suzuki and while he rode up and down the straight stretch of road a few times, nursed the Yamaha back to life.

"I'm not feeling very steady on this," she said. "Let's walk them both through the stream then ride until we find a good place to hide the Suzuki. I'd feel much better sitting behind you for now. The ground still keeps moving under me."

On the far bank they mounted the bikes and rode slowly side-by-side, their dual headlights piercing the blackness of the covered road until Nisha signaled for them to stop. On the left side of the path a boulder the size of a boxcar had broken loose from the hillside above ages ago and now stood covered in moss and thick vines with broad, hand-shaped leaves. Thick brush hugged the rock on one side, but a faint path skirted it on the other. They rolled the Suzuki along the side of the boulder and propped it against its back.

"Check the odometer," Nisha said as she climbed onto the Yamaha behind Nolan. "We may want to direct someone back to this spot."

For the next hour they rode in silence, Nolan gaining confidence as he got a feel for the bike, and Nisha clutching him around the waist as she fought dizzy spells that threatened to topple her if she let go. As they looped around a hillside beside what was now a small river, the light caught a path as wide as the one they traveled that left the road to the right, cutting diagonally up the hill into the trees. Nolan slowed the bike and the faint smell of wood smoke drifted down to them on the night air, accompanied by the sound of syncopated drumming.

"Let's try it," Nisha said into his ear and he steered up the path, slowing to a crawl and steadying the bike with his feet as they bounced through washed-out cuts in the path and over downed limbs that had gradually been worn into its clay surface. Several hundred yards from the smugglers' road the trees opened onto a small village of open-sided wooden huts, each raised on a poled platform so that the mat floor stood chest-high above the ground. Thickly thatched roofs of dried grass and palm fronds covered the rooms and villagers rose from low woven benches and came to the edge of the platforms as the bike rolled through the darkness into the village. Each hut glowed with the light of an oil lamp and the men came forward first, dressed in t-shirts and loose-fitting pants or shorts. Behind them the women of the village gathered to see who was coming this late at night, each displaying a bright headdress of reds, yellows and blues, with a plain white blouse and patterned woven skirt. Layers of gold rings wrapped their necks like an extended spring, forcing the head upward and collarbone down so that some of the stretched necks were as long as the woman's head. Children clustered around the mothers, even the youngest girls wearing the elongating rings.

"Padaung," Nisha whispered. "The long-neck Karen tribe from Burma. Most of them are refugees here."

A man descended a set of steps from one of the platforms and stood in the center of the road that divided the village, bringing the bike to a halt in front of him. He didn't speak but waited for Nisha to dismount while Nolan adjusted the kickstand.

"Do you speak any English?" she asked. The man nodded.

"We have come from Burma and need a place to stay for the night. And we need some food. Is there a place we could eat and sleep?"

The man remained silent then shook his head. "No place to stay," he said finally.

"We can pay you," she assured him. "And we will leave early tomorrow. We have been traveling all day and are very tired."

Nolan swung from the bike and joined Nisha. "We can give you a motorbike like this one if you allow us to stay," he said. A second man descended from one of the other huts and the two spoke for a moment, then the second man turned back to Nolan.

"How will you give us this motorbike?"

"We were both riding and she fell and hit her head." He lifted Nisha's hair to show the men the knot behind her left eye. "We had to leave the bike along the road. We will take you to it in the morning and you may have it."

"These are not your motorbikes," the first man said. "You use them only for today."

Nisha reached into the back pocket of her jeans and pulled out the bill of sale for the Yamaha while Nolan fumbled for the Suzuki papers, holding them out for the men to inspect. "We bought them in Toungoo in Myanmar," she said.

The men studied the papers and conversed again for several minutes, then the second man waved for them to follow him. "You stay with me. Tomorrow she will stay and you go with me to get motorbike. Then you can go."

Nolan nodded and the man barked instructions up to the women who hovered on the edge of his home platform. The oldest of the women relayed instructions to the rest of the household and each scurried in different directions, readying a meal and finding mats for two guests. As they followed their host up the steps to his hut, Nolan turned and whispered to Nisha, "Fascinating people. And what women won't do to meet some arbitrary standard of beauty!"

He knew immediately from her look that he had said the wrong thing.

"You think?" she said. "Maybe it's more a matter of what women won't do to keep food in the mouths of their children. I've heard these villages compared to human zoos. If the zebra becomes a horse, no one wishes to come look at it anymore." Nolan let it drop.

They sat on mats on the floor around a low table and ate rice with a meat curry and baked whole fish. It took Nolan only a single taste of the fish to get over having the milky eyes staring back at him as he peeled away the flesh, setting the blackened skin to one side. One of the children slid over beside him, looked at him intently for a moment, then reached for the skin and slipped away, popping the charred scales into his mouth. When it was evident he wasn't going to do anything with the head, another child, a young girl who already sported six rings around her neck, lifted it from the flat wooden board that served as his plate and began to pry it open, gobbling up the eyes and any soft matter she could find.

"They must really be hungry," Nolan murmured, pushing what he had not eaten of the fish over to the two remaining children.

"You've left some of their favorite parts," Nisha smiled. "We enjoy eating what we were raised to eat, and we were raised to waste what they consider to be some of the tasty parts of the fish."

By the time they finished their meal and nodded their satisfied thanks to their hosts, an entire family and a number of neighbors were sitting silently around them, staring curiously. Nolan tried speaking to some of the women and children but they simply nodded and smiled, seemingly curious to see what these foreigners would do when they weren't parading through the village to have their pictures taken with the "long-necks."

"I think if we're going to keep this from being too awkward, we'll need to talk to each other," he said finally. "I don't think it's quite bedtime."

Nisha glanced at her cell phone. "It really isn't that late. Only about nine-thirty. I have no idea when they go to bed."

"This may be a good time to talk about tomorrow then," he suggested. "What are you planning to do with me?"

Nisha thought for a long moment before answering. "Do you have a copy of the manuscript?" she asked finally.

"Yes. It's in a deep inside pocket of my rain jacket."

"You are lucky it wasn't stolen."

"When they checked the jacket, they were looking for packages of money. They didn't even notice it."

"Were you able to read it?"

He nodded. "It's an amazing document."

"Have you told anyone about it?"

"No."

"What do you plan to do with it?

Nolan shrugged. "When I acquired it, my plan was to make it public, of course."

"And now?" The ring of villagers followed the conversation as if watching a tennis match, turning from one of their guests to the other as they exchanged comments. Even the children sat in complete silence, tracking the flow of strange words with amused enjoyment.

"I'm not certain, but I think I will take it to the village and find someone to give it to."

"You think they may not already be aware of it?"

"I have no idea. If they are, no harm, no foul."

"And if they are not?"

Nolan shrugged. "From the interest everyone seems to have in this village, they probably should be. I'll decide that when I get there-- assuming you allow me to go ...." He paused while Nisha considered his comment, then said, "and I think this is the time for me to ask. Tell me about the village."

Nisha continued to think, but her eyes reflected a shift in thought. "There is nothing mysterious about it," she said finally. "It is not some Shangri La or hidden place. In fact, thousands of people visit it every year."

"I was told by the caretaker in Yangon that it is called Mae Aw. That sounds a bit mysterious."

"That's the old name. The Thais call it Ban Rak Thai, the 'Village that loves Thailand.'"

"Hmmm .... Sounds like a refugee village. Are the people there Burmese like these people?"

"Chinese," Nisha said. "Most were Kuomintang soldiers who came here when the nationalist supporters of Chiang Kai Shek and his army fled the country. They didn't all go to Taiwan—what was then Formosa. Many who were in western China fled west. One group came here, including a large group of Thomas Christians from Xian."

"Mae Aw. What does that mean?"

"I'm not certain." Nisha glanced around at the smiling circle that clearly had no idea what they were talking about but anticipated an answer. "Something about rice, I think."

"And what will I find there—in Mae Aw?"

Nisha's face relaxed into a contented, faraway smile. "Peace," she said. "It isn't like any place I've ever been. Friendly, happy tea farmers who seem completely satisfied with their lives and make you feel the same."

"Tea farmers?"

"They produce some of the best oolong teas.... One they process with milk has a soothing, creamy taste that is like nothing I've ever tasted."

Nolan smiled at the transformation that had come over her pretty face as she spoke. "And why have you been there before?"

She raised a brow as if it should somehow be obvious. "For members of the Disciples—and for some other Thomas Christians—it is our Rome. Our Mecca. We try to go there at least once during our lives."

"Because ...?"

The faraway smile faded from Nisha's face and he could see that she had decided she may have said too much. "Why are you headed there?" she asked, looking again at the circle of faces as if each was wondering the same thing.

"The caretaker in Yangon .... He said that was where Thomas ended his journeys."

"But you visited the place in Chennai where he died ...."

"Or is said to have died," Nolan corrected. "Perhaps he died here. Or if you believe the letter ...."

"Do you believe the letter?" she asked, and the circle of Padaung turned again to Nolan.

"Let's say that I have become increasingly intrigued by the letter—or by the idea of the letter."

"The idea?"

"That someone exists on earth who is a preserver of peace. Whose presence keeps us from completely destroying ourselves. We seem to have come so close several times."

"It *is* an intriguing idea," Nisha said.

"That's why I want to go to the village."

"To expose it?"

"Expose? You mean let everyone know what I find there?" He turned the idea over for a moment. "No. In fact, once I've been there, I really don't have anywhere else to go. I'm hoping that if peace resides there, perhaps I can stay."

"And do what?" Her tone showed a trace of skepticism. "Raise tea?"

"Perhaps. Or teach Aramaic. Be the Mae Aw tourist greeter. Whatever is needed."

Her skepticism spread across her face and she cocked her head to one side. "You would leave a life as a happily married distinguished professor?"

"Married? Yes. Happily? No. Professor? Yes. Distinguished? Definitely not. In fact, my interest in coming to Kochi to begin with was partly to get away from that marriage for a while and largely to become 'distinguished.' I came closer to becoming 'ex-tinguished.' I think now I'm looking more for redemption—and a little peace."

"Redemption? From what?"

He shrugged. "From being weak. From being dishonest. From being a man who lived off the work of others. Who knows? Perhaps it really *is* destiny."

"Destiny?"

"A woman I met on the boat. She thought my coming here was destiny."

"The Disciples don't accept pre-destination," Nisha said.

"Call it 'guided intervention' then."

Nisha sat for a long while without speaking as the ring of villagers watched her expectantly, sensing that it was her turn. She studied his face with such care that the entire circle seemed to lean forward, turning from her to him, then back to see what she would say. Nolan could see that although they knew nothing of what was being discussed, they understood that the conversation had reached an important moment.

"Tomorrow, I think you should go to Mae Aw," she said finally.

Nolan nodded. "How far is it from Mae Hong Son?"

"About forty-five kilometers. Thirty-five or forty northeast up toward some of the other Karen villages, then another five or ten kilometers into the hills."

"I think I would like to walk that last five or ten," he said. "I don't want to just arrive there like a tourist. I feel like I've been working my way toward it for a week now—or maybe for my whole life—and need to take it in a little at a time as I approach. A *Camino de Santiago* kind of thing. Does that make any sense to you?"

"Perfect sense. I wish I had done the same when I visited before."

They nodded to each other and exchanged understanding smiles and the Padaung all nodded and smiled with them, rising as if by signal and readying the hut for sleep.

"I think it's bedtime," Nisha said.

Their host shook Nolan awake before daylight.

"We go now to get motorbike," he said, and rode behind Nolan as they traveled the distance he had measured back to the rock. The Suzuki was still in its hiding place and quickly changed hands. The villager was on the bike, out of sight, and back on his platform with Nisha beside him when Nolan again rolled into the Padaung settlement.

"He likes it," she said with a smile, descending the steps with a lightness in her step that showed she had fully recovered from her fall.

"No longer dizzy, I see," he laughed.

"No, and I'm driving. We don't have all day to get to Mae Hong Son."

How far is it?"

With me driving, forty-five minutes."

"What do we do when we get there?"

"That depends," she said, swinging onto the bike in front of him, "on who else is there."

CHAPTER TWENTY-NINE

The small plane descended into the valley in tightening circles, drawn like a swirl of water into the funnel created by the mountains surrounding Mae Hong Son. Marcus pressed against the window, entranced by wisps of morning mist that rose from the valley floor and drifted upward, shrouding and then releasing a gleaming gold pagoda that crowned a hill above the town. He had never flown on a propeller-driven aircraft, let alone a twelve-seater like this Beechcraft, and the hum of the engines and blurred circle created by the spinning props added to his sense that he was traveling back in time.

He and Kanta had reached Bangkok the day before with just enough time to rush through customs and get to the domestic terminal for the last flight to Chiang Mai. The trip north had been an hour-long hop on a fully loaded 747, followed by fifteen minutes through dark streets in a taxi that took them to the Royal Princess Hotel. The general lack of conversation with Kanta convinced him it was not the time to complain again about too much luxury, and he was too tired to argue anyway. But he hadn't slept. He lay awake fighting off visions of Nisha lying injured somewhere in the mountains of Myanmar, abducted by smugglers, attacked by jungle animals, or just lost to him forever in some great green expanse of forest.

At 8:10 a.m. the following morning they were aboard Kan Air flight 721 for the forty-five minute hop across the mountains to Mae Hong Son. Marcus had now been in two of Thailand's most celebrated cities and hadn't seen anything of either. And he was moving across vast distances with such speed that time seemed almost irrelevant. But boarding the Beechcraft and staying low over the mountains as they flew northwest back toward the border with Myanmar reminded him of scenes from the Indiana Jones movie where a red line streaked across a map of Asia as an ancient Goonybird aircraft flew the fabled Burma Hump between China and India. As the plane circled in toward a landing in Mae Hong Son, the mountain community added to the impression of other-worldliness.

The runway seemed to fill half of the valley, with ragged, tree-covered mountains rising on every side, the heavy green forest spilling down the slopes to the very edge of the airstrip. The Beech taxied to a stop beside a small white terminal with a red terra cotta roof. As the steps were lowered and the twelve passengers clambered onto the apron, Marcus felt the first twinges of relief. The air was cool and smelled of damp leaves with a trace of pine, and even this far from the trees, the whistle and chatter of birds were the only sounds that broke the quiet of the mountain air. There was no sense of danger here.

He stood on the steps of the arrivals gate for several minutes before entering the building, looking at the sweep of the valley and wondering again what had become of Nisha. He wasn't sure what direction he was facing, but somewhere out in those mountains she was trying to make her way here. As much as he was frightened for her, the feeling of this place told him she was alright. And if anyone could navigate the border crossing, his Nisha could.

By the time he entered the terminal, Kanta had disappeared. As he made his way toward the exit, he saw her standing at a counter that rented motorbikes, keys dangling from her hand as she pushed a yellow sheet of paper across to the clerk. She turned quickly and walked toward him as he approached, giving the impression she did not want the attendant at the counter to know they were traveling together.

"Nisha found Lemay," she said coolly, as if she had hoped it might not happen. Marcus' heart swelled almost to bursting and tears welled in the corners of his eyes. He reached to hug Kanta but she stepped away. "They are on their way here. You wait. I have business to take care of."

"Are they both okay?"

"That's all I know. I had a text when I got off the plane. She said to wait here."

"But you're not waiting ...?"

"As I said—I have business." And she was gone.

·   ·   ·

As soon as they turned onto the road to the airport, Nolan could see the imposing figure of Marcus Branscomb towering above a busload of Japanese tourists who were clustered around a guide who held aloft a pink umbrella. An involuntary squeal escaped Nisha's lips as she goosed the Yamaha, throwing him back so unexpectedly that he had to grab the back of her shirt to keep from tumbling off. As she braked at the curb in front of the main terminal doors, Marcus swept her from the seat and lifted her against his chest, leaving Nolan to steady the bike.

"You are a crazy, wonderful woman," Marcus whispered in her ear, loud enough for anyone in the unloading area to hear. She kissed his neck and squeezed him until he protested.

"Easy! You already take my breath away!"

She slipped back to the pavement and both turned toward Nolan.

"You've had us worried," Marcus said, then seemed uncertain what to say next.

"It looks like you two have become better acquainted," Nolan smiled, looking from one to the other. "Guess I haven't been much of a chaperone ...."

The couple stood in embarrassed silence, realizing that he knew nothing about their growing relationship and that perhaps he should have.

Nolan broke the awkward silence. "Anyway, you look good together. But one of Nisha's friends scared me into leaving town and before I knew it, I was on a pilgrimage."

"Quite a pilgrimage," Marcus said. "You look different .... And you're lucky you made it this far."

"More than you know. Nisha here probably saved me."

"We sort of saved each other," she said. "And I think we've resolved some of our issues."

Nolan felt the corner of his eyes moisten and his chest swelled with an overwhelming affection for this young woman. She looked up at him and smiled, acknowledging the sentiment, then turned and looked expectantly toward the doors of the terminal. "Where is Kanta?"

Marcus followed her gaze. "She left. Rented a motorbike and said she had business."

"Did she say where?"

He shook his head. "No. Just told me to wait for you and left. We haven't had a very friendly two days."

Nisha leaned back against the seat of the bike and looked at Nolan. "We may not have all the issues resolved. Kanta can be a little obsessive."

Nolan remembered the piercing black eyes and how coldly she had warned him about sharing Bartlett's fate. "Where would she go? To the village?"

"I don't think so. It's not a place that accepts her kind of obsessiveness. But I think you need to change your plan about walking the last few kilometers to Mae Aw."

Lemay shook his head dismissively. "I've come this far. I'm not going to let her frighten me again. Let's rent another bike and I can ride behind you. Drop me off a few miles before we get to the village and wait for me there."

He and Marcus stayed with the Yamaha while Nisha arranged for a bike rental.

"We go north out of town on Rt. 1095," she instructed when she returned with the second bike. "In about ten kilometers, you will see a sign to Ban Rak Thai. That's Mae Aw. We'll stop about six kilometers from the village for you to begin your walk, Doctor Lemay."

"I need to get to an internet café first," he said. "There are a couple of messages I need to send before I go to the village."

Nisha unstrapped her roller bag from the Yamaha and opened it on the seat, pulling her iPad from the zipper pocket in the top. She checked settings and found that the airport had wi-fi that could be accessed by the hour for a small fee.

"I assume you haven't kept any credit cards—or that what you had were taken with your money. Let me log in here and you can send your messages." She accessed the network and paid for an hour of time, then handed the tablet to Nolan.

He sat on a low wall in front of the terminal and entered his university email account, typing in Regina's address.

Dear Regina:

I trust you are finding your stay in Italy all you had hoped for. I will follow this note with a letter as soon as I have an opportunity to get something on paper, but I am sending this message now to let you know I will not be returning from India. I have found a new life here for which I am much better suited, and suspect you will find your own life less burdensome without me. Tell your friends whatever you wish about my decision. I'm sure you are thinking as you read this that it can't be from me—that I would never make an independent decision of this magnitude.

And to a degree, you are right. The old Nolan would never have dreamed of it. The new Nolan knows it is the right thing to do for both of us. Feel free to take your life in whatever direction you choose. I will be doing the same.

Respectfully,
Nolan

When the message was on its way, he returned to his inbox, found an unanswered note from his dean, and hit reply.

Dear Dr. Arnold:
Please accept this note as my formal resignation from the department and as confirmation that I will not be returning to the university at the end of this sabbatical. You have my permission to send any remaining salary and benefits to my wife Regina at my home address. A written copy of the resignation will follow as soon as I am able to send one. I have enjoyed my time at the University and wish you well in finding a suitable replacement.

Sincerely,
Nolan Lemay

He marked and deleted the rest of his unanswered messages, started to exit his account, then pulled a card from his shirt pocket and entered another address.

Dear Kavitha:
To say that my time since I left the ship has been an adventure would be an understatement. I cannot say whether destiny, dumb luck, or a guiding hand has brought me to this place, but I wanted you to know that I am keeping my eyes forward. I believe I am about to complete the final leg of my journey and if you are interested in how it turns out, I will be delighted to hear from you and continue a correspondence. I hope Port Blair is all you had hoped for.

With warm thoughts,
Nolan

He returned the tablet to Nisha. "Thank you," he said. "I believe I am now ready."

As she steered the rented bike into the mountains with Marcus and Lemay close behind, Nisha remembered how enchanting she had found this drive three years earlier. At this altitude the forests were laced with pines and bushes covered with sweet-smelling flowers. The air was cool and much drier than in the central river plains and the veil of grey smoke that hung over Asia's rice-growing deltas hadn't made it into the mountain valleys. The ride to the village was a gradual immersion in serenity and she tried to recapture some of that feeling.

But her memories couldn't overcome the present reality of Kanta. Every cause has its zealots and among the Disciples, it was Kanta. Nisha feared her—not out of any sense of personal danger, but because Kanta had become so narrow in her personal interpretation of what it meant to "protect" that she had ceased to be rational. She had lost all wisdom. And Nisha had made the mistake in her text to Kanta at the airport of telling her she thought the professor was safe—that he was anxious to redeem himself and was planning as a form of penance to walk the final few kilometers into Mae Aw.

As she turned off Rt. 1050, checking her mirror quickly to confirm that the other riders stayed with her, her eyes scanned every side road and path, every turn-out and abandoned hut for any sign of the rogue Guardian.

The paved road ran up the side of a narrow valley with thick forest covering the hillside to her left, almost to the edge of the asphalt. On her right she could see into the valley below where small farms with thatched wooden houses raised on stilts huddled along a river, the farm boundaries marked by natural screens of bamboo or crudely constructed pole fences. She slowed as she reached the crest of a long upgrade, hearing the lowing of cattle on the road ahead. The odometer showed they were about six kilometers from the village. She pulled to the side at the brow of the hill where she could see the three animals on the road in front of her, and Marcus could see her from behind.

The second bike rolled to a stop beside her.

"This would be a good place to begin your walk," she said, looking ahead to where the road disappeared around a gradual bend. "As I remember, the last few kilometers are mainly downhill, so it should be pleasant."

Professor Lemay swung from behind Marcus and stretched. "This has been breathtaking," he said, looking about him. "As anxious as I am to get to the village, I hardly want this to end. I'm not sure I've ever been in such a beautiful place."

"There is a bridge as you enter the village," she said. "We'll wait for you just beyond the bridge."

"Do you mind if I leave my bag on the bike?"

"Not at all ... but your jacket is in it. Don't you want to have the letter...?"

Lemay shook his head and looked off across the valley. "No. You keep it with you. If for some reason ...." His voice faded into nothing.

He knows, Nisha thought. And he's not concerned. This is not the Professor Lemay who came to her parents' home in Kochi.

"Be alert," she said. "The tourist vans that come along this road aren't expecting anyone to be walking. These cows are taking a major risk."

"Thank you. I'll be watching."

Nisha turned to Marcus. "You ready?"

"I can't wait to see this place," he said, and they eased their bikes back onto the road.

Nolan stood on the crest of the hill where he could see in every direction. In almost every way he could imagine, he was as far from where his journey had begun as he could possibly be. How close was this, he wondered, to being exactly on the opposite side of the world? He was still in the northern hemisphere, of course, but still .... When he was a boy they would say that if you drilled a hole through the middle of the earth you would come out in China. He thought it would probably be closer to here.

But the greater distance was in how far he had come from being the Nolan Lemay of Charlotte who wanted everything, and wasn't willing to do much to get it. He now wanted practically nothing—and was willing to do whatever it required to be rid of that former self. He had become a thief to learn this, and that now ate at his insides like a cancer. He hoped that at this village there would be a surgeon ....

Plus, he had killed a man—and much to his surprise, that didn't eat at him at all. He tried to picture Regina but found in the midst of all this beauty and simplicity, it was hard to get a clear image of her. Would she like this new Nolan? He didn't think so. There was something about the weak and needy old Nolan that suited her perfectly.

The cows had moved to the uphill side of the road when Nisha and Marcus passed, but now stood again in the center of the pavement, watching him curiously. He started down the hill, conscious not to skirt the ragged brown animals but walking straight toward them. They lowered their heads cautiously and one scraped nervously at the pavement, then moved resentfully to the side and watched him pass.

He walked for half an hour and was passed by a dozen tourist vans and an occasional person on a motorbike. They waved as they passed as if they had expected to see him and weren't at all surprised at a lone hiker strolling along the road to Mae Aw. The road looped along the hillside in a narrow turn and Nolan hugged the side of the road, ready to jump into the trees if a van came around the curve too quickly. He was halfway through the turn when he heard her behind him.

"Well, Professor. You have been a difficult man to find."

Though he had anticipated this moment, he still felt a chill raise the hair on his arms and neck and his heart quicken. When he turned, she was standing a few steps back into the trees on a foot path that climbed the hillside.

"You did remarkably well at following me," he said, drawing a slow deep breath to steady his heart.

"You were given a warning."

"Indeed I was, but unfortunately after the fact. I had already made my deal with the devil."

"I need the copy of the manuscript."

"I don't have it." A van swung around the corner and he thought fleetingly of waving it down, then let it pass.

"Manisha said you had it, but had shown it to no one."

"I did have it, and no one else has seen it."

"Where is it now?"

"Where you have no further reason to worry about it." He wondered what she would do if he suddenly began to run down the road—or down the slope on the far side toward one of the distant farms. She answered by pulling a small revolver from her handbag, waving Nolan toward the path on which she stood.

"I have to assume that you read it. You are an Aramaic scholar.... I can't allow you to enter the village."

Nolan didn't move. "I did read it. That's why I'm here." He looked at the gun with nervous amusement. "How did you get here with that thing—with all the security inspections you had to pass through? And somehow, a gun doesn't seem your style."

Kanta's perfect lips curled into a disdainful sneer. "You are a naïve man. You don't carry things like this. You just need to know where to go when you arrive. And my style, as you call it, is to use whatever is necessary. Come. We're going for a walk."

"I don't think so."

"You don't understand, Professor. I will not hesitate for a moment to kill you where you stand."

"Then a walk doesn't make much difference. But before you do, I at least have a right to know why you are doing this. I've broken no oath and I've shared what I learned with no one. In that respect, I'm just like you and Nisha and a hundred others."

"They are all sworn to protect the secret," she said coolly. "And I have no confidence that you will."

"Hmmm," Nolan mused. "And you are the person who has a right to make that judgment?"

"I am someone who, like your friend Nisha, is sworn to guard the secret. But she has no courage."

"Perhaps she has much more than that," Nolan suggested. "Discernment? Compassion? An understanding of some higher principle?"

Kanta hesitated for a brief second. "No principle is higher than the oath we take," she said quickly.

"I know you serve the Second Son. But both he and you also serve the First Son. And He presents some principles I think Nisha understands better than you seem to."

"And those would be ...?"

"One might be that God will forgive whom he will forgive, but we must forgive all people."

"I don't have time for your pathetic sermons," Kanta glared, again waving with the pistol. "I can't let you enter the village."

"I think," Nolan said slowly, "that people there are expecting me...

and I don't mean just Nisha and Marcus. When I don't arrive, they will know that you have been the reason. Are you prepared for that?"

Kanta's dark eyes lost their piercing focus for a brief moment as the thought passed behind them. Nolan took that moment to turn and began to walk down the hill. "Do what you have to," he said back over his shoulder. "I am walking to Mae Aw."

CHAPTER THIRTY

The village of Mae Aw nestles in a valley of mountain pines and tea farms within a stone's throw of the Thai border with Myanmar. Its colorful adobe houses frame a small, man-made lake and are capped with the grey leaf thatch typical of villages throughout the northern hills of Thailand and Burma. But travelers entering the village immediately sense that they have arrived at a place that is uniquely different. Brightly colored Chinese lanterns hang from trees that line the road into the village and ornate Mandarin calligraphy decorates the mud walls of shops and homes. Every third building seems to be a tea house, offering the delicately-flavored oolongs that draw thousands of visitors each year to tables along the lake shore where the order of the day is beauty and relaxation. Even the peeling paint on hand-planed wooden doors and shutters seems intentional, giving the village an air of timelessness and graceful aging.

There was no breeze as Nolan began the long descent toward the bridge that spanned the village stream, and the glassy smooth surface of the lake mirrored the village in perfect relief. Across the lake, visitors clustered around the tea houses or walked aimlessly about the village, reflecting a conviction that there was no need to hurry.

As he approached the bridge, an old man tottered out to greet him, bracing himself with a gnarled wooden cane. He was an elderly Chinese gentleman with a thin, grey beard that left white flakes on his black, high collared jacket. A black skull cap crowned a head of equally thin and equally long white hair. He bent forward as he walked but moved toward Nolan with such energy that Nolan wanted to rush to meet him.

The man stopped when he was a few paces away and bowed deeply, his hands tucked together against the front of his long black shirt. "Welcome to Mae Aw," he said and looked up at Nolan with a wide toothless smile.

"I didn't know I was expected," Nolan said, returning the bow self-consciously. "But thank you for the welcome."

"We are a small community," the man said, then added quickly, "... the Thomas Christians. When someone seeks to locate and visit each of our important sites, word travels. It has been many years since anyone has found us here as you have. Come. Let us have some tea and you can tell me about your journey."

At the far side of the bridge, Nisha and Marcus waited in an open tea house and joined them as the old man led Nolan into the village.

"I am so relieved to see you," Nisha said, handing him his jacket. "I was afraid ...." Nolan silenced her with a quick glance at his escort.

"We met along the road," he said simply. "I think we managed to come to terms."

Nisha looked over his shoulder at the road descending the hill into Mae Aw. "Is she coming ...?"

"I don't think so. I heard her leave in the other direction."

"Your friend and I will be visiting for a while," the old Chinese gentleman said. "I will return him to you when we have finished." He continued on down the street for a hundred meters, then turned up a flight of rough stone steps that climbed the hillside between two homes. Despite his age and the cane, the man moved with such agility that Nolan had to hurry to stay with him. At the top of the steps, he entered the doorway of an adobe home, painted a bright saffron with green framing about the door and windows. As he beckoned him through, Nolan noticed that carved into the lintel were two fishes, one smoothly formed and the other rough, the heads overlapping so that they shared a common eye. They passed directly through to a balcony that looked out over the lake where his host seated him beside a round table, its mahogany top inlaid with graceful lotus blossoms carved from a creamy yellow wood. As soon as they were seated, a young woman in traditional Chinese dress appeared with a porcelain tea set, serving them both without speaking.

In typical Chinese fashion, the first twenty minutes of the conversation helped the men become more comfortable with each other.

"The people here call me Master Chen," the old man said. "You may call me Chen." With that he launched into a detailed description of the history of the village—how Nationalist soldiers and their families had fled China in 1948 for Burma, then moved across the border into the more accommodating Thailand.

"Ban Rak Thai, the name given to this village by the Thais, means 'The Village that Loves Thailand.' We were most grateful for the protection they gave us here."

"And how did the Thomas Christians end up in Mae Aw?" Nolan

asked, easing the discussion toward the reason for his own journey.

"We were concerned that the Cultural Revolution would not be kind to us. Though we are largely pacifists, we fled with the army."

"This village seems much more suited to pacifists than to soldiers," Nolan observed. "It has a sense of serenity about it that removes it from the rest of the world."

Chen smiled and stroked his thin beard. "Is that why you have come?"

Nolan sipped at his tea and looked out over the lake, then directly back at his host. "It wasn't my reason to begin with. You may or may not be aware that I managed to get a copy of a manuscript the Kochi Disciples hold very sacred."

Chen nodded.

"Are you familiar with what it says?" Nolan asked.

"Generally, yes."

"My first thought was to test its veracity. To be the scholar who revealed a document from the first century claiming that Thomas still lives, and trace his journey east as far as I was able."

"And does that remain your intent?"

Nolan had placed his jacket on the back of his chair and reached to pull it in front of him. He felt deep into an inside pocket and retrieved the photocopy of the letter.

"I have come to return this, and to ask forgiveness."

Master Chen took the paper, unfolded it, and scanned it quickly. "And what do you think of its contents, now that you have traced the journey to this place?"

"I'm no longer seeking to refute or validate the letter. I am now more intrigued by the idea of a 'Sustainer of Peace.' My life could use some peace."

"And you expect to find that here?"

"I admit that I am a little confused," Nolan admitted. "The caretaker in Yangon said that if I wanted to find the end of Thomas' journey, I needn't go to Xian but should come here. Yet this village was only established sixty-five years ago ...."

Chen's face opened again into a broad toothless smile. "Were you really expecting to find the living Thomas?"

Nolan shrugged, his face flushing slightly. "I was beginning to hope...."

"And what would that be like? That 'hope?'" Chen asked. "Would it be a place that, in a world of turmoil and chaos, maintains the peace and serenity of a perfect world?" He answered before Nolan could reply, holding his hands apart in front of his chin as he spoke. "If that is what it would be, then you have found the living Thomas in this village."

"Then I have found what I have been seeking," Nolan said.

"And where do you go from here?"

Nolan tried to formulate into a single question the thousand thoughts that had passed through his head as he walked the six kilometers to Mae Aw.

"Can the village use another tea farmer?"

Chen extended the copy of the manuscript back to Nolan. "I believe we have all the tea famers we can manage," he laughed softly. "But this is not the only manuscript of its kind. A number of others are here. But we have no one who knows how to care for them as they need to be preserved. We could use what I think you call an 'archivist.'"

"A much better match than being a tea farmer," Nolan said, bowing his head gratefully. "But that may not produce anything that will help sustain the village."

"Nor do I," Chen said. "Those who work with their hands tolerate those of us who work with our minds. But they tolerate us without complaint. There is a small cottage near here where you can stay."

"I have enough in my bag to keep me for a few months and help the village," Nolan said. "I am most grateful that you have accepted me."

Chen stood slowly. "This can be a solitary life. We do travel from the village and friends visit us here, but it is a remote place. Some attachments to the outside world can be difficult to maintain, and others difficult to sever. I have been assured that your heart is sincere, but you must consider what you are about to do very carefully."

"I've been thinking about nothing else for the past week," Nolan said. "My past is the past. I am ready to begin again."

"Then let us return to your friends," Chen said. "I think they are anxious to know what has become of you."

On the hillside above the village a farmer worked along a row of green, waist-high plants, selecting some of the newest growth to use in the tea-leaf salads that were especially popular with tourists. Though he was dressed as the other workers and wore the same woven bamboo hat, he was not Chinese. If asked to describe the man, a visitor to the village might say that he was Middle Eastern or from southern Europe, firmly built without being heavy, and perhaps forty or fifty. His hair and short beard showed early traces of grey and as he stopped his work and surveyed the village below, his golden brown eyes reflected a life of great struggle but of infinite contentment.

He watched as Master Chen led the American back toward the bridge and his companions. This must be the new man—the one they all had been told was coming. Chen had met with the village elders the night before, describing the journey this man had followed. He had asked if they wished to accept a new person into the community and with a single voice, they had assented. Master Chen had been looking at him directly when the vote was taken and when he raised his hand and declared his support, Chen nodded his satisfaction. The farmer did not have to give his consent, of course. They were a community of consensus, and if any member expressed reservation, he would be asked if he objected strongly enough to be unable to support the majority. Few did. But the farmer lived with Master Chen and had been the only member of the community who was not Chinese. It was important to the community leader that he accept this new man. Now there were two.

CHAPTER THIRTY-ONE

In the stone chamber behind the chapel in the foothills near Coimbatore, the three Guardians sat on plain, straight-backed chairs and faced the senior elders of the Disciples of Thomas.

"Much has happened since we met here a year ago on the Day of St. Thomas," the senior elder said. "Much that has involved each of you. We are most grateful for your service and for what you have done to safeguard the sacred trust that has been given to us." He paused and for several moments, those seated looked across at each other like two rows of stone statues, without sound or motion. The room seemed unusually cool but none of the elders made an effort to pull his wrap more tightly about his shoulders. The Guardians remained perfectly still beneath their colorful silk scarves. At last the senior elder spoke, reciting the litany they all now knew by heart.

"This is the day that we come together to renew your vows. You have known from the time of your initiation that you can choose at the beginning of any year to forsake your vows and return fully to your former lives. Should you choose to leave, it will be without disgrace or recrimination. The Guardianship is a covenant of choice." Again he paused and the room became so silent it seemed that no one was breathing. A muffled cough escaped one of the old men, encouraging his senior to continue.

"Do you, Kanta, choose to continue as Guardian of Thomas?"

Kanta sat with head covered, looking straight ahead without focusing on any of the five men. She did not answer immediately and the same hush seemed to squeeze the very air out of the room.

"I do not, *Babaji*," she said finally, her voice strong and direct. "Forgive me, but I realize I am no longer equal to the trust that you have placed in me."

"You are too hard on yourself, Kanta. You have fulfilled every assignment you have been given."

"Not as I believed I should," she said. "I do not have the discernment needed to be a trusted Guardian."

"That admission shows that you have gained discernment," the elder suggested. "We will not try to dissuade you, but you continue to have our trust."

"The discernment is that I no longer trust in myself," she said. "I ask to be released from my vows."

"Then you are released," the old man said. "Go with our blessing and with the blessing of the Second Son."

Kanta stood and bowed respectfully to the five men, then silently left the room.

"And Meera, do you choose to continue as Guardian of Thomas?"

"I do, *Babaji*," she said, and moved forward to kneel before the five men.

"Do you, Manisha, choose to continue as Guardian of Thomas?"

"I do not," Nisha Pillai answered without hesitation. "I have—with great difficulty—honored my vows through this past year. But I do not wish to continue."

"We know you have struggled," the senior elder said, his voice expressing the understanding his words left unsaid. "We release you from your vows. Go with our blessing and with the blessing of the Second Son."

Nisha rocked forward onto her knees and kissed Meera's cheek. "Go with God," she said, then stood and bowed to the elders.

When she walked from the building the sun was reaching its zenith and a hot, humid day immediately soaked away the chill of the stone chamber. She paused on the step and lifted her face to the sun, pulling back her scarf to feel its warmth against her cheeks, then hurried across the road to her parked Honda. She had spoken to Marcus that morning on the phone before going to the church, only to tell him that she would call again that evening and give him an answer about coming to Charlotte. He wanted her there until he completed his dissertation. Probably for another year. Then they would return to India—or possibly to the Village that Loves Thailand.

Author's Notes

This book is entirely a work of fiction. All of the characters, with the exception of the historical religious figures, are creations of my imagination and are not based upon any real person. Similarities are completely coincidental.

The underlying idea for the story does come from references in early Christian literature that Thomas, one of the twelve original disciples of Jesus of Nazareth, was called Didymos or "the twin." The Gnostic text discovered at Nag Hammadi, the *Book of Thomas the Contender*, suggests that he was the twin of Jesus, a tradition that was maintained by some Syrian Christians. The *Gospel of Thomas*, also a Gnostic text, indicates that Jesus passed three secret truths along to Thomas that were so inflammatory that Thomas was not at liberty to share them with the other disciples. These early apocryphal teachings form the basis for this plot.

Although there is a strong Christian community in southern India that traces its origins to missionary visits from St. Thomas, and by tradition, Thomas established a series of churches across southern India, there is no sub-group similar to the Disciples of Thomas. They were a complete creation for this story. The Nagar Glass Factory in Yangon (Rangoon) actually exists and is a wonderful place to visit, though not managed by a man named Arun and not adjacent to the ruins of a Thomas church. There is no evidence of Thomas visiting Burma. Some legends do have him going as far as China, though the route of his journey is uncertain if it occurred at all.

The Thai border with Myanmar is scattered with villages of Karen tribal refugees, including "long-neck" Padaung who have become a major tourist attraction around Mae Hong Son—probably to the detriment of the women who continue the ring-neck tradition largely to remain an interesting oddity. Forty kilometers from Mae Hong Son near the border with Myanmar there is a village called Mae Aw, or Ban Rak Thai. It was founded by expatriate Nationalist Chinese soldiers and is one of the most picturesque and peaceful places I have visited, but is not a home to a community of Thomas Christians. It just seemed to me that if a place existed in the world where peace prevailed, it would be like

Mae Aw.

I have attempted to describe other places much as I perceived them from my experience and memory. My apologies to those communities, hotels, rail and road systems if they are unhappy with my descriptions.

Other Novels by Allen Kent

The Unit 1 Series
The Shield of Darius
The Weavers of Meanchey
The Wager

The Whitlock Saga
River of Light and Shadow
Wild Whistling Blackbirds

Domestic Mystery
Backwater

Cover Design by Jillian Farnsworth

63458685R00133

Made in the USA
Middletown, DE
26 August 2019